ONE EGYPTIAN SUMMER

ONE EGYPTIAN SUMMER

Iris Collier

The
Leisure
Circle

Copyright © Iris Collier 1986

All rights reserved

This edition specially produced for
The Leisure Circle Limited
by Century Hutchinson Ltd,
Brookmount House, 62–65 Chandos Place,
Covent Garden, London WC2N 4NW

Printed in Great Britain by
St Edmundsbury Press, Bury St Edmunds, Suffolk

To my mother

1

Paul Tomlinson was late for his own reception. By the time he had battled his way through the Cairo traffic, which grew more and more chaotic each week, the guests had already arrived. They had deserted the sitting-room, and were now standing awkwardly around in his garden. Fortunately, he could trust his wife Patricia to keep them happy, and the drinks were circulating freely.

He cursed his luck that the wretched Frenchman had called in just as he was leaving. He was too important to be got rid of quickly, and, as everyone else had left the office, he was forced to listen, to proffer whisky and soda, and, after he'd left, make notes to remind himself of the meeting next Monday morning.

A tough, terrier of a man, Paul Tomlinson was in charge of the Embassy's commercial section. A late entrant to the Foreign Office, he'd come in from Shell at the age of thirty-three. But his knowledge of the Middle East, and his considerable business experience, made him an indispensable member of the Embassy team.

He was a bit of a misfit. He was just a bit too outspoken, just a bit contemptuous of the other diplomats who had brought their classical degrees to the Diplomatic Service, but little else. His wife, too, wasn't quite at home with the other wives. She was too forceful – too severe with the servants. She was critical of the other women and the way they filled up their days. She had a lot of energy which she channelled towards the poor of the city. She spent three mornings each week looking after expectant mothers in the sprawling suburb of Bulac. She didn't go to church services either.

Every Friday, the Tomlinsons invited local businessmen and their wives to their comfortable villa in Zamalek – the island in the middle of the Nile, much favoured by the local western community. Most of the senior diplomats lived here – and the local journalists and the BBC correspondent. White villas surrounded by flame trees, and well-watered lawns, provided an oasis of peace for the returning diplomats when they had forced their way through the nightmare of Cairo's traffic. Paul's wife loved the garden. Despite protests from Mohammed and Ahmed, his two resident suffragis, she tried to grow English plants and vegetables. Tonight the guests were admiring her fine crop of tomatoes. She was even successful with parsley.

Mohammed put down the tray of drinks he was carrying, and took Paul's coat. He also handed him a weak whisky and soda, with lots of ice. The evening was stiflingly hot; not the pleasant dry heat of June, but the sticky heat of late July, when the Nile was rising. Paul had never learnt to slow down, in spite of all his Middle Eastern experience. He still moved at his London pace, but then he'd always had to move quickly. It was the only way he'd reached his present position. Coming from a poor background – his father had worked for British Rail – he had had to fight his way to the top. Fighters tend to be energetic. He drank the whisky and soda straight off.

'Thanks. Everything all right?'

'Yes, sir. They are all outside. We're still waiting for one or two more – not everyone is here.'

'Who's here from the office?' He always suspected his colleagues of avoiding his receptions. He expected them to work – to talk to local businessmen and write reports on their conversations for him to read first thing Monday morning.

'Miss Peel is here. And Mr Leigh. Miss Peel came early.'

'She's a good girl. Thank you, Mohammed. Tell my wife I'm here. I shall just have to change this damned shirt. I presume everyone is in shirtsleeves?' He was still not confident enough to wear what he liked. He needed that security which comes from following the herd.

'Oh yes, sir. It's very hot tonight.' The Sudanese grinned at Paul showing a row of white teeth. His black face was puckered with tribal markings. He and Paul shared a sartorial joke. When the weather turned hot and humid, Paul Tomlinson threatened to turn up to one of these occasions wearing one of Mohammed's gallabiyas. The flowing white cotton robe was designed for coolness. The westerner, in his shirt and tie, and trousers with a tight waistband was ridiculously uncomfortable...

The odd thing was that Paul Tomlinson, an old Middle Eastern campaigner, always wore woollen socks, hand-knitted by his wife. He wore them throughout the year, whatever the temperature. He'd even worn them during a Baghdad summer. He believed that one's feet should be allowed to sweat freely. But the sweat had also to be absorbed fully. The servants treated these socks with veneration. Most of them went barefoot round the house, if they could avoid Mrs Tomlinson's hawk-eyes. Ahmed, the junior suffragi, dearly wanted a pair of these socks for himself. One day he would summon up enough courage to ask Mrs Tomlinson for a pair of her husband's cast-offs – if he could stop her handing them over to the poor of Bulac. But she knitted them with good British wool, and they didn't wear out. She even washed them herself which made them still more desirable in Ahmed's eyes.

Paul went out onto the terrace to meet his guests. He kissed his wife.

'Sorry Pat,' was all that he needed to say. She understood.

Most of the guests were there – Günther from Mercedes, Frank from Qantas, Peter from English Ford. It was mostly a male gathering. He liked to talk business on these occasions. He despised the 'socialites' of the Diplomatic Service, never understanding that much information could be gleaned from a purely social evening, or that a man's wife could often be very indiscreet, especially after two strong gins and tonic. His job was to help British businessmen get local orders: it was only a part of his job to extract information about other countries' commerce.

He nodded to David Leigh – an eager Third Secretary who always came to his receptions. David wanted to be useful. The quicker he was promoted from Third Secretary to Second, and given some responsibility, the better. He hated being at everyone's beck and call, but as a new arrival to the Foreign Office from university he couldn't expect anything else. But it is the nature of young men to be impatient at having to learn the trade. David Leigh was anxious to get his apprenticeship over as quickly as possible.

'Thank you for coming, David. You've got a drink? Good. Look after old Günther for me. Your German's better than mine. He needs cheering up. Are you sailing this weekend?' he added as an afterthought. He felt a twinge of guilt at handing over Günther to David. He wanted to relax with his squash partner – the man from Ford's. He'd had a long hard day, and really couldn't face Günther Miessen. David understood the reason for the question.

'Yes; I'm going to Alexandria tonight. The weather's perfect for a weekend's cruising.' David sailed with two law students from Cairo University; both were useful contacts for information about Egypt's political affairs. The Ambassador approved of David Leigh.

He turned to Charlotte Peel – one of the brighter diplomats. Tall and slim, he always thought her waif-like, and despite her intelligence he felt protective. His face softened when he looked at her. She appeared so vulnerable with that long brown hair, held back like a schoolgirl's with two tortoiseshell combs. Her brown eyes melted his heart. She was a good worker though, and an expert Arabist. He got on with her, whilst most of his colleagues felt uneasy when left alone with her. The Foreign Office had its fair share of women diplomats – but a lot of the older men in the Service couldn't get used to them. They patronised Charlotte, and then were nonplussed by her replies. She was used to them, but they never got used to her.

Tonight she looked anxious. She was too tense. The hands that gripped the glass of lemon juice were too tightly clenched. Her eyes were fixed on the door leading from the sitting-room into the garden. She seemed to be only half-listening to what people were saying. Not for the first time, Paul wanted to see her relax – to forget herself. He wanted to hear her laugh loudly, without restraint. She had the alert air of a watchful animal – one who was wary of human beings. But she knew her job. Men talked to her because she was a good listener, and they thought she wouldn't understand what they were saying. They didn't realise that she had inherited a superb memory from her journalist father; that her brain never stopped sifting and filing away information and impressions. She never made lists, but she never neglected the smallest detail. She had a real respect for facts; she never forgot a single figure. Had she not entered the Diplomatic Service, she would have made a good journalist. People always underrated her. But not the Ambassador.

Suddenly her face brightened. The brown eyes came alive. Paul turned to see who was responsible for this transformation. Coming down the steps onto the lawn was the dapper figure of Hassan Khatib, a local businessman. He always came to these receptions. Paul liked him, though he didn't trust him. He exported cotton; but Paul often wondered what else he exported. It was for that reason he was invited to Embassy receptions. Paul Tomlinson wanted to know more about him. Certainly Charlotte seemed to be on familiar terms with him. She crossed over the lawn and linked her arm through his. Paul watched her face light up as Hassan greeted her. A waiter came up and Charlotte handed him a drink. She didn't have to ask what he would like. He watched her change from a shy, watchful girl into a self-confident woman. He felt uneasy.

'I ought to see Anthony on Monday,' he thought suddenly. 'We can't have Charlotte mixed up with a local chap. Not when we know so little about him. I wonder how far it's gone. Not too far, I hope.'

He kept an eye on the couple for the rest of the evening. He was expert at talking to a guest, but keeping tuned in to another in a different part of the reception. She talked to no one else, and this annoyed him. She was here to do a job, not to enjoy herself. He wasn't too worried about Hassan Khatib. He doubted whether there was in fact much to learn about him. He was just a local businessman; undoubtedly rich, with a house in Alexandria, and a house-boat on the Nile. No one had ever seen his wife. He supposed he was married. Rich Egyptians usually were, but it was also quite normal for them to keep their wives hidden away. He wondered whether he ought to warn Charlotte – but, being at heart a shy man, he jibbed at interfering with the private lives of his colleagues. That was Anthony's job. As Head of Chancery he had the unenviable task of keeping a watchful eye on the staff. But Charlotte did seem to be very indiscreet. Openly talking to one man for an hour did seem to be a bit excessive. Even if she wasn't sleeping with him, people would start talking. Anthony wouldn't like that.

Around half-past eight people were starting to drift away. It was quite usual for people to eat dinner between nine and half-past. Most of the Egyptians ate around ten o'clock. The nights were the best time of all. Most people in Cairo worked in the mornings, slept in the afternoons, worked again from four until seven, and then played at night. Most people didn't go to bed until the early hours of the morning. Even the city's workers stayed up until all hours of the night. But the streets were empty by two o'clock in the afternoon.

Charlotte and Khatib were among the first to leave. This too, annoyed Paul, because the unstated rule was that the staff were always last to leave on these occasions. It was bad manners to leave the guests standing around on their own. Diplomats were supposed to work, not to enjoy themselves.

Patricia came over to join him as the guests came to say goodbye. They shook hands and drifted away into the scented darkness. Several were reluctant to leave and hovered, hoping to be asked to stay to dinner. Paul was adamant. The invitation said six-thirty to eight-thirty. There had been no mention of dinner. He looked forward to a quiet meal with his wife. They were a good team, and he actually enjoyed talking to her. He found her work at the clinic interesting, and wanted to hear her opinion about the guests that evening. Sometimes she showed an unexpected shrewdness, and then he felt that she would have made a better job of his work than he did! But there was no rivalry. She seemed quite content with her lot. As the last guest left by the side gate, she turned to her husband.

'What a lovely night. Let's eat outside. The mosquitoes seem to have given us up for once. A nice evening. You ought to persuade more people to come along from the office, though. Old Günther was standing on his own for too long. David did his job, but you can't expect a young man to talk too long to that old bore. He can speak English perfectly well, you know. He just likes to put people at a disadvantage by expecting them to speak German. David did very well.'

They walked towards the small table that always stood out

on the terrace. Mohammed had laid up two places, and now stood behind Patricia Tomlinson's chair ready to serve the prawn curry.

'By the way,' said Patricia, as she unfolded her linen napkin, 'I think you should have a word with Charlotte on Monday. She's seeing too much of that Egyptian. They went off together, and I noticed that they drove off in his car. They must have arranged to meet here. She's asking for trouble.'

'Don't worry,' replied her husband, as he helped himself to the prawns. 'I'll have a word with Anthony on Monday. It's his job to speak to the staff. I only hope it hasn't gone too far, that's all.'

Anthony Maitland glanced down at the file in front of him. He hated this part of his job. He respected people's privacy. He wanted the staff to be happy. Too many diplomats were bedevilled by emotional problems. But the fact remained that his senior staff were not ordinary citizens. Cairo was not Tooting or Guildford. The place was teeming with dubious characters – dope-peddlers, Israeli spies, Russian spies, informers for the Egyptian government, informers ready to sell any scrap of information to anyone wanting to buy it. Even the wastepaper baskets in his own house were searched. He gave his own suffragis a pound every time they told him that the Egyptian police had called.

Everyone expected to be watched. No conversation was private. No servant was fully trusted. Even the most loyal could succumb to temptation. All the work in the Embassy was confidential. Everyone was expected to respect certain unwritten rules, the most important being that emotional attachments to local Egyptians should not be embarked upon. The staff were discouraged from falling in love with locals – whether male or female. It was the only safe way. On the rare occasions when this happened, the person concerned always resigned. Fortunately, this was before Anthony Maitland's time in Cairo.

Now, he'd come to the office on a Monday morning only to be told by a senior member of his staff whose opinion he respected, that one of the diplomatic staff was being indiscreet with a local Egyptian – a dubious character named Hassan Khatib. He cursed his luck.

It was not the first time he'd heard the rumour. Charlotte Peel had been under surveillance for some time. He liked the girl. He respected her ability. He also thought her unhappy, and in need of a friend. But not Khatib. He was almost certainly married, although no one had ever seen his wife. And no one knew very much about him. He had warned Charlotte before. He glanced down at the file – a month ago, during June. So it was still going on. This was going to be serious. He liked her, but he didn't want to risk being accused of negligence. In his experience, nearly every puff of smoke concealed a fire. Too many people turned a blind eye to the peccadillos of the staff. She would have to be stopped. He would have to deliver the final warning.

What was he up against? What sort of person was she? Forget her sex – look at the facts. Again he glanced down at the slim file in front of him.

'*Charlotte Emily Peel* – born thirty-five years ago.' 'Old-fashioned family,' he thought, 'or literary.'

'*Father* – Reuters Correspondent' – 'Ah! that was it.' He'd worked in the Middle East and North Africa. So she'd had a turbulent childhood. Eventually, she'd been brought up by grandparents who lived in Woodbridge, Suffolk. Or did – they'd died several years ago. Both parents had been killed in a car accident in France only six years ago. So there was no family left – no immediate family. There was no mention of brothers or sisters.

'*Education* – a girls' boarding school in Haywards Heath.' A traditional girls' school with a record of high academic standards. She'd 'won a scholarship to Newnham College, Cambridge – read History – a First Class degree. Spoke German and French fluently.' She was all set for an academic career, but took the Foreign Office exam instead. She came very high on the list. She'd then been sent to Beirut to the School for Arabic Studies. She'd come top in her year.

'*Posts* – Rome, Ankara and . . .' and now she'd been two years in Cairo.

'*Personal* – highly intelligent – excellent memory – valuable member of a team.'

'*Socially* – adequate. Tendency to shun company. A bit of a loner.' 'That's interesting,' he thought. 'They're always the ones who give us problems. Why can't they all be cheerful extroverts and go to Scottish dancing in the evenings, instead of sitting alone in their apartments brooding over their personal problems?'

'*Friends* – few but loyal.' There was no record of 'attachments'.

He sighed, and closed the file. So that was it! A highly-intelligent, emotionally-starved girl. Still immature; not used to the Ways of the World. Fair game for types like Khatib. He saw trouble ahead.

A knock on the door, and Charlotte came in – a neat figure in a white sleeveless cotton dress. She was carrying a report she was working on; she thought that was what he wanted to see.

Anthony looked at his watch. He would have to get this over with. If she was cooperative, then it would only take a few minutes. He would take her word that she didn't intend seeing Khatib again.

'Charlotte – good morning! Come and sit down.' A brisk man – he'd made his decision. He wouldn't beat about the bush.

'I'm wearing my Head of Chancery's hat today. It's a security matter.'

Charlotte looked surprised. What was her secretary up to? She seemed extremely well-adjusted. She was getting on rather well with David Leigh, and that was a thoroughly good thing. Both were well-suited.

'You've been seeing too much of Hassan Khatib. We don't know him, and he's not security cleared. In any case, he's almost certainly married, and has no business escorting you around Cairo. We can't tell *him* we think he's undesirable, but we can tell *you*. I think we warned you before,' he added, a little sharply.

Charlotte went white. She pushed the hair back behind her ears and her eyes blazed with indignation.

'I think my private life is none of your business, Anthony,' she said.

He sighed. This wasn't going to be easy. The girl looked like a tigress.

'Oh yes, it *is* my business, and the Ambassador's, and the Personnel Department's in London. You are not an ordinary citizen, Charlotte. You knew this when you accepted a Foreign Office career. This was explained to you. You handle confidential work – you are always under surveillance, by us, and by other countries – some of them not friendly to us. Any misdemeanour will be reported to them. You know the rule – no relationships with locals unless approved of by us, and necessary for the conduct of your work.' He paused and gave her time to order her thoughts.

'Hassan and I have known each other for several months now. He has never once asked me about my work, or what I do here. He is a kind and gentle man, and likes the British.'

Anthony leant over the desk and looked keenly at Charlotte. 'Do you love the man?'

He watched the colour come flooding into her face. He saw her eyes grow huge with desire, and then blaze at him in anger. The girl was in a highly-emotional state.

'Yes, I do,' she said. 'What harm is there in that? Are we to be deprived of normal instincts because we work for the British Embassy? What harm can come through loving?'

'Most of the harm that is done in the world comes through loving – either too much, or not enough. As a diplomat, you are expected to love wisely, preferably one of your own countrymen. Your job is not a normal job. You are not Miss Peel from Dorking, working in a nine to five office job. You know that.'

'What are you asking me to do?' The colour had left her face, which had resumed its usual pallor.

'I am asking you to give me your word that you will not see this Egyptian again – not on your own. You will obviously meet him at receptions. But you will not talk to him exclusively.'

'I can't do that. We love each other, and he has mentioned marriage. I can't give him up.'

Anthony looked at her in astonishment. He was finding this all beyond his comprehension.

'Charlotte – wake up! How can he talk of marriage? He almost certainly has a wife.'

'Even Egyptians are known to divorce if necessary.'

'Yes, but it's highly unlikely in his case. There's something about this whole business I don't like. I must ask for your word that you won't see him again.'

'I can't say that. I love him, and would marry him if he was free to do so. Meanwhile I shall go on seeing him. My work is not affected. My loyalty to my country is unquestioned. I have a right to my own private life.'

'Unfortunately, you forfeited that right when you joined the Diplomatic Service. If you continue to see this man, then I have no alternative but to ask for your resignation. We can't make an exception in your case. As a wife of an Egyptian your loyalty to your own country would be bound to take second place. I'll give you twenty-four hours to come to your decision.'

'I don't need twenty-four hours. My mind is made up. I don't intend to stop seeing Hassan Khatib. If loyalty to my country means giving up my friends, then I am not prepared to make that sacrifice. I will give you my resignation.'

The girl was rigid with tension, and utterly determined. Anthony saw that there was no alternative. Someone as unbalanced as Charlotte would be better out of the Service. If this had happened once it could happen again. Next time, she was quite likely to fall for a glamorous Russian. He would have to enter an account of this interview in her personal file. No one in London would blame him for what he had to do.

'Very well. I'm sorry to have to do this. I'll see the Ambassador this afternoon. Meanwhile, I should like your resignation in writing. If you change your mind, then you have the rest of the day to think about it. Remember, once you have made up your mind to see Khatib again, these doors will always be closed to you. You will have given up a promising career – lost our good-will, and our protection. For what? In Heaven's name – for a middle-aged Egyptian with a wife, and probably a bunch of children.'

She stood up, and left the room, leaving behind her report. He glanced at it. A beautifully concise account of an interview she'd done recently with the editor of one of Egypt's main daily papers. The Ambassador should see it, and it would have to go to London. What a waste of talent! He almost dashed out to call her back – but he knew it would be useless. Maybe, after she'd calmed down and thought about it, she would change her mind. But he doubted it.

Anthony Maitland didn't dislike women. He knew how capable they could be. He didn't blame the female sex for Charlotte's obsession. He blamed Nature. That was why the security services had always to be on the alert. People were only people – the highest in the land were still susceptible to human passion.

2

Suffolk in early spring. A bleak landscape, a biting wind, straight from Russia, a potato patch, and Charlotte leaning on a hoe. Her woollen hat was pulled down over her eyes; the anorak buttoned up to her chin. She dropped the last seed potato into its hole, and stood up, involuntarily rubbing her back as she did so.

It was the end of March – a month of frustrated expectations. Every day she looked for signs of spring; every day she was disappointed. Only a handful of crocuses near the back door had managed to pierce the earth; flashes of light in a harsh landscape. Yet they signalled better things were on their way.

For a month now, the wind had been blowing steadily from the east. It seemed as though summer would never come. The flat landscape, the hard soil, the plaintive call of the seagulls as they followed the solitary tractor in the next field, created an impression of utter desolation. It was time to go inside. It was freezing cold. The wind cut through the thick clothing like a knife. She braced herself to pick up her basket and hoe, and prod the mud off her boots. Winter in Suffolk was an endurance test.

A last look over the fields to where the river widened out towards the North Sea. There was the spire of Harwich church. Opposite, the black loading cranes of Felixstowe Docks – Wellsian monsters outlined against the sky. Charlotte loved this part of Suffolk. In spite of the stark landscape, the bare fields and the dead salt marshes, she felt at home here. She loved the sense of space, of freedom. Overhead, the black clouds raced across the huge vault of the sky – the perfect back-cloth for this harsh landscape.

In summer this part of Suffolk – the estuary of the Orweil, was a water-colour artist's delight – a mixture of blues and greens. Now in the white light of spring, the river was a grey lowering reptile, lying in its coils between the mud-flats – a monstrous relic from the ice-age.

Was it only last summer she'd sat on Hassan's house-boat on that other river? The sun setting behind the pyramids, flooding the Nile with a rose-coloured light. She remembered that wind, a whisper of a breeze, laden with the scent of jasmine. Was it only last summer she'd drunk Turkish coffee at a restaurant which looked out over the pyramids of Giza? A particularly fierce blast nearly knocked her off her feet. It was time to forget that other river, and the house-boat with the purple cushions, and Hassan. She ought to go back to the cottage. That life was over; it was sheer self-indulgence to dwell on it. She ought to go indoors and stoke the fire up for the evening.

She was tired. She picked up her basket, and plodded up the path to the back-door of the tiny red-brick cottage where she lived alone with her cat. It was a typical Suffolk cottage, built in the nineteenth century by the local farmer for his game-keeper and mole-catcher. In fact the date, 1876, was carved on the surprisingly ornate chimney. The locals called it 'the mole-catcher's cottage', and Charlotte had kept the name. She'd driven over from Cambridge last September, and had fallen in love with its solitude. It had given her the peace she needed.

It had been a tough year, with little money, and no friends. She would need those vegetables next summer. Unless she got a job soon, she would be in trouble with her bank.

The short day was coming to an end. It was time for tea, and a hot bath to ease her aching back. She wasn't used to heavy work, and planting potatoes had been a strain. She tugged off the wellington boots, and shook out her hair from under the woollen hat. It fell around her shoulders like a brown curtain. It was her best feature – the only part of her appearance she was proud of. As a child she had hated her hair. Her grandmother, always practical, had insisted on having it kept short – cut in a straight fringe across her face, like the picture of the Norman baron in her history book. At Cambridge she'd let it grow – mainly because she couldn't be bothered to go to the hairdressers. She had liked the effect. It softened her sharp features, and added colour to her sallow skin.

She caught a glimpse of her face in the mirror. As usual she looked away. It looked as bad as it had yesterday. Her skin was grey in this light – cold and pinched by the wind. In Cairo she'd been able to lie in the sun for hours at weekends. She was never bothered by sunburn. Her skin had turned to the colour of ripe chestnuts after a few days. With her dark hair, and brown eyes, she had felt beautiful for the first time in her life. Now, back in this climate, her skin was yellow again. She felt plain, dried up. 'Withered spinster' was the expression that came to her mind. She turned away from the glass.

The cat wanted attention. There was no full moon to draw him out tonight, so he'd stay by the fire as long as possible. He looked up at Charlotte with his great luminous eyes, and stretched luxuriously. They were very close. She'd found him the day she'd arrived in this part of Suffolk. He was the strongest of a litter she'd seen at the local pub. She had been waiting for the agent, and the basketful of kittens had entertained her. Thomas, she called him Thomas, was the boldest of the bunch, springing up and flexing his claws on her trousers. His coat was interesting – a haphazard arrangement of black and white patches apparently painted at random. It was as if the artist had become bored with his subject and wanted to get the picture finished off as quickly as possible. By the time the agent appeared, Thomas and Charlotte were great friends, and the pub owner had pressed her to take him. So she had come to the mole-catcher's cottage with Thomas in a cardboard box.

She would have bought the cottage on the spot. But the agent had been nervous and insisted she spoke to her solicitor. He couldn't believe his luck. He was expecting a difficult sale – the cottage was two miles from anywhere. This lady, with a certain elegance, was not the type he was expecting to buy the place. She hadn't bothered to have the cottage surveyed. She knew she'd found her refuge. She gave the agent a deposit on the spot and had driven off to Cambridge.

Thomas was now fat and sleek. He slithered off the chair by the fire and made a playful grab at Charlotte's stockinged feet. But she was tired and cold. She gave him a perfunctory stroke and went upstairs to the tiny bedroom with its low ceiling and oak beams. Thomas would have his moment at supper-time. Later on, the frosty night would call him out into the Suffolk countryside. Then he would forget the soft carpets and the food, and turn into a silent instrument of deadly destruction.

She ran a hot bath. Once again, she thanked her stars that she had found this sanctuary in this remote part of England. Her previous life was slowly fading away. Sometimes, the strains of Arab music over the radio would make her catch her breath. That stupid film the other evening on television, a 1930s film about Caesar and Cleopatra – ludicrous, but the glimpse of the Sphinx had brought the memories flooding back. Sometimes, when exhausted after digging her garden, or returning from the fore-shore with a pile of driftwood, she would stand in her kitchen and say 'Thank God, he's gone. It's over. I'm through the experience.'

Feeling light-hearted once again, she would go upstairs and brush out her hair in front of the mirror on her dressing table. Then she would catch sight of the little inlaid jewel box, and the memories would come flooding back. Why didn't she get rid of that box? It was the only present he'd ever given her. Every night it reminded her of him – the occasion when he'd given it to her, in one of those open-air restaurants outside Cairo, where the air was warm and still and smelling of jasmine.

Then he'd told her he'd loved her – that she was beautiful and desirable. It was all nonsense, of course. He'd called her his Cleopatra because of her dark hair and eyes. He'd said he couldn't live without her, that he needed her, and that he would leave his wife. He'd wooed her with platitudes, and she'd believed every word he said. She hadn't asked any questions. She wanted to believe him, and was grateful for every sign of affection. She'd been an easy conquest. But part of her still lived in a sort of remote hope that she would see him again.

They'd met once more after that dreadful day when Anthony had asked for her resignation. She'd taken the extreme step of telephoning him that evening on his house-boat. He had always forbidden her to phone him. He had been the one to decide on when they should meet. They'd met in a small bar on the island, and she'd told him what had happened. At first he'd looked alarmed, and then concerned. He'd put his arm round her, and calmed her down. Then he'd suggested she came back to England, and one day he'd come and find her. He had promised marriage once he'd managed to divorce his wife.

That was all. She'd taken his word that they would meet again. She'd left the Embassy that August. Her few friends had given her a small drinks party in the office – a sad occasion, because everyone thought she was making a big mistake. She'd cleared up her papers, and left at the end of the week. She would wait for Hassan – forever if necessary. She knew she would never find anyone else like him again. She wanted solitude – the life of a recluse. Like a princess in a mediaeval romance she would wait for her Prince Charming.

But now it was March, and there was no sign of the Prince. She'd told him that she was going to buy a place in Suffolk. She hadn't given him her address, believing that if he wanted to contact her, he could always find her. Now she felt like a fly trapped in amber; this would be her life for ever if he didn't come. She could try to forget him; it would be better if she did. Then there was a chance she could get back into some sort of public life again. The Foreign Office might even reconsider her; if not for a senior post, then in some sort of lesser capacity. But she would probably be better off trying to get an academic job in Cambridge. She did have friends there.

The bath water was going cold. She had to chop wood for the fire and prepare supper; something complicated which would require all her attention.

She reached for the towel, and stood up in the bath, deliberately avoiding looking at her body as she did so. Her friends were right; she was spinsterish. Egyptian women of her age would be full and soft, with two or three children. She couldn't put on weight however hard she tried. In spite of the fact that she liked cooking, her body remained obstinately thin. Through the steam, she glanced at herself in the mirror over the wash basin. Her shoulder-blades were too pronounced. Her chest was all bone, and no flesh. The ribcage was clearly outlined. Waist and hips ran into one another with no undulation. She should have been a model; she could wear designer clothes. She would be a good clothes horse.

But Charlotte, the intellectual, wasn't interested in clothes. She mourned the fact that she wasn't round and sexy. Her best feature was her eyes — huge and brown which the locals said made her look tragic. She seldom smiled, and her air of self-sufficiency repelled most people. They left her alone. She was known as 'Miss Tragedy from below the church' — the mole-catcher's cottage stood below the church at the foot of a hill.

She impatiently pulled the blue woollen caftan over her head. It suited her. The full skirt and the long sleeves gave substance to her figure. The deep kingfisher blue of the material complemented her hair and eyes. She'd made the dress herself. She'd bought the material last month in Cambridge, and had spent the winter evenings sewing it by hand, as she didn't have a sewing machine. It looked like a winter version of an Eygptian caftan.

She brushed out her hair, put on legwarmers, and went down to the kitchen. There were bacon and mushrooms in the fridge. Somewhere she had eggs. She'd make an omelette. Thomas began to wrap himself round her legs.

The telephone rang in the sitting-room, shattering the silence, and bringing Charlotte back to reality. She didn't feel like talking to anyone tonight. The ringing continued. It must be someone who knew about her anti-social habits. She pushed Thomas aside, and reluctantly picked up the receiver. It was James, her old supervisor from Cambridge. She was relieved to hear his quiet voice. Nice things happened when James telephoned. She'd been one of his brightest students, and they had kept in touch. He knew a little of her affair in Cairo, but wisely asked no questions. Tonight he offered her dinner on Saturday. He lived alone, but from time to time he enjoyed entertaining people he liked. He would cook curries, and entertain his friends with Mozart opera. Charlotte looked forward to these evenings. They were always civilized; no one asked questions; it was comfortingly familiar.

'Charlotte, my dear, I hope you can join us. I've got an Egyptian coming — a research student from Cairo University, interested in the Third Crusade. I know you like this period — do come and help me out. He sounds a bit exotic for me. His name's Edward Wassim. He's a good chap, but I'm a Renaissance man, as you know, and I shan't know what to talk about.'

This was nonsense, of course. James was one of the most cultured people she knew. Whatever he didn't know about the Third Crusade today, he would certainly have made up for by Saturday night.

'He's obviously a Copt,' said Charlotte, a trifle pedantically. It was a spontaneous remark — she didn't mean to sound patronising.

'I expect so. I shall need some light relief. Also, I need someone with your diplomatic training. I'm bound to say the wrong thing about the Third Crusade. Did the Crusaders massacre any Copts, do you know? I expect they did. Oh yes, do bring your guitar along. We could take his mind off his subject with the music of the English Renaissance.'

She laughed. 'It sounds fun. The usual time?'

'About half-past seven. I think I might ask Brian and Sheila. They don't know Cairo, but they looked at Crusaders' castles last year. The most interesting thing about the Crusades was how much of Western Europe was involved in them.'

James was already off. He liked a new subject. By Saturday night, he'd know as much about the Crusades as the Copt — maybe more. She looked forward to seeing him again. His house was full of interesting objects which he'd collected over the years, mostly from Italy, a country he loved best of all.

She knew he wouldn't ask questions. He didn't know about Hassan and her dismissal from the Foreign Office. He thought Charlotte was taking a long mid-tour leave. Diplomats often bought houses and lived in them before they returned to this country for good. She also knew the food would be good. James had never married, but had developed a talent for cooking. His menus were international. Holidays abroad were gastronomic investigations. Once, Charlotte had come across him in Rome, sitting peacefully by himself in a restaurant — a little book in front of him in which he was writing down the ingredients of the dish he was eating. He was actually sketching the strange squid-like creature on his plate, writing down the colours of the flesh, as he had no coloured pencils with him. One day he'd probably write a cookery book, probably a collection of recipes from the Ottoman Empire of the sixteenth century!

He rang off and Charlotte prepared her meal quickly and without interest. Her mind was on James, and whether she might one day return to Cambridge and do some research with him. The idea was appealing. She knew he would offer her a post. He had been delighted with her appointment in the Diplomatic Service, but he'd always hoped that she'd return to academic pastures. He knew she would make a brilliant lecturer in Middle Eastern history. He had always helped and consoled her. When her parents had been killed in that dreadful accident in France, he had come to stay with her and helped her through those first nightmare days. Perhaps she would talk to James. A life of quiet study in Cambridge had a lot to be said for it. Perhaps she would even marry James, and help with his students – sherry parties on Fridays, and holidays in Italy.

She switched her mind away from the future. She was thirty-five; the Foreign Office had dismissed her. But it wasn't the end of her life. She hadn't done anything disgraceful. She hadn't betrayed her country, or sold secrets to shady characters in grey macintoshes. She'd only been human. She'd loved too fondly; that was all. Never once had Hassan asked for information about her job. In fact he didn't like politics. The subject bored him. He'd made her laugh. The relationship had been essentially frivolous. He liked his food, dancing on the house-boats along the banks of the Nile; and he liked well-dressed western women. Charlotte had blossomed under his influence. Life had been fun. She'd welcomed each day with open arms. Her own youth, with her serious journalist father and harassed mother hadn't been fun. The constant travelling, the packing and unpacking, often at short notice, had exhausted her mother. There had been no time for frivolity. Life was serious. She knew about the world's calamities – the sudden disappearances in the night. Then the hasty drive to the airport. The childhood days spent with her grandparents hadn't been fun either. They had disapproved of her father's roving life, and had lectured her on responsibilities. They had paid for her school fees, and expected good reports on their investment. Holidays were spent in study, and they had been delighted when she got her scholarship to Cambridge. Hassan had brought laughter into her life, and irresponsibility. But she had to pay for her pleasures. The Calvinistic grandparents would have approved of her punishment had they been alive to see her now – isolated and jobless, in a remote part of England.

Charlotte pushed aside the tray, and reached for her guitar, an instrument which she played very well. Tonight, she played Dowland, and the music of the other Elizabethan composers. She played from memory; the delicate notes weaving and dancing under her long fingers. She sang the airs of Orlando Gibbons, melancholy tunes with delicate harmonies. They sounded well in that house. James had tried to persuade her to record her songs. She had a lovely clear alto voice – as pure as a choirboy's with no trace of vibrato. But she didn't value her talent. She sang for her own enjoyment, and was shy about singing in public. Occasionally she would take her guitar along to James' evenings, and then she didn't mind playing the sad melodies to his friends. She felt at home in his house in Trumpington Street.

When she played like this – the firelight flickering on her long hair and mediaeval face more boyish than ever when she concentrated on the music, she looked her most attractive. On one of James' evenings, a guest had discreetly produced charcoal and paper, and had sketched her dark, withdrawn face. She had hated that portrait. It seemed to emphasise all the features which she most disliked. The face in the portrait was that of a Magdalena; she wanted to be a Madonna. She wanted soft pink flesh and full outlines. He had emphasized her long neck and slender sloping shoulders. She seemed to epitomize the intellectual; she would have given anything to have been an Aphrodite.

On and on she played, whilst the fire burned down to its last few embers. It was growing late and cold. Thomas stirred at her feet, and stood up, arching his back and flexing his claws in anticipation of the night's hunting. Charlotte put aside the instrument, and closed down the front of the fire. Thomas led the way to the back door and stood there patiently waiting for her to open it. She stood there for a few minutes looking up at the frosty sky, and smelt the air filled with the scent of the newly-ploughed earth, and the damp, salty smell of the sea. The night air of Cairo was sweet and cloying; jasmine mingled with the stench of drains; incense and garbage festering in the open sewers.

She closed the door impatiently. She had to forget him. Suffolk was light years away from Cairo. Tomorrow, she'd think about the early cabbages. There was more wood needed. The exercise would take her mind off him.

She climbed the steep wooden stairs to her bedroom. She slipped into her narrow bed. She always left the curtains open so that she could look out at the stars. At least the sky was the same as Egypt's. Why had he not contacted her? Had he gone back to his mysterious wife whom he hardly mentioned? Soon she was asleep – the deep sleep of the physically exhausted.

3

'What a nice man he is!' thought Charlotte, as she looked across to where James Hamilton was talking to the earnest young Copt. James had the great art of making people immediately comfortable. Edward Wassim was enjoying himself. A shy man, he was at home in that academic circle. His face, straight out of an early Egyptian tomb painting, was relaxed and happy. Charlotte was fascinated by his appearance. She'd met Copts before, of course; they were the main prop of Egyptian commerce, but never before had she seen a face quite as timeless as Edward Wassim's. Small, brown, slightly pointed, with slanting eyes, it was a face that had gazed down at her thousands of times as she studied the frescoes in the tombs of the Pharaohs. These little men had worked the boats along the Nile, tilled the fields and built the pyramids. Models of them had been found in the tombs clustered round the sarcophagus of the Pharaoh, to look after him in the next life. The Copts prided themselves on being the real Egyptians, and looking at Edward she could see why.

James, in his dark grey suit, looked very Anglo-Saxon. The blue eyes and curling grey hair were unmistakably Northern European. He felt her interest. He smiled at her inviting her to join them. Edward politely made way for her as she approached. They'd finished with the Crusades over dinner, and were now talking about Norman castles. Brian and Sheila, fellow lecturers, had joined the group and were describing their trip to the Crusader castles in Syria. They'd been over difficult country, and had felt uneasy because wherever they went, the army seemed to be there in force.

'Yes,' said Edward quietly. 'We're now fighting an endless crusade. But this time they're not building castles, but launching rockets.'

Charlotte was able to study James now, without appearing rude. Inevitably the conversation led on to Arab-Israeli politics, and because of her old training, she preferred to listen and not join in. James understood. He glanced at her and smiled, his blue eyes lighting up with affection when he met her glance. She knew he admired her. Should she marry him? And forget Hassan and the Egyptian involvement? In spite of the obvious difference in their ages, it would be a very suitable match. Probably she needed a stable father-figure like James. He would be a devoted and kind husband. They would have attractive and intelligent children who would not have the insecurities of her own upbringing. They could live in James' elegant town house, or move out to Grantchester, and live in an old house with lawns going down to the river. They would own a punt, and take the students out for afternoon picnics. Her life would be safe and predictable – a busy husband during the University term; travel in the long holidays to places like Greece and Turkey. She would be busy and occupied doing things she liked doing. But would she be happy? Was life meant only to be a safe and secure haven with a safe and predictable companion? She knew she had experienced excitement and rapture. How long would she remain content with the kindly James?

He now turned to her. Dinner had been cleared away. The coffee was served, and the guests were moving towards the comfortable armchairs. Edward made for the fireside and sat cross-legged on the little prayer mat, looking more and more like one of the guardians of the tombs.

It was now time for Charlotte's guitar. James put an arm round her. 'Charlotte my dear; do you feel like playing us some of your Elizabethan music? You will have an appreciative audience. Edward here is all ready and waiting. You can't disappoint him.'

Charlotte fetched her guitar and sat quietly in a corner on a high stool which James had bought specially for her. The company relaxed and gave themselves up to the spellbinding music of Dowland and Orlando Gibbons, and the musicians of the seventeenth century. Her melancholy beauty perfectly matched the sadness of the songs. The heavy folds of her vivid blue caftan, her brown hair cascading down her back reflected the flickering candlelight. Small jewelled slippers glinted from beneath the hem of her dress. She looked apart from the solid university dons and their comfortable wives. James, looking at her, saw a Mary at the foot of the cross; a Magdalena at Christ's feet straight out of a Zeffirelli film. Her eyes were expressionless. They looked across the room unseeing like a Byzantine icon.

James decided to propose to her at the next suitable occasion. He wanted to see those melancholy eyes light up with happiness. Someone produced a camera and took a photograph. She appeared not to notice the flash of light. Edward seemed hypnotized by her haunting beauty. He would never forget this evening.

She left at half-past eleven to drive the forty odd miles to her cottage. She shook hands with everyone, thanked James with genuine warmth for his hospitality, and slipped a scarf over her shoulders.

'Thank you for playing so beautifully,' said James. 'I'll see you soon.'

'Thank you for being such a kind audience. If I ever need a job I can always play my guitar,' she said with a laugh as she made towards the door.

'If you ever need a job, come and see me,' replied James seriously.

She drove off into the freezing night. The guests talked about her when she left, and James resolved to telephone her as soon as he could.

At the same time as Charlotte was intriguing James' guests, forty miles away at the Queen's Head in Shotley a foreigner was drinking whisky and water, very conscious of the curious stares from the locals. His appearance was unexceptional, except for the dazzling row of gold fillings in his white teeth. The regulars were fascinated. They only went to the dentist when extraction was urgent. To pour all that money into one's mouth was unthinkable.

A well-tailored brown suit, with a discreet stripe; a brown silk tie with a hint of amber, indicated a man of wealth and taste. His accent was perfect, that of an educated Englishman. Yet, he was undoubtedly foreign.

The three men round the bar silently drank their beer and summed up the newcomer. They had seen him arrive in a Rover, seen the expensive suitcase he'd brought in with him, and glimpsed the sheepskin covers on the front seats of his car. Such a display of wealth was unusual in this essentially rural community. Bill Davies, the local garage man, finally put down his glass and looked at the foreigner. He decided to take the lead.

'Are you looking for anyone special around here? We don't see too many new faces in Shotley, particularly at this time of the year.'

The stranger smiled – a charming smile that lit up his face and treated the three men to another glimpse of his expensive dentistry.

'Thank you, yes. I'm looking for a lady, as a matter of fact. I think she came to live around here. She's a friend of someone I know in Cairo, and he wants me to convey his regards.' The English was perfect, but too correct. The locals needed thirty seconds to grasp his meaning. Bill hesitated. He didn't want to make trouble for anyone by saying too much. He left it to others to continue the conversation.

The stranger came to their aid. 'But first, let me fill up your glasses. It's a cold night, so why don't you join me in this excellent whisky?'

The men at the bar immediately drained their glasses and looked alert. They sensed an evening's good drinking at someone else's expense.

'Why thanks,' said the second man. 'I'm a brandy man myself. I always drink it on cold nights.' The others agreed.

'An excellent idea. It's always nice to drink with men of taste. Landlord, bring over that bottle of Rémy Martin and the rest of the whisky, and we'll help ourselves.'

The three men couldn't believe their luck. It needed several brandies and a lot of flattery before they were willing to tell the Egyptian what he wanted to know. By then they had learned that his name was Ahmed el Azhar, and he wrote it out for them on a beer mat, laughing at their pronunciation. They insisted on writing out their names as well, and then the stranger tried again.

'Do you know of a young lady who lives near here? I expect she lives on her own. She's beautiful, I believe.'

'We don't know anyone who's beautiful,' said the garage man. 'There's only Miss Tragedy below Shotley Church. She's new around here – came from somewhere overseas, so I hear. She's far too stringy and jumpy for my taste. I like them a bit more . . .' The gesture he made was quite explicit. The others laughed.

'She's all right, though,' said his companion. 'She needs a man, that's all. She'll soon fill out with a couple of kids. All that digging and playing that guitar does her no good. Someone will have her one day, no doubt. But not me. I like them like Bill here. I expect you do too, sir. Oriental ladies are usually a bit more curvaceous, I believe.'

Ahmed noted the 'sir'. They were all mellowing. 'Yes, I like them full and soft, like a box of Turkish Delight,' he said. The men looked startled at this imagery, and then roared with laughter. The next quarter of an hour was spent in discussing women. As the level of brandy in the bottle went down, so the volume of noise in the bar increased. Ahmed chose his moment.

'So where does she live, this skinny lady?'

'About a mile away – maybe two. Go down the track opposite the pub, and she's at the bottom of it, near the river. Your car can just make it. A bit awkward to turn round, but you can pull into Mr Hastings' field, if it's not too wet, and do your turn there. Nowhere to leave your car, though. He'll be needing that entrance tomorrow, or Monday, to park his tractor. Still, maybe you won't want to stay the night. Miss Peel is hardly a piece of Turkish Delight.'

Ahmed nodded amidst the laughter. 'No fear of that; I just want to send greetings. I have a present for her, that's all.'

They all looked interested at this piece of information. Maybe Miss Tragedy was going to come into a fortune. Maybe this Egyptian was going to give her a fabulous necklace. There was enough here to keep them amused for the rest of the winter.

The bottles were nearly empty. The landlord was beginning to clear up the glasses. His wife came over to join the men who had moved over to the fire.

'You won't be able to see Charlotte Peel tonight. She's gone to Cambridge for dinner. She came here to buy a bottle of wine for the party. She won't be back until late, so I should go tomorrow morning. She's bound to be there on a Sunday.'

The landlady was fond of Charlotte in a maternal way, and was uneasy about the foreigner going to that remote place tonight. She was well brought up on the *News of the World*, and could imagine unspeakable things happening.

Ahmed knew what she was thinking. 'I wouldn't dream of troubling her tonight. I was hoping I might stay the night here. I have enjoyed your hospitality, and the company of these good friends.' He waved his hand towards Bill and his friends, who were settling down in a comatose heap in front of the dying fire. They weren't used to so much brandy, and it wasn't even Christmas!

Mrs Potter looked at them disapprovingly. 'And it's time you were out of here,' she said. 'You've drunk the best part of a bottle of brandy, and your wives will give you hell if you don't sober up quickly. That cold air will pull you together. Come on, it's closing time.'

She looked at Ahmed. She didn't like him. She didn't approve of strangers flashing their money around. He must want to see Charlotte very badly to waste a bottle of the best brandy on these layabouts. She felt uneasy. Nevertheless, money was money.

'Yes, I've got a spare room you can have for ten pounds, with breakfast. It's over the bar, so it'll be nice and warm. When these gentlemen go, which they will be doing in thirty seconds as the bottle's empty, I'll take you up there.'

The pub emptied – the men promising to be back the following evening for more of the Egyptian's generosity. They went out into the freezing night, arms linked, and singing 'For He's a Jolly Good Fellow'. Ahmed picked up his suitcase, and looked at Mrs Potter. He was quite sober.

'I'd like to go up to bed straight away, if you please. The whisky will make me sleep well. I shan't need breakfast before nine-thirty, as I expect Miss Peel won't get up early on a Sunday morning.'

She showed him the way to the spare room, at the top of the

stairs which went up from the corner of the bar. They were almost vertical, unchanged since the pub was built four hundred years ago. He had difficulty steering his suitcase round the bends. Mrs Potter was more concerned about the suitcase; she'd never seen one like that before – with the owner's initials picked out in gold letters on the expensive leather. In fact, she'd never seen so much gold before in her life – and all in the space of one evening!

Just an hour after Ahmed el Azhar fell asleep in his small bed under the sloping roof of the Queen's Head, Charlotte arrived home. She opened the door of the mole-catcher's cottage and breathed a sigh of contentment. The stove was still burning, and she undressed in the kitchen in front of the pot-bellied iron stove. For a few minutes she thought of Edward Wassim and James' kindness, then she climbed the wooden stairs to her bed. Wondering whether she ought to marry James, she fell asleep. Thomas guarded the house; the silent sentinel behind the chimney. Only the owls disturbed the silence with their eerie cries.

She woke up at nine o'clock the next day. It was freezing cold. Frost covered the windows, blocking out the pale spring light. It was the persistent tapping of the cat on the window which finally forced her to get up. There he was, sitting on the roof outside her bedroom, his fur puffed up around him like an eiderdown; his face indignant at being kept waiting.

Reluctantly she got out of her warm bed and groped for her dressing gown. With any luck she could give him his breakfast and bring her tea back to bed for an hour. The garden could wait.

She was hungry. James' food was delicious, but not sustaining. He was a fastidious eater – fussy in the way it was served, but underestimating his guest's appetites. Charlotte felt like eggs and bacon and lots of coffee. The kitchen was warm; the stove still burning. It only needed a rake through, and the front left open, and soon the flames were radiating heat into the small kitchen. She dressed quickly in jeans and pullover. The *Sunday Times* had arrived. The local shop delivered it to a hole in the garden wall. A generous tip at Christmas had persuaded the boy to ride his bicycle down the track. She needed her newspapers; without them she would be totally isolated, as though she was in another age, another world.

She put the bacon under the grill. There were plenty of eggs. The coffee was steaming in the percolator. She braved the cold and collected the newspaper from the hole in the wall. She glanced at the headlines, whilst she waited for the bacon to cook. Nothing much had happened since yesterday. She wasn't interested in sport; a famous football team had won a spectacular victory in Ipswich on Saturday afternoon. A bunch of thieves had robbed a jewellers' shop in Knightsbridge last evening. She read the item with some amusement. They had simply knocked on the door of the exclusive shop, and had been admitted. Then they had produced guns, pointed them at the terrified staff, and made off with several hundreds of thousands of pounds' worth of bracelets and rings and necklaces, including a very valuable diamond bracelet belonging to one of England's oldest aristocratic families. She reluctantly admired the cheek of the thieves. Not owning much jewellery herself, she didn't envy those who did. At least no shots had been fired. The thieves would be well out of the way by now. The beating up of old ladies for their small savings was quite a different matter. That sort of violence horrified her. But like a lot of people she admired the nerve of a good honest piece of thievery, where nobody got hurt, except the pride of the aristocratic owners. The police were watching all airports, but there were no fingerprints left on the doors of the shop, and the sales assistants had only a very hazy idea of what the thieves looked like. They couldn't even guess at their nationality, except they were all certain that they weren't black.

'Probably the Mafia,' thought Charlotte as she turned her attention to the eggs.

She had just finished her breakfast, and had turned her chair round towards the fire, when a loud knock on the front door made her jump. Thomas slithered out of sight under the armchair, and Charlotte sat there motionless. Perhaps the caller would go away. She wasn't expecting anyone; no one came to see her now. It could be the paper boy, or the local farmer, who dropped in sometimes to offer her firewood, or to leave a couple of cabbages on the front door step.

Again came the loud banging on the door. She ought to go and see who it was. There couldn't be many people out on a Sunday morning in this part of Suffolk. She stopped when she reached the door. Perhaps he had gone away. But again there was a loud knock, and this time a cultured voice called out, 'Miss Peel, are you there?'

The voice was reassuring. It sounded normal; the person wasn't drunk. It could be one of James' friends. She opened the door, leaving the chain fastenend. She saw a middle-aged man, well-dressed and well-shaven. His car, a Rover, was parked outside the front gate. He smiled at her.

'Miss Peel, I am so glad to have found you. May I come in? I have a message for you from Hassan Khatib.'

4

'She'll come.' Ahmed el Azhar looked down on the dapper little man lounging on the shabby velvet cushions. He felt uneasy on the house-boat. He didn't like confined spaces, and although Hassan Khatib's boat was one of the more luxurious on the river, he still felt unsafe. The shutters were open, and the rattle of the bead curtains irritated him. He couldn't understand this passion of the wealthy Cairenes for their house-boats. In high summer they were oppressively hot, and the smell from the river unbearably pungent – sweet, sickly, redolent of decaying offal and unspeakable remains.

The swish of a skirt behind him made him turn round uneasily. There was someone in the kitchen. He could smell Turkish coffee. So Hassan had a woman with him! He felt a prickle of irritation, maybe envy; Hassan seemed to have everything.

'She's a good girl – very sad,' said Ahmed. 'They call her Miss Tragedy in the part of England where she lives.'

'She was always sad; she takes life too seriously,' said Hassan. 'Why don't you sit down here?' He patted the cushion next to him. 'Coffee's nearly ready. Annette will bring it to us.'

Ahmed sat down uneasily. An Alexandrian, he wanted to get back to his own house, overlooking the Bay. There, the sea air was fresh, smelling of salt and fish; not this sickly stench from a river backwater off the island of Zamalek. It always made him think of rats; his scalp tingled at the mere thought. Once, he'd had to spend a night on this boat, and he'd been unable to sleep, imagining hordes of the brutes invading the boat. He'd spent the night sick with terror.

Hassan looked at him curiously. 'You don't seem easy. Relax. All the jewels have been disposed of. The bracelet is the last. Soon you'll get your cut, and then you'll be a rich man. That yacht will soon be yours. When is my little Charlotte going to come?'

'In two weeks' time. On April the tenth. I'll meet her at the airport and bring her here. She's expecting you to look after her. She'll bring the books in her hand-luggage, and I'll see she gets the parcel only on the morning she leaves.'

'How will you arrange that? We don't want her looking into the parcel to admire my choice of textbooks.'

'There's a boy who brings her newspapers. He leaves them in a hole in the wall. For ten pounds he's agreed to go to Ipswich Railway station and pick up the parcel. George will leave it there, suitably stamped. Charlotte thinks it will get there by an express service, called 'Red Star'. The boy has got a small motor-bike to get him to Ipswich. I didn't want to make too big a thing of it. In the sort of country area where Charlotte lives, they are all used to other people collecting shopping and parcels. It seems to work out well enough. The parcel will be well-sealed, so no one will be tempted to peel off the wrapping paper lightheartedly. Charlotte won't have the time, as she will be setting off for Heathrow, and the paper boy won't have the time or the patience to open it.'

'Good; it all sounds well under control. Bring her straight here, and she can then hand the parcel over to me without delay. Ahmed has got a buyer for the bracelet – a rich American who wants it for his girl-friend, and is not asking any questions about where it came from.'

Ahmed looked relieved. 'So it will soon be over. Stealing the stuff is the easy bit; getting out of the country is the worst part.'

'Not as difficult as getting the other into England. At least I don't have to steal heroin. It's always available in the bazaars. But it's getting very difficult to find carriers to take the stuff to London. Fortunately, good entrepreneurs are not easily defeated. We like a challenge.'

Both men fell silent as the girl came out of the kitchen carrying the tray of coffee. She was breathtakingly beautiful – very young, no more than sixteen, Ahmed thought. Her skin was tanned by the sun; her figure slender beneath the long cotton skirt, and the small bodice. She had not ripened yet. Long blond hair fell to her waist, and when she looked up at Hassan to see if she wanted her to pour the coffee, he saw that her eyes were a cool green. Hassan spoke to her gently in

French. As she leant forward to pour the coffee, he stroked her breast gently as though caressing a cat.

'My lovely Annette. She has breasts like nectarines – ripening in the summer sun. Not quite ready for the table though. I like to feel them swelling to my touch. Isn't she beautiful? She comes from France. Her father's an important man in the Army. She doesn't understand much English. She's learning, though, aren't you darling?' With a swift, and thoroughly professional movement, he leant forward and untied the lacing of her bodice. Ahmed saw a perfect breast, full and satin-textured; the nipple pink and delicate. As he watched, Hassan leant forward and licked it, his tongue curling like a cat with a saucer of milk.

'She likes being licked,' he said as the girl shuddered with pleasure. 'But back to the kitchen. We have business to discuss. Later, my darling,' he murmured in French. Reluctantly, she left them to their coffee.

'What is she doing in Cairo? She looks so young; no more than sixteen.'

'She's a student. She lives with three other girls in Garden City. I met her at the French Cultural Attaché's party the other evening. She'll do anything for me – anything. I have never known anyone with such a natural talent for giving pleasure in bed. I might send her to London one of these days when the regular carrier lets me down. She ought to have the opportunity to learn to speak English.'

Ahmed was amazed. Why had Hassan this fatal attraction for women? Outwardly, he was undistinguished – rather on the short side, a little too fleshy, and rather swarthier than the normal Egyptian. His eyelids were particularly dark, as though touched up with a blue paintbrush. But women loved him. He was uninhibited in their company. Ahmed had seen him lean towards a formidable English lady at an American dinner party, and, in the full view of her husband, nibbled her ear. If Ahmed had done this, he knew he would have been slapped round the face, and the lady would have left the table. Instead, she had looked fondly at Hassan as though she'd known him all her life, and had whispered something to him which had made him laugh.

'Why do women love you?' asked Ahmed impulsively.

'Because I love them,' was the obvious answer. Then, after a few seconds' thought, 'I also desire them, and that's the secret. They must feel desired, and then loved; that's all.'

Ahmed thought for a moment of his own wife in Alexandria – heavy after three childbirths, living only for the next spending spree in Venice or Rome. She was always bored, indolent, indifferent to his advances, and sinking into hypochondria. Where had he gone wrong? Where could he find an Annette?

He thought of Charlotte when he had left her on that freezing Sunday morning, in that tiny labourer's cottage. Why had she given up everything for this man? Her intelligence was razor sharp. She wasn't beautiful, but attractive enough to make some important man happy. She would look well in expensive clothes. She'd had an important job, a good income. Yet, this man had ruined her life, and might be responsible for her going to prison if she was stopped and searched at the airport. He couldn't understand sexuality. Hassan was no better-looking than himself. He'd heard it rumoured that he really preferred very young girls, on the brink of puberty. He knew he hired small boys for an evening's entertainment. Ahmed had picked them up for him at a certain silversmith's in the bazaar, near the University.

Ahmed finished his coffee, and stood up. He wanted to get away from this man, and this place. If he left now, he could be back in Alexandria by nightfall. It wasn't yet too hot. The Cairo spring was short, but delightful. Next month the desert road across the Delta would be like an oven.

'I'm off. I'll let you know the time when I can bring Charlotte to you. I know all will be well. She still loves you, you know, and would do anything for you. The sad thing is that she even trusts you.'

'Then it's time she grew up. Don't worry; I will give her a good time when she comes out. I'll put her in the Garden City flat, near her Embassy. Her friends will look after her, when I leave.' He shook Ahmed's hand. 'Goodbye; you have done well. I'll give you the money when I receive my parcel from Foyles Bookshop. I always liked that shop when I was in London. Be careful how you walk across the plank. You know what the British say about our river? One swim in the Nile, followed by ten injections?'

Ahmed remembered his nightmare, and shuddered. The rats were there, waiting for him under the plank. He dashed over the frail piece of wood, and walked swiftly to his car. He couldn't wait to get back to his modern apartment, made of clean concrete!

Bach's violin concerto in E Major came to an end. Charlotte looked across at James. It was the third of April, a week to go before she went back to the country she had left so abruptly, and never expected to see again. James was sipping his wine; he leant forward to stir up the embers of the wood-burning stove with a little brass poker.

They both loved Bach, preferably when played by a small orchestra. This recording of the violin concertos, conducted by Christopher Hogwood was one of their particular fravourites. James had taken Charlotte to concerts in London the previous autumn, and was hoping to persuade her to go to Cambridge at the end of the month for a performance of the 'Mass in B Minor'. He couldn't believe that Charlotte was going back to the country which had been the scene of so much unhappiness. She had just told him that evening about Hassan. Also that she was going back to this man who had caused all her past misery. He couldn't bring himself to think about what might happen to her in that huge city, this time without the support of her friends. He wouldn't accept it. Now was the time to force her to become rational. Surely the violin concertos, the embodiment of rationality, must have calmed her highly emotional state.

'You cannot go back to see this man – not willingly, Charlotte,' he began. 'How can you leave all this?' He waved his hand round the room – at the comfortable furniture, the Bang and Olufson record player, the one luxury she had insisted on buying when she returned to England. He wanted to include himself, but the time was not yet right.

Charlotte looked round her with distaste. The music had moved her more than she wanted to admit. Bach always calmed her. The discipline, the logical sequence of notes, the controlled sustained emotion was always cathartic. The last week had been a strain; for once, this evening, she felt calm and able to think clearly. Ever since she had opened the door on that Sunday morning, and had heard Hassan's name, she had been walking round in a dream. She had frequently to look at her airline ticket to reassure herself that it had really happened.

Ahmed hadn't stayed long; just long enough to arouse her emotions, and make her want to leave this peaceful and intellectual existence. He had said Hassan still loved her. She believed him. He had said that Hassan had finally persuaded his wife to divorce him, and she believed that. It was always what Hassan had wanted her to believe when she was in Cairo. She had left before he had been able to sort out his personal affairs. Now this was accomplished, he had sent for her. It all fitted together.

'You can't go back there,' James persisted. 'Not after all the misery he's caused you. How do you know he really wants you back? He hasn't bothered to contact you up till now. Why should he change his mind so suddenly? Without being rude, you haven't a job – your money is limited. How are you going to live out there?'

Charlotte silently rose to her feet, and turned the record over. Then she went to the desk drawer, and took out a brown envelope, which she handed to James. Inside was a British Airways ticket, a normal scheduled flight to Cairo. It was only a single ticket.

'There; it's dated for the tenth of April. He has booked my seat. All I have to do is turn up at the airport and Ahmed will meet me at the other end.'

James looked up. 'Is that all? Where will you stay?'

'I leave that to him. His friend assured me that I shall be well looked after. I will only need a small amount of money. If his divorce is through, then we can get married immediately.'

'He doesn't mention marriage,' said James, eager to grasp at any straw. 'Why doesn't he send a note? Why isn't he going to meet you at the airport? That's the usual thing for suitors to do.'

'Ahmed gave me the message. Hassan is busy that day;

besides he doesn't like airports. The ticket is enough. Why should he bother to spend all his money, if he intends to use me, and send me back again. The ticket is only one way.'

James was silent. The music went on inexorably, ordering his thoughts. He was used to persuading his students not to rush into matrimony. He used to think that was why he hadn't married. He knew all the reasons why he shouldn't. He never understood the overpowering obsession which overcame the most rational of people, to rush headlong into that state. He saw now that his gentle Charlotte was beyond reason. She had reached that obsessive state, almost bordering in madness. He also knew, with an alarming flash of intuition, that what she was about to do was destructive. He doubted whether he would ever see her again if she maintained her present course.

'My dear, I see you are determined. I cannot approve, but you have long since left my influence. Let me just say this; and then I'll go, and not contact you again. You were, and are, one of my brightest students – a star with a shining intellect. You would make a first-rate tutor. Any school or university would be proud of you. Don't waste these talents. Don't throw your life away. I know nothing about Egyptians. So far, this Hassan has not made you happy. In fact, you lost your job through him. He hasn't even contacted you to see if you were all right. For all he knew, you might have been living in utter destitution. You might even have died, for all he cared. Why does he want to see you again? You are too precious to become his plaything, or any man's plaything.' Even the logic of Bach could not control his emotion.

'Oh Charlotte; I have cared for you ever since you were my student. I know I'm an old bore. I haven't many interests outside my academic life. But I would do anything you wanted to make you happy. I have a passable house in Cambridge, and a cottage in the Dordogne. We could make our life together, if you wanted me. Don't go rushing out of my life for an Egyptian who has so far brought you nothing but unhappiness.'

Charlotte stood there, the air ticket in her hand. What could she do? The violin concerto was urging her to be rational; to think before she jumped over the cliff. Yet the air ticket was the magic talisman, luring her towards the unknown. She looked at James; his kindly worried face, his blue eyes looking at her with such affection. He really cared for her. He was offering safety and security – a calm anchorage after the storm of the previous year. Yet she knew she wouldn't accept his offer. She had to see Hassan again. She knew her life would be impossible without him. She could never be happy with James.

'I have to go,' was all she said.

James stood up. 'Then go you must. I wish you every happiness. But, my dear, if it all goes wrong, if this man turns out to be not what he seems, then don't hesitate to contact me. There must be telephones in Cairo. Just pick one up and call me – reverse the charges if you haven't any money. I will get to you on the next available flight. You are much too precious to waste your life in a strange land. When do you leave?

'On April the tenth – a Wednesday. I've got to get to Heathrow, but I might get a mini-cab to run me there. I have to wait for the paper boy, that's all. He's picking up a parcel for me from Ipswich station which I said I would take out to Hassan. Jimmy will meet the train.'

James looked curious. 'What parcel is that?' he said.

'Some books Ahmed ordered from Foyles when he was over here. He couldn't wait for them to be delivered, as he had to get back to Cairo. He asked me whether I would mind putting them in my hand-luggage. They should be here by the tenth. Jimmy said he'd go and pick them up. I can't understand why Hassan needs textbooks. He was never a great reader.'

James was used to people ordering textbooks. He'd often been asked to pick up books for his foreign students when he'd gone out to Rome or Athens. He nodded his understanding.

'He's probably ordered them for a friend. It's difficult to get good textbooks in those countries. They're very expensive out there as well. I only hope they're not too heavy for you to carry. Some of these overseas students have no idea how much books weigh. I hope they get to you safely.'

'Ahmed didn't seem concerned. If they don't get here in

time, it doesn't matter. He'll chase them up next time he comes over. He hoped they'd get here in time, that's all. It'll save him a journey later on.'

James fell silent. They listened to the end of the record. He knew he was beaten. Nothing could stop Charlotte now. She had never really left Egypt. She had always kept Hassan locked away inside her. He hoped desperately that she would be all right. She was too intense for her own good. But James was not worldy wise. He still believed in romantic love, and maybe this man was right for Charlotte. She probably needed a non-intellectual – a man to take her out of herself. James could satisfy her mental life, but deep down, he didn't really believe he could satisfy her emotionally.

He kissed her gently on the forehead. It was a brotherly kiss. He got his coat from the kitchen and picked up his umbrella. He always carried an umbrella. He detested getting wet. Charlotte had only once seen him lose his temper when an unexpected shower caught him without his umbrella. It was the anarchy of it which upset him.

She looked at him affectionately. She wished she could love him. He looked so safe, so normal. Why was she rushing off into the unknown?

'Goodbye, Charlotte. A safe journey, and a safe landing. I hope you find your pot of gold at the end of the rainbow. Don't forget though, that this is the twentieth century, and the telephone is very efficient. I'll be at Cambridge until the end of this month. By then you'll know if everything is going to work out for you. Don't rush into marriage. See what's offered. You're much too intelligent to spend the rest of your life in purdah. From May onwards I shall be in the States, but will be back again in September. If I were a priest I would pronounce a blessing, but as I don't believe in God, all I can say is "Look after yourself". I know it sounds trite, but you are the only one who can. At the end of the road we are alone. Just make the journey as nice as possible. Goodnight, my dear.'

He left without looking back, as he always did. She heard the car door slam and the sound of the engine starting up. Thomas slunk in to enjoy the last of the fire. She stood there for a moment with the door open, looking up at the stars, aware that she had rejected a good man's love. She still clutched her air-ticket, as if it were a lucky charm. At that moment, she had no doubts that the charm would work.

5

Charlotte detested air travel. She had travelled all over the world, but she still couldn't control that sick feeling as she walked towards the low door of the British Airways jet. The entrance into Hell! A step into a metal tube containing packed humanity. The door closing; the shrill crescendo of the jet engines as they revved for the take-off. The mounting feeling of panic as the plane waited for starter's orders. Then the rush into the air – the feeling of a power outside her control. She was trapped!

Other people seemed to be settling down; ordering drinks, opening books, looking out of the window. She sat there rigid with terror. She knew her fear wasn't rational. Her friends had explained the aerodynamics over and over again. She knew that the plane was in its element: it had a right to be thousands of feet above the earth, just as a boat had the right to be on the water. She knew that the machine had been designed for this purpose; but still her heart pounded, and her hands were damp with sweat.

Gradually, she relaxed, and asked for a tonic water. She wouldn't drink any alcohol, believing that if one actually needed it, then it was safer to refuse. Otherwise she would only be able to get on a plane if she was drunk. She never smoked cigarettes for the same reason. She suffered through this self-imposed discipline. She liked to be in control. Stress should be controlled by mental effort. There should be no need for props.

Only five more hours, and then she would see Hassan again. That morning had passed in a dream. The mini-cab had arrived on time, and the paper-boy had only just turned up as the car was about to leave. He had thrust the pile of books at Charlotte – remarkably heavy, but then books were heavy – taken the pound note, and then stood at the gate, waving them off. His mother would look after the house whilst Charlotte was away. She wanted to sell it, but James had been adamant that she should hold on to it, until she in fact married Hassan. For once she had given in. It was the only piece of advice she'd taken from a friend. She had kept single-mindedly on her course, her heart singing with joy.

So she simply walked out of the front door of her cottage, locked it behind her, and went to the waiting car by the gate. She handed Thomas over to the paper-boy. His cottage was similar to Charlotte's, so the cat would feel at home. He would have to get used to a different life-style, though. Jimmy's mother had neither the time nor the money to indulge a cat.

She felt a wave of nostalgia for Thomas and her cottage. This metal tube crammed with people was an alien world – a hostile one. She tried not to think of the jagged heap of charred metal if the plane fell out of the sky. She imagined the heaps of torn bodies, the piles of limbs. Once again she felt the mounting panic. She wanted to go to the lavatory, but nothing would induce her to stand up and walk along that metal tube. She tried to read. She'd bought herself a popular novel at the airport – something easy and funny to keep her mind occupied. She read without understanding; her brain tuned to the hum of the engine, ready for any change of note. The steward, reassuringly British, brought her the drink. The iced tonic water pulled her together. She checked her thoughts impatiently. The panic subsided, and she looked out of the window. She then glanced at her neighbour. Gradually, she felt herself relax. She began to look ahead to what she might find when she landed.

April was a tricky month in Cairo. It could be beautiful – not too hot; and the flame trees would be about to burst into a riot of scarlet blossom. The nights would be cool. It could be a perfect month, but the wind could change. Normally, the prevailing wind was from the north, keeping the air fresh. But sometimes, in the spring, it could blow from the south, bringing with it clouds of penetrating sand from the Sahara. The old-time fogs of London were nothing compared with the Khamsin of North Africa. Cairo would be covered in a suffocating layer of desert sand. The temperature would rise, but there would be no air to breathe. The dust covered everything

– chairs, tables; shutters couldn't keep it out. It filled eyes and ears. People wore masks in offices, to keep the dust out of their lungs. Psychologically, it was a bad time. Tempers were short. There was always an increase in the crime rate. Charlotte always felt unwell. Maybe the Khamsin would be late this year. She wanted a north wind with cool nights and clear bright days. Hassan would look after her, though. He always left for Alexandria when conditions in Cairo became unbearable. He liked the sea air when the air in Cairo became saturated with the sand. He always looked after his physical comfort; she really shouldn't worry.

But she couldn't stop the niggling anxiety. She hoped she hadn't lost too much weight. The yellow cotton blouse she'd bought in Cambridge for this journey had only been a size ten. The white skirt was also a size smaller than her usual. She didn't want to lose weight. Hassan had teased her about her 'boyish' figure. She now had doubts about the blouse she was wearing. Her skin was still sallow from the English winter, and the yellow was probably too bright for her. She pushed away the worry. Soon, she would become tanned in the long lazy days at the Gezira swimming pool. She'd spent hours there, lying in the sun waiting for Hassan to join her. She'd get out her Indian cotton skirts, and her emerald green bikini. She'd put away all those layers of woollen clothes, needed to survive an English winter on the East Coast. She'd given them to the paper-boy's mother.

She had wanted to buy a gallabiya – the national dress of Egypt, but Hassan had angrily dismissed the idea. He liked western women in western clothes – preferably expensive clothes from the great fashion houses. The gallabiya was the dress of the poor and ignorant *fellahin*. He contemptuously called it a 'nightshirt', and had forbidden her to buy the beautiful and graceful garment.

She checked this morbid preoccupation with her appearance. Of course she was different from eastern women. Hassan had admired her intellect – her trained mind. They had talked for hours. She remembered the conversations, the fun, the activity. Hassan had taken her sailing on the Nile. They had ridden horses in the desert – wild gallops across the sand, with the pyramids in the background. They had eaten at expensive restaurants; danced to western music. There had been picnics under the stars, and always the love-making back at the house-boat, or in her own flat. They had made love in the desert, under those stars. It had all been Heaven. Her first, shattering love affair! Nothing in her disciplined academic life had been remotely like this. She forgot her worries, and lost herself in daydreaming.

The engine note changed. They were going down. Charlotte's heart began to pound. She hadn't been able to eat a mouthful of food. For five hours she had sat in a tense, introspective trance, unaware of the piped music, the attempt at conversation from her neighbour, and the solicitous enquiries of the stewardess. Finally they had all given up, and Charlotte was left to her own thoughts.

She put away her book, still open at page five. She combed her hair, and dabbed her face with a wet tissue paper. She felt hot and clammy. Her face in the small pocket mirror was white, with dark rims of exhaustion under her eyes. She shivered and put the mirror away. She didn't look like a bride about to meet her groom.

The plane bumped along the runway. The potholes were still there. The airport was only a strip of the desert, and the runway had a habit of subsiding. The engines were now screaming into reverse gear. Charlotte couldn't breathe with terror. Finally, the plane came to a stop, and the engines reverted to their subdued hum. They had arrived.

After five hours of sitting in a cramped position, Charlotte's body was stiff and aching. She felt dehydrated, as she had been too terrified to ask the stewardess for more liquid. Her mouth felt thick and unsavoury. But her terror subsided as she stepped out into the Cairo sunset. It was only a short walk to the lounge where Ahmed would be waiting for her. She clutched her hand-luggage, and followed the others over to the cluster of lights which indicated the airport buildings.

Cairo! She remembered her previous impressions when she landed there the first time four years ago. The smell; it was unforgettable. Even though they were outside the city, the prevailing wind wafted the stench of the ten million inhabitants of Cairo towards the airport. The smell was unique – a mixture of raw sewage, open drains and the decomposing remains on thousands of rubbish tips. The people of Cairo lived on a steadily mounting pile of rubbish. The sewers, built by the British nearly a century ago, were quite unable to cope with it. Rubbish disposal systems were primitive and inadequate – men carrying baskets and dumping the contents into the open spaces of the city. In the western sectors, the roads were kept clean and the sacks of rubbish collected daily. But in the populous quarters of the city rubbish collecting was haphazard and infrequent.

That evening, however, Charlotte smiled at the familiar smell. This was the smell of her city. This was Hassan's city, therefore she loved it, and loved its smell. There were overtones of Oriental spices mixed with the sweet smell of decay. It reminded her of Arab cooking, and the scented oils used in cosmetics. Now, as they approached the airport buildings there was another scent – the pungent aroma of Turkish coffee.

There was the usual bedlam in the arrivals lounge. But she was familiar with this scene, and knew she had only to wait, and someone would come for her. Today, however, it wouldn't be a British Embassy official, but a local suffragi – a servant of Hassan's. Sure enough, a small figure in turban and gallabiya, with Sudanese tribal markings on his face, was pushing his way through the mob. She liked the Sudanese. They had always been friendly. Many of the Embassy servants had been Sudanese, coming to Cairo to work, and leaving their families behind in the villages along the Nile. This one, sure enough, was smiling his welcome. He shook her hand, and reached out to take her hand-luggage. Charlotte, remembering the precious books, shook her head, and held on firmly. She shook his hand, though, and asked his name. His English, she knew, would be good. It was, as expected, Ahmed – the popular name in Egypt, and in fact throughout the whole of Islam.

Once through the formalities, they went out into the last lounge, where the noise and the crush of people were unbelievable. But there was the other Ahmed waiting for her, and smiling his welcome. She let him take her luggage, and the suffragi put the suitcases into the boot of the waiting black Mercedes before melting away into the dusk.

'A good flight, I hope?' asked Ahmed.

'Uneventful, thank heavens. I hate flying. It seems the most unnatural way to get around.'

She got into the seat next to Ahmed. There was no chauffeur. The Mercedes moved off into the deepening twilight. She'd forgotten how quickly night fell in North Africa. She was used to the long evenings in England. By the time they had reached Bulac, the crowded suburb to the north of Cairo, night had fallen. She knew the road though, and waited impatiently for the glimpse of the Nile. They would cross it by the July the Twenty-Sixth Bridge, as Hassan's house-boat was on the west bank of the island of Zamalek. The car moved quickly along the wide sweep of the Corniche, then over the bridge. She caught a glimpse of a *felucca*, the sailing boat of Egypt, making its way towards Upper Egypt, against the current, but with the wind filling its distinctive triangular sail – 'Not unlike a Thames barge,' thought Charlotte.

The wind coming in through the car's open window, was not like the Suffolk wind, though. This was soft and warm. Outside, the sky was dark and velvety and the stars seemed enormous. The scent of jasmine was everywhere. She felt her excitement mounting, as they left the bridge, and turned along the leafy streets of the residential quarter of Zamalek. Here were the villas of the wealthy – the foreign diplomats, and the businessmen. Off now along the edge of the river, along a small road that petered out into a dust track. The Mercedes stopped beneath a palm tree, and Charlotte caught her breath at the sight of the familiar outline of Hassan's house-boat. She could see the lights shining through the frail structure of the cabin. There was the gleam of copper through the unshuttered windows. Her mouth was dry with excitement. This was the moment she had been waiting for over the last few months. The moment she had dreamed about, but never expected to see in reality.

Ahmed walked round and opened the car door for her. He smiled reassuringly. They hadn't talked much on the journey from the airport. He wasn't at ease with this reserved girl. He felt vaguely guilty at the part he was playing in this comedy. Somehow, it was all turning into a tragedy, as, unbelievably, he was feeling sorry for Charlotte. He was a hard man, and he knew that after the next day, he wouldn't ever see her again. She had the bracelet in her bag, and he would get his money from Hassan. He always paid promptly. But he wished she didn't have such large eyes. She looked like a lamb going to the slaughter, as she timidly walked over the gangway to where Hassan was waiting for her.

'He's inside, my dear. Don't be scared. He'll be delighted to see you again.'

His voice gave her courage, and she walked the last few feet with greater confidence. She remembered this boat so well. She walked across the wooden deck and pushed aside the bead curtain which covered the entrance to the cabin. Down the little companionway, past the kitchen. The sound of music greeted her – the westernized version of Arab music, which Hassan liked, more typical of the old Beirut than Cairo. It was the same voice of the French singer which he had always played in the past – smooth and seductive. Only the drums in the background were Oriental. Her senses were finely tuned to every detail. She heard the soft music; she smelt the spices of the cooking; she felt the man's presence.

There was the man himself, rising up from the cushions with the grace of a cat uncurling itself after a long sleep. He bowed. His face smiled a welcome. Ahmed watched him, and then looked at Charlotte. She was transfixed – mesmerized by this man. He looked away. He couldn't bear the thought of the pain she was about to suffer.

He used joviality to hide his embarrassment.

'Here she is. I've brought her to you safe and sound. Now can I go? I've got to get home, and I'm coming again tomorrow to take Charlotte to her apartment. What time do you want me?

'Not early,' said Hassan, still looking at Charlotte. 'She'll not want to hurry away. Has she got the books?'

Ahmed felt sick with loathing. 'Of course – why not?' Here is your bag, my dear. You forgot to bring it from the car.' He wanted to tell her to run whilst she still could; to jump into the car and he would drive her to Alexandria, to his wife, who was a good woman, although not beautiful. She was too young, too vulnerable for this man. He would kill her, and she would disappear without trace, as so many had in this teeming city. But, like the snake caught by the snake-charmer, Charlotte was beyond reason. He doubted whether she was physically capable of running to the car. Her eyes never left Hassan's face. She scarcely noticed Ahmed's departure. Hassan advanced slowly, and took Charlotte's hand. It was a formal handshake.

'Welcome back, Charlotte,' he said. 'Welcome home.' Ahmed had had enough. He backed away towards the bead curtain.

'I'll come tomorrow at twelve. Then you should have things sorted out.' He left them together. For the first time in his life of shady dealings, and the single-minded pursuit of money, he felt ashamed. He hated Hassan. The quicker he got that man on the boat leaving Alexandria tomorrow night, the better. He didn't want to see him again, ever. As for the girl, she would have friends in the Embassy. She'd probably come to no harm – but she would suffer. She looked born to suffer.

6

Hassan was the first to break the spell. He put his arms around the transfixed Charlotte, and gently kissed her on the forehead. This was not the moment for high passion. Besides, she looked so ill; her small face was white with exhaustion. Her eyes, when she finally looked up at him, were enormous. He hadn't remembered her eyes. They could haunt you.

'Come and sit down. Don't bother to unpack your suitcase. I have found you a beautiful apartment in Garden City near your friends in the British Embassy. Tomorrow, we'll take you there. You will be able to look out over the Nile towards the pyramids, and there are two balconies for you to relax on. You look tired – a rest will do you good. You need to eat more as well; you're so thin! What have you been eating in that primitive part of England you were so fond of? You need good Egyptian food.'

He led her gently to the windowseat. The velvet cushions were the same as she remembered them – purple with rose-coloured tassels. She hadn't remembered the tassels. Her legs felt weak, and she sat down gratefully. She couldn't speak. Hassan grew alarmed at her silence.

'Let me fetch you a drink.' For a good Moslem he kept a well-stocked bar. He poured two whiskies, and she drank hers quickly. She felt the warm liquid burn her throat, and the colour poured back into her face. Hassan looked at her approvingly. 'That's better.' He refilled her glass. This time she drank it more slowly. She was beginning to come out of her trance.

Hassan decided to be matter-of-fact. It would make her relax more quickly. He resorted to platitudes, knowing that the English middle-classes were at home with small talk.

'Was the journey pleasant? Did they feed you well? Tell me about your cottage in Suffolk. Is that what they call that part of England? I should have offered you tea – China or Indian?

Milk and sugar?' she smiled, looking up at him – her eyes more enormous, washed by the rising tears.

'Oh, Hassan how English you are! Yes, of course the flight was all right. Yes, they fed me, but I wasn't hungry. Yes, I've left my cottage in Suffolk, and my cat Thomas. I shan't go back again.'

Silence, as she drank her whisky. Hassan picked up her canvas bag, her hand-luggage in the plane.

'May I? My books, I mean. Thank you for bringing them out to me. They're on English architecture, for a friend of mine at the University. He admires your buildings, particularly the English colleges. He especially wanted the Pevsner. He will be most grateful.'

He took the parcel out of the bag, and walked with it to the inner room, his bedroom. She heard a drawer open and shut. She was glad to have been of use. She was too tired to be curious.

'Now my dear, food. You look famished.' He had become brisk and cheerful, firmly in control. He went into the little kitchen and reappeared with a dishful of batarikh, 'caviar' made from the roe of the grey mullet. He piled some onto a plate in front of her, and much to her amusement, passed her a dish of Bath Olivers. He reached forward and filled her glass with more whisky. It went down well with the batarikh. Russians would have drunk vodka.

'Where on earth did you get these?' she asked as she spread butter on the biscuits, and heaped the 'caviar' on top. Suddenly she felt hungry.

'From friends in your Embassy. When anyone goes to London I always ask for Bath Olivers. I love them. I eat them with marmalade for breakfast. They're better than toast. When in England I eat real toast, made with English bread. But that's difficult to get out here. So I eat Bath Olivers instead.' She laughed; the ice was broken. Hassan watched her relax. Soon, she would sleep for hours.

He got up to change the cassette. The Arab music had come to an end. The other side was softer – the liquid voice of a Lebanese singer. He knew she loved music. She actually listened to it – it wasn't just background music for her.

'Fairouz,' he said. 'You remember?' She was the Arab singer she had admired when she was last with him. 'This was recorded in the Lebanon – at the Baalbeck Festival – a few years ago, now.' The voice was like honey – a sweet cascade of Arab harmonies. She listened, speechless with pleasure. It was all she had imagined – the food, the music, the scent of jasmine and spices, and the man. But the reality was better. The nightmare of the aeroplane had all been worthwhile.

Hassan smiled to see her relaxing. He liked happy faces around him. He didn't like tragic heroines with reproachful eyes. What had Ahmed said the locals called her in England? Miss Tragedy? He would change all that. For this evening anyway.

He took the plates into the kitchen and reappeared with a plateful of spit-roasted pigeons, steaming hot and swimming in a rich brown sauce. The smell of roast meat and spices made Charlotte feel faint with hunger. She hadn't eaten a proper meal for ages. During the last few days at the cottage, she had been too excited, and too nervous to eat much. Now, the combination of the whisky, and the relief that she had actually arrived, and that Hassan was pleased to see her, released her appetite. She ate as though she was starving.

Hassan looked at her approvingly as she gnawed the small leg bones, and mopped up the sauce with the tough Arab bread. He brought over a bottle of the local red wine. She smiled when she saw the name – Omar Khayyam. It looked like a joke, but she remembered how good it had tasted before. All the Egyptian local wines were good. It was strange how they were not exported to Europe. They were far superior to the rough wines of Greece.

He spooned more of the rice stuffing onto her plate – rice, soaked in the juices of the pigeon, and mixed with currants, nuts, and chopped liver. She ate greedily. Finally, she washed her fingers in the little copper bowl by her plate and leaned back on her cushion. For the first time she looked confidently across at Hassan. He hadn't changed; the same laughing eyes, the same white teeth, the same taut, lithe body. He was probably older than he looked, but tennis, and the daily game of squash kept him fit. He was always full of energy. A rest after a game of tennis at the Gezira sporting club, and then he was ready to dance, or ride horses, or order his guns for pigeon shooting. She saw his muscles outlined through the thin Egyptian cotton shirt. He liked English tailored suits too, when the weather turned colder in the winter. She had only seen him in shorts at the swimming pool. She looked again at those strange, blue-lidded eyes. His lips were full and red with health; his hair, thick and black, had a strong natural wave. He was a beautiful male animal. He exuded health, sexuality and confidence. She would give up everything to stay with him. She wanted him more than anything else, and would have been glad to be just his servant. Marriage was beyond her wildest ambitions.

He brought over the bowl of grapes and handed her a small bunch. This time he stayed with her, relaxing by her side, and looking at her in a provocative manner.

'So – you've come back to me. Are you glad to be here?'

'Yes. This time you will never get rid of me. I am here for ever. England has no more appeal. I'll become Moslem if you want me to.'

He laughed. 'That won't be necessary. Besides, you'll then have to stop drinking this,' he indicated her glass. 'And also you'll have to agree to me having at least four other wives.'

'You won't need anyone apart from me. I'll keep you happy.'

'Is that a threat or a promise?' He leant over and stroked her cheek. The touch sent a shiver of desire through her body. He drew back. He needed her more relaxed. These English girls were far too inhibited! Yet, release the tension and they could become lionesses. This one, he remembered, liked to bite. She'd left him last time with outlines of her small teeth all along his shoulder. They had laughed at him in the changing rooms after squash.

'Aren't you going to look at your books?' she suggested playfully. He shook his head.

'Later. They're not for me. I'm not all that interested in

architecture but I do like to study the symmetry of the human body. Take your clothes off.'

He grew suddenly tense. She saw the pupils of his eyes dilate with sexual arousal. The abrupt command took her by surprise, but she felt the answering ripple of desire flood through her body. She remembered the hardness of his athletic body, and pushing aside the bowl of grapes, she stood up, and unbuttoned her yellow blouse. The voice of the Lebanese singer ululated softly – the drumbeat had become slow and seductive. The blouse fell to the floor, and she kicked it aside. She wore no bra; her small breasts needed no support. They were unformed, like a boy's, but the nipples were brown and prominent. Hassan gazed at her. She had the appeal of a boy. He thought of the number of teenage boys he had enjoyed from the bazaars. They had bodies like this.

Now he couldn't wait. He pulled her to him, and in one brutal gesture ripped off the white skirt, breaking the zip fastener at the waist. He bit through the frail lace of her white bikini pants. He sensed her anxiety. He was too rough. He laid her gently on the rug, and began to lick her all over, as if he were the lioness, and she the cub. She had forgotten his tongue. It was rough and prehensile. He liked to taste his women, and this one was different. She didn't wear any perfume, and he liked that. She tasted of the western world, of soap, talcum powder, and the faint odour of cigarettes from the air travel. He liked her thin muscular legs, the thick bush of coarse brown hair between her legs, and the hair under her armpits, which she never shaved. Her arms and legs were covered in a soft down which he also liked. He had tired of the smooth, full flesh of Egyptian women. He turned her over, and licked her small tight bottom, so unlike the backside of an Arab woman. He parted her flesh and licked vigorously along the inside of her thighs. She began to moan with pleasure. He would like to have taken her like he took the boys of the bazaars, but he knew she wasn't ready for that. That wouldn't be his pleasure tonight.

She had turned over, and was sitting up on the rug, her eyes huge with love and arousal. 'My darling Hassan. We shall never leave each other.'

With a groan of pleasure, he pulled her to him. She stretched out her legs on either side of him, and it was in this position that he took her. He knew how to use his penis, large and thick, and he waited for her to cry out with pleasure again and again before he came himself. She lay back exhausted, her brown hair streaming around her shoulders, her eyes closed. She looked lovely like this. Her body, in a strange way was beautiful. The lines were long and graceful, the muscles firm.

He got to his feet, and fetched a rug from the chair.

'Don't get cold, my darling. Remember the air in Cairo is very treacherous.'

She was already shivering, so he lifted her onto the couch, and brought her some more wine, and the bowl of grapes. This time, he fed her with the fruit. She kept her eyes closed as he dropped the grapes into her mouth one by one. She offered him one from her own mouth – the games that all lovers play. He laughed and offered her one in turn, except he wouldn't let her take it, but kept her mouth pressed on his, and together they drank its juice.

The cassette had come to an end, but neither of them noticed. Hassan began to bite grapes over her body, lapping up the juice as it trickled over her stomach. She laughed with pleasure. He turned her over, her head pressed sideways onto the cushion. Now he was licking her shoulders and back. On and on went the tongue, now licking vigorously, now playfully flicking along her spine like a snake's. She felt sick with pleasure.

'Now you must lick me,' he said, as he knelt in front of her, his penis tilted like a spear. She kissed his lean body, tracing the outlines of the muscles with her own tongue. She bit him along his shoulders, and he cried out in pain as she bit his ears. Gently, he guided her lips to his penis, and she took the huge organ into her mouth with a cry of joy. She wasn't expert. She had never done this before, but so great was her desire, and so strongly had he aroused her, that all inhibitions were gone. She sucked and licked until Hassan groaned aloud with pleasure. He was surprised at her energy. With a shout as if in pain, he released himself over her tiny breasts. He fell on top of her, feeling the semen ooze over his chest. She was in an ecstasy of pleasure.

They lay there a long time, listening to the water lapping along the side of the boat. He got up to make some coffee; she got up to wash in the tiny bathroom. He began to think of tomorrow; she thought only of him.

When she came back, she was wearing Hassan's dressing-gown, looking very beautiful in the blue silk. She'd brushed her hair, and now sat back on the couch gazing at him with love. Together, they drank their coffee.

They sat like this for a long time listening to Fairouz. Charlotte's body felt relaxed, her brain clear. Hassan had got dressed. He'd even put on his tie. He looked composed and correct, as if at a business meeting.

'You must sleep now. Tomorrow, I won't wake you, but let you sleep your fill. Then Ahmed will take you to your apartment. I think you'll like it. There you must wait for me to send for you. I still have things to arrange with Stephanie, and my divorce is not yet through, so it would be better if we don't see too much of each other straight away.' (Stephanie was his wife. Charlotte knew this.)

'Why do these things take so long to arrange?' murmured Charlotte, nearly asleep.

'Lawyers are great procrastinators – especially Moslem ones. Also, my wife doesn't agree to the divorce, so that makes it complicated.'

Charlotte didn't doubt him for one moment. Idly she wondered if there were any children by his marriage. She'd never enquired about his personal life. He had never offered the information.

'Are there any children to organize?' she dared to ask. She sensed his displeasure at the question. His body became tense. She didn't want to annoy him.

'I'm sorry. I wanted to know, that's all.' She reached up to kiss his dark face, but found him suddenly withdrawn.

'There was one – a boy, but he died when he was still a baby. We don't talk about him.'

She wanted to hug him; to comfort him as one would a hurt child, but he looked withdrawn, almost hostile. She decided not to risk the gesture. He stood up.

'Come, I'll show you your room. You must get some sleep now.'

She looked bewildered. 'Why can't I sleep with you? Who will clear away all the plates?'

'How English you are! Annette comes tomorrow, and she looks after all that. She musn't find us in bed together; she'd be very shocked.'

She felt disappointment. She wanted to sleep in his arms – to feel the comfort of his body, and be reassured of his love. She had given up so much to be with him. She didn't want to be separated for one night.

'Of course not – I forgot. But I love you so much, and can't bear not to be with you.'

Hassan hated clinging women. He actually disliked sleeping with anyone. Love-making and sleep were two different things; two entirely separate activities. He didn't like the proximity of a body, except during the actual sexual act. The 'togetherness' of married people irritated him. Sexually expert, he disliked physical contact. He didn't like being touched by people at parties. Outwardly gregarious, in reality he kept a wall between himself and his fellow men. Having used Charlotte to relax his body, he couldn't get rid of her quickly enough.

'You are everything to me, Charlotte,' he said. 'But now, I insist you retire to your room. It's all ready for you.'

He helped her to her feet, and led her to a small room next to his. He kissed her gently, and stood watching as she took off his dressing-gown, and slipped between the sheets of the couch he had had prepared for her. It was a cool night. She felt relaxed and very sleepy. Her body was at peace, and her mind at rest. She had not imagined such happiness.

'Goodnight Charlotte, sleep well. I shall come for you tomorrow. Rest now.'

He turned off the light, and went to his own room. Charlotte lay there, listening to him moving around. Then she heard the sound of the water lapping against the sides of the boat, and the voice of a fisherman calling to a friend. A dog barked, and there was a scuffling in the reeds along the bank. Then silence, and she was asleep – a deep sleep of contentment. She had come home.

7

The door slammed; she heard the creak of the lift as it went down to the ground floor. She went out onto the balcony, and looked down to the road below. There was Ahmed, now ant-like in size, walking out of the building and getting into the black car parked outside the block of flats. She saw the car move off along the Corniche towards Old Cairo. She was alone.

She went back into the sitting-room and gazed round her new home. Hassan had done her well. The flat was large and modern – the type of accommodation suitable for a foreign diplomat or businessman. The parquet floor had been polished recently – probably that day – and there was a strong smell of furniture polish. She remembered the smell. It was because the servants made up their own polish using turpentine. The sofas and chairs were made of some sort of light wood. The quality was good, and the upholstery clean and light. She touched the material. It was silk – a strong silk, cream with a pale blue stripe. The wooden standard lamps with white shades looked as though Heal's had just delivered them. Charlotte was fussy about lighting, but she thought they would be adequate. She probably wouldn't be there long.

A dining-room annexe was at one end of the sitting-room: a rosewood table suitable for six people; six chairs covered in the same material as the sofa.

Windows were on two sides of the room. There were no curtains, but Venetian blinds would keep the sunlight out, and as the flat was at the top of the building, they couldn't be overlooked. She supposed there was a kitchen. Ahmed had shown her the bedroom that afternoon, and there was also a modern bathroom. He had said there was a spare bedroom, too.

She looked inside the sideboard, and someone, she supposed it was Hassan, had left her a bottle of whisky. On the desk by

59

the door there was a huge box of Italian chocolate liqueurs. She smiled at his generosity. She poured herself a glass of whisky, feeling guilty as it was only early afternoon, and she had been brought up to believe that alcohol before six o'clock in the evening was sinful. Now, she needed a drink. She had hated saying goodbye to Hassan. She had clung to him like a child, and Ahmed had had to prise her away from him, and lead her gently to the waiting car. She was also suffering from shock. She felt weak and unconfident. She wasn't at all sure what she should do. Up till now, her life had been ordered for her. Embassy officials had met her at airports, and had taken her to flats and colleagues. Her social life had been organized. There was always an office, a desk, and a waiting secretary.

Now everything was changed. She had placed her life in the hands of one man she hardly knew. 'Never put all your eggs in one basket,' James had once said. Now there was only one basket, and one egg.

So far, everything was wonderful. The flat was almost certainly the most expensive in the block. It was the best she had ever stayed in. Probably Hassan owned it; he might use it to put up visiting businessmen. It might be his company flat. She would probably be able to use it as long as she liked – at least until her marriage.

The whisky made her feel bolder. She went outside onto the balcony again and gazed around her. The view was overwhelming. She was eleven floors above the city. On the far horizon she recognised the unforgettable silhouettes of the Giza pyramids. They looked remote and aloof; awful reminders of man's immortality.

The Nile, then the desert. The boundary between the two was startlingly clear. There was the cultivated strip along the Nile's edge, with its palm trees and rice fields, and the cluster of mud huts which made up a village. She remembered how she and her friends had once stepped over from the irrigated fields to the desert. It was almost as if an artist had drawn the line with a ruler.

Immediately below her was Roda Island with its strange, garrison-like building. She didn't remember having seen it before. It couldn't be a garrison because there were no signs of soldiers, only a queue of Egyptians in white gallabiyas waiting patiently outside the gates. They were very orderly. Lots of them carried baskets of food. She didn't think it was the prison. She thought that was in another suburb of Cairo. It could be a hospital.

The waterseller was doing well. She heard the clinking of the metal cups as he poured water out of the bag on his back when called. She smiled as she saw him. She'd always wanted to taste this water. Sometimes it was flavoured with liquorice. But her friends had always stopped her. Europeans hadn't acquired the immunity to local germs.

She sat down on one of the cane chairs. Egypt was spread out before her. She felt like Christ on his mountain, tempted by the Devil. For thousands of years people had lived in this land. The Pharaohs had built these pyramids whilst the British were still in neolithic times. Their irrigation techniques had been amongst the most advanced in the world. It was strange to sit there and gaze out towards those monuments of man's longing for immortality, and at the same time hear the weird call of the muezzin from the minaret of a nearby mosque – 'There is no God, but Allah, and Mohammed is the Messenger of Allah.' This was proclaimed from every mosque, yet she could sit there and be acutely aware of the ancient gods of the Pharaohs.

All religions came together in this fascinating city. She could just see the towers of Old Cairo – the stronghold of the Copts, the ancient Christians of Egypt, whose rituals had been fossilized back in the seventh century. All the other Christian sects had settled in this city – Anglicans, Armenians, Greek Orthodox, Roman Catholics. There were the Jewish quarters and, of course, it was the chief city of Islam. The mosque of El-Azhar, which she had visited many times before, was devoted to the teaching of the Prophet. It was a city where one was overwhelmed by the past. Spread before her was the huge canvas of man's struggle to understand the meaning of life. . .

Charlotte shook off a growing depression. The Egyptians had always been preoccupied with death. She had experienced life only yesterday on the house-boat. She could look forward to life and children. Yet everywhere, there was this sense of death. She got up to explore the rest of the flat. She kicked off her sandals. She would have liked some music, but there was no record player, not even a radio.

A small flight of stairs led to the top of the building. The flat was really a penthouse, and on this next floor, there was her bedroom and a modern bathroom. She turned on the shower, and was pleased to find there was plenty of hot water. She admired the marble walls and floor, and decided to take a shower before she went any further.

Soap and talcum powder had been provided. She got under the scalding hot water and rubbed her body, and washed her hair. She smiled at the bite marks on her stomach and shoulders. She remembered with a shiver the passion of the night before. She pushed away the memory; it was too powerful a sensation to think about now. She needed to distance herself from that scene. An intellectual, she liked to analyse sensation. But last night had been too overwhelming to understand. Another night's sleep, and then she would go over the details again.

Dressed only in a large towel, she went into the bedroom, and began to unpack her clothes. She hadn't brought many. Just enough to see her through the first few weeks. Then, as Madame Khatib, she would have to buy another wardrobe. She smiled at the thought of herself as Hassan's wife. She'd never wanted to be a wife before, always preferring her independence. But she was now quite ready to submit to anything Hassan desired, even the servitude of being a Moslem wife.

It didn't take Charlotte long to hang up the few dresses and fold the tee shirts away in the chest of drawers. She put on the blue cotton dress — a shift, with no sleeves. Then she brushed out her magnificent hair, and went down to the kitchen. She thought it was by the front door.

There was not much to see — a large fridge, a small primitive cooker, which seemed to work from a large container of gas underneath the stone sink. There was only one cold tap for water. She'd have to boil water or carry the washing-up to the bathroom.

She poured herself another whisky. She felt herself relaxing. This was a beautiful apartment in a beautiful city. She had a wonderful lover, who was soon to be her husband. She would make friends, and entertain. Perhaps James would come from England. He could stay in the spare room. She didn't think he'd ever been to Egypt. He would love Cairo, and haunt its museums and churches.

Thinking of James, she decided to look at the spare room. She went upstairs, carrying her drink, and opened the door of the small room next to her bedroom. She was surprised to see a door leading out to another balcony. So there were two balconies, one looking west from the sitting-room, and one to the east from the back of the flat. She would be able to watch the sun rise over the Moqattam Hills.

She stepped outside. The balcony was larger than the front one. This is where she would sunbathe in the mornings. The view was even more spectacular. The Old City of the bazaars and mosques lay beneath her, with its labyrinth of dark streets. She was above the incessant hooting of the cars stuck in a perpetual traffic jam. Yet, above the noise, she heard a donkey bray. It was a wail of despair and protest – from a creature doomed to a life of kicks and curses. She hated the sound.

There in the distance were the towers of the Mohammed Ali mosque, and the outline of the Moqattam Hills. All around her wheeled the sinsister shapes of the kites – forever hovering over the city in search of food from the rubbish tips and the cemeteries. She remembered these birds; loathesome scavengers, preying on human decay.

She shivered and went inside. She wouldn't use this balcony. Outside there were too many reminders of man's mortality. This was not the city of the Arabian Nights. It was a city weighed down by its ten million inhabitants. Out there in the old city one could decay and die, forgotton by friends. One could sink without trace; one's body, food for those repulsive birds.

She went downstairs and opened the door to the other balcony. There she would sit and wait for the sun to set behind the pryamids.

She must have dozed off, because when she woke up, she was startled to hear a key turn in the front door. For a moment, she thought it was Hassan. Maybe he'd decided to come early to see how she was. Perhaps he'd finished his business sooner than expected.

She got up and went into the sitting-room, hoping to see the brisk figure of her lover. Instead, there stood a little man, smiling at her shyly.

'Good evening, lady,' he whispered in broken English. 'Is there something I could do for you?'

She looked at him in astonishment. She liked his shy smile. His blue and white gallabiya was clean, and the turban round his head was spotless. He was obviously her servant, or suffragi. Hassan hadn't told her about him. He probably had thought she would take it for granted that there would be a servant with the flat.

'Good evening. What is your name?' A pause whilst he thought for a moment.

'My name's Mohammad. I am a suffragi. I come every day except Friday.'

'And what do you do?'

'Everything. I cook, clean and buy food. Is the apartment clean enough for you?'

'It's perfect.' So he had done all the polishing. 'What time do you come?'

'At eight o'clock. But tomorrow is Friday. I must go to the shops now, if you want me to buy food for tomorrow.'

Charlotte approved of his efficiency. He'd be far more expert at shopping than she would be. Her other suffragi had done everything. She didn't ever find out where he did the shopping.

'Are you employed by Mr Khatib?' she asked. Once again, the pause. She wondered whether he understood the question.

'Yes', he said. She wanted to believe he understood.

'Good; then I shall need something for breakfast tomorrow. I'll probably be out for dinner. Just get some bread for now, and some eggs – oh, a chicken would be useful.' She thought perhaps Hassan would eat with her tomorrow in this flat. 'Get some cucumbers and tomatoes, and a couple of bottles of beer.'

Once again he paused, and smiled at her. He looked at his feet. She waited, not understanding.

'You give me money, lady. I have none.'

Of course, he wanted his house-keeping money. She'd forgotten. Fortunately, she had some Egyptian pounds with her. She'd need to change some traveller's cheques after the weekend.

'I'm sorry. Please wait.' She ran up the stairs to her bedroom and picked up her handbag. She gave him a handful of pound notes.

'Come to me when you want more. Write down what you spend.' She wrote imaginary lists in the air. He understood.

'Lady, what is your name?' He looked embarrassed as the question was rather too personal. She smiled and told him. He looked relieved that she wasn't offended.

'Thank you. I call you Miss Charlotte.' She nodded. He went into the kitchen and extracted a straw shopping bag from the cupboard. So he knew the kitchen. He obviously went with the flat. She felt relieved. At least she wouldn't starve.

She watched him go silently out of the front door, and ring for the lift. He smiled reassuringly at her. She went back into the sitting-room, and heard the dungeon-like clang as the lift doors closed.

She felt mistress of her own house. It was only a matter of time before she would have a husband coming home in the evenings. She, independent Charlotte Peel, who up till now had resisted matrimony, was actually looking forward to a life of domesticity and socialising in a strange city. Soon she would have servants to manage, and entertaining to organise. She was beginning to look forward to this new life. It was going to be exciting and rewarding. Perhaps Hassan would let her help him with his work. After all she could type, and answer the telephone. He had told her that a lot of his work was in English. She ought to revise her Arabic. She had been very fluent when she'd come here before. She could have spoken to Mohammed in his own tongue. She'd surprise him when he came back. She wished Hassan would telephone. But he'd told her that he had business to see to that night. She'd have to change all that when she was his wife, Charlotte thought.

She occupied herself for the next hour, by imagining herself as Hassan's wife. She'd be happy to stay in this flat. The two of them would have a marvellous life here. Maybe, if there were any children, they would have to move to something more suitable. But somehow she couldn't imagine Hassan with babies. There would probably be a nanny.

It was dark when Mohammed returned. His shopping basket was full. She went into the kitchen to see what he had bought. It was mostly European food — butter, milk, eggs, a strange-looking cheese, and some tough white bread. There was also a bony chicken. It looked very undernourished. It might make good soup, though.

He'd shopped carefully, and all the prices were written down. She only glanced at them out of politeness. She hadn't any idea about the cost of living. Mohammed was delighted when she spoke Arabic. He congratulated her on her accent. He told her about the iniquities of the bus service. He lived in Bulac, not far away, but it took him over two hours to get to Garden City in the morning. She finally propelled him towards the door. She wanted to be by herself. She'd cook her own omelette, and get to bed early.

'Thank you for all your work,' she said to him. 'We shall get on very well. Now, I shall see you on Saturday, and you could make me my tea when you come. Leave the tray outside my door.'

'Yes, lady. I shall come on Saturday. Enjoy your first day in our city.'

He left her to her thoughts. Already she was feeling at home in her flat. She found a small frying pan, and made a passable omelette with some of the small eggs, the cheese and tomatoes. She didn't like the bread. He'd bought the white bread which Europeans always ate, as it looked like the bread they were used to at home. It was tough and tasteless. She ought to tell him to buy the local bread which the bakers carried around on their heads in flat baskets. He would be shocked. All the suffragis thought that Europeans should eat their own food. On Saturday, he'd probably try to cook her bacon and eggs, and toast the bread over the naked gas flame. Somehow, they managed. Her own suffragi had made excellent toast.

She finished the omelette, and put the plate in the sink. As there was no hot water, she'd leave the plate for Mohammed to wash up on Saturday. She felt guilty. Already, she was behaving like a lazy European. But she knew Mohammed would expect to find the washing up left for him.

She sat out on the balcony, and breathed the cool night air. There was the sound of the radio playing softly on the other side of the wall. So someone lived in the next flat. The music was western. She wondered what the radio station was. Perhaps it was a cassette, but then a voice spoke, and it was in Arabic. It must be the local station, or more likely, from Alexandria.

Cigarette smoke drifted over the wall. She found it comforting. There was another human being near her. Tonight, though, she didn't want to meet anyone. She wanted to breathe the air of this great city, and think of her life with Hassan. There would be plenty of time to meet the locals tomorrow.

8

Charlotte woke late the next morning. She hadn't slept well. She didn't mind sleeping alone, she was used to it, but last night she had been lonely. She missed the womb-like security of her cottage in Suffolk. She had dreamed a lot – uncomfortable dreams, lurid with sexual detail. She had been racked by anxiety. Again and again she had woken up in the night, trying to get her body comfortable. Perched on the top of a modern block of flats, she had felt like an eagle in its eyrie. She had wound the sheet around her body like the wrappings of a mummy, trying to find security in its tight folds. All that happened was that she had got too hot. She groped her way out of bed and opened the balcony door, but the sight of the full moon, and the vast expanse of the sky with its sprinkling of stars had overwhelmed her. She was terrified of so much beauty; she couldn't cope with it.

She closed the door, and drew the net curtains to block out the unearthly light of the full moon. She lay down on her sarcophagus, and drew the shroud-like sheets around her body. She was stiff with tension. Despite the temperature, she felt herself shivering. Her brain worked away ceaselessly, filing the events of the last few days into its memory bank. Some things she didn't dare think about. The last night with Hassan was still too powerful for her brain to digest. From celibacy in Suffolk to the overwhelming eroticism of the scene on the house-boat was too great a leap for her brain to cope with. She felt uneasy, almost sick, when she thought momentarily of the previous evening. She turned restlessly on her hard mattress.

When daylight came, Charlotte fell into the deep sleep of utter exhaustion. The pale Egyptian dawn gave way to the yellow light of a perfect day in early spring. She slept through the sounds of the city waking up – the blare of the car horns, the call to prayer from a nearby mosque, the scream of the donkey kicked into life to start the daily round of collecting the rubbish from the European dustbins, and the shrieks from the ever-circling kites.

It was eleven o'clock when she finally opened her eyes, and gazed up at the white ceiling. It was very hot. A fly had got in under the sheet, and was hurling itself against her bare leg. She tried to slap it away, but found that her arms were pinned to her sides by the winding-sheet. She was damp with sweat and very thirsty. She struggled to free her feet from the wrappings, tearing the sheet with her toenails as she did so. She felt tired, and ill-at-ease. The next night, she thought, she'd leave the sheet off, and the door open. No one was likely to climb in on the eleventh floor, and she would have to face up to the sinister moonlight.

But with the strong daylight, the demons of the night were banished, and she jumped out of bed, ready to face the day. She wondered if Hassan had telephoned, and cursed her laziness. The telephone was downstairs, so she wouldn't have been able to hear it. She had to be ready in case he called.

It was Friday, so there was no Mohammed. She made her own tea, and carried the pot with a dish of sliced lemons onto the front balcony. She wasn't strong enough to face the back balcony. She preferred to look out towards Pharaonic Egypt rather than mediaeval Cairo. The ever-wheeling kites reminded her of her nightmare – it was her flesh they were after.

She'd found some yoghurt in the fridge and remembered how good the local variety could be. She ate half the carton and put the rest aside to make the sauce for the chicken that evening. She expected Hassan would want to eat at her apartment that night.

The food tasted good in the clear air. The view lifted her spirits. The lemon tea, heavily sugared, restored her energy, and dispelled that feeling of menace. Everything felt normal. After her light meal, she would get a towel from the bathroom and spread it out on the balcony. Whilst she waited for Hassan to ring, she would soak up the sun. She expected the call at any moment. She remembered that Egyptians seldom telephoned in the early afternoon. Hassan, she knew, liked his siesta. He woke up when the sun went down. Mornings were for work;

afternoons for sleep, and evenings for play. She thought she would lie in the sun, and later on take a stroll along the Corniche. The Embassy was just a short walk away, and she would enjoy looking at the building again, although she knew that she could never enter those elegant gates again.

She stretched out in the sun, tucked up in the corner of the balcony, feeling her English body open up to the foreign sun. She tanned very quickly; she could spend hours soaking up the heat. She would only need sun-oil for the first two days; after that she could bask like a lizard, and watch the English pallor fade rapidly.

There was no sign of the cigarette smoke of the night before. Whoever it was did not spend the days at home. Perhaps he was still alseep. Friday was a holiday for Moslems. She didn't even know if he was Egyptian. Cigarette smoke is international.

She drifted off to sleep as the sun moved over the building on its path towards the pyramids. Her sleep that afternoon was deep and restorative. There was no moon to look at her disapprovingly. The food had given her energy, and calmed her nerves. She knew Hassan would phone that evening. She worshipped the sun and relaxed in its heat.

At half-past three Charlotte awoke with a start. Her first thought was whether she had missed Hassan's phone call. She cursed her laziness. Jumping to her feet, she went upstairs and ran the shower, noticing with approval that her skin was changing colour from the hated yellow to a pale milk chocolate.

The sun was losing its fierceness, and Charlotte thought she would walk along the Corniche towards the Embassy. She needed activity. Her body, now rested was demanding action, and she found herself waiting with sickening anxiety for the telephone to ring. He had to contact her today. She couldn't stay a prisoner in this apartment, comfortable though it was. He had forbidden her to visit the house-boat, so she had to occupy her time as best she could.

It was time to get to grips with the lift, and venture outside. She was procrastinating. In her Embassy days she had been over-protected. The comfortable umbrella of the Foreign

Office had shielded her from realities. There were always friends to go with her to parties, and sightseeing. There were always Embassy staff to call taxis for her. She had never had to walk alone around the streets of the city. Perhaps she really wanted to look at the Embassy again to reassure herself that life was still normal. She felt she was in a world of fantasy – a world she couldn't really understand.

Charlotte picked up the key and her bag, and went to the lift. It wasn't there. She pressed the button and waited for the clank and groan of the metal cage staggering its way from the first to the eleventh floor. There was no sound, and for one moment her heart pounded. Where were the stairs? What if there weren't any? There was no one around today. Usually these blocks of flats were alive with people rushing around – the bustle of the suffragis, the cries of the children, the black-cloaked figures of the nannies, looking nun-like and inscrutable. Today, all was silent. She felt suspended at the top of the world, unable to get down.

Then she heard the groan of the approaching lift, like a wounded animal. Why were Eygptian lifts so reluctant to be summoned? Why did they stop so unpredictably, and then, for no reason start with a jolt and gallop off into the unknown?

Next to flying, lifts were her second fear. It required an enormous effort of will to get into one of these monsters on her own. She hated that moment when the doors closed. Once again she was trapped. Technology had taken her over. The machine had captured her, and could grind her to pulp.

Some lifts were less frightening. The old-fashioned lifts which she had met with in Paris had not caused this terror. There, one got into a cage, open on all sides. One could look out at the passing floors, and wave to people if one felt like it. The French lifts were ornate affairs, friendly and solid, not like this one – a metal capsule which only held four people. Inside there would be no escape. If the electricity failed, which was a real risk, as Cairo was prone to power cuts, then she would be in complete darkness. She began to sweat with fear at the thought.

The capsule arrived. She stepped inside, her heart pounding. She pressed the button, and as she feared nothing happened.

'Thank God,' she thought, 'now I can go and find the stairs.' She moved forward, and at that moment, the doors slid shut, and the contraption set off at a sickening speed to the bottom of the building. Her heart thudded. She couldn't breathe with terror. She had put herself at the mercy of a machine and she couldn't escape.

At the bottom of the building, the same sickening delay before the doors opened. She had once before, in Brussels, been trapped for a few seconds in a lift in the Charlemagne building. But the Belgians had been quick to start up the monster again, and the delay had only been thirty seconds, hardly time to raise the blood pressure. This lift didn't inspire confidence. There was doubt whether it would actually want to go. When it went, would it stop?

The doors were reluctant to open. Desperately she clawed at the metal to force it open for the last remaining inches. As soon as there was space she jumped out, trembling with relief. Better the house-boat with its rats and dampness than that metal box.

Already, she was worrying about the return journey. Suppose it stuck on the way up, and she missed Hassan's phone call? She should never have left the flat, especially on a Friday.

Outside, the air was warm, and the Corniche deserted. She crossed the road, and looked down at the river. There were small children playing at the edge of the water, naked brown figures, laughing and splashing the water at each other. One of these tiny figures was on duty. He was looking after a very large buffalo, which the locals call a 'gamoose'. She had just drunk its milk, and eaten its yoghurt. The gamoose was a creature of general usefulness.

The small boy was on the creature's back; his only means of controlling it, a stick. With this weapon he was hitting the animal, trying to make it hurry up with its drinking. The gamoose took no notice. With a swish of its ear it brushed away the stick as if it was a fly. Slowly it subsided into the muddy waters of the Nile, ignoring the child's screams, and the irritating stick. With a groan like a woman in the last stages of labour, its knees gave way, and it collapsed in the mud, the boy, beside himself with rage, sliding off the shining back at the last moment.

With cries of glee, the other children joined in the fun, using the black back of the animal as a diving board. The one in charge continued to grumble, but gave up the battle, and helped the animal with its bath. He pulled up a handful of reeds and washed and scrubbed the great back, the beast groaning with ecstasy.

Charlotte smiled at the sight. The boy gave the animal shelter and took it to the food and water. In return, the gamoose supported the family – milk, meat and, finally, leather.

Strolling on towards the elegant colonial façade of the Embassy Residence, she looked out across the river towards the graceful shapes of the feluccas on the other side of the island. There was no one about. People were either asleep, or shut away in their houses and offices. This was the European suburb – the diplomatic quarter. Her old flat which she had shared with another girl was not far from here.

She arrived at the white wall of the Embassy. She stood looking at it from the other side of the Corniche. She could just see the top of the colonnaded front door. It was a splendid, colonial-style building, built for another age, when there was no doubt as to which country controlled Egypt.

She thought of the garden parties she had been to on that beautiful lawn, watered by hordes of servants. She remembered standing under that flame tree talking to British people who had come out of their apartments, and dressed themselves up in their finery to talk to the Ambassador. It was a yearly ritual to confirm national solidarity.

She remembered how she had called on the Ambassador's wife, an exotic figure in flowing caftan and bare feet. They had drunk China tea under the flame tree, and talked about Marks and Spencer's, and where to buy cheap plates for buffet suppers. It all seemed light years away. Now she was excluded from that magic circle. Her new life would still be in this city, but not centred on that kindly couple who had controlled her previous life. Now she would be one with the boys and the gamoose. They would be her people. The mosques and the bazaars would be her new setting.

Impatiently she turned away from the buildings. Here was

her Egypt below her. A felucca had drawn into the shore, and a team of workmen, their backs bent double beneath the load were carrying stones to pile up against the bank. The sight was timeless. She'd seen it depicted on the walls of tombs – teams of thin brown men, staggering along a narrow plank from a boat to the shore, carrying huge slabs of stone. These people were the real pyramid builders. Their backs twisted by the colossal weights they had to carry. They were the heroes of Pharaonic Egypt. Kings could order the monuments, but these tiny men literally carried the stones into place.

Remarkably agile, they jogged over the plank with stones piled into baskets which they carried on their turbanned heads. Women did the same work – pregnant women, and with a couple of toddlers clinging onto their own gallabiyas. On one side of this wall she had toasted the Queen's health, whilst on the other side, human beings were leading lives in the same way as they had done for thousands of years. Here, in this great city, the Space Age and the Bronze Age lived side by side.

She didn't notice the man come up to her.

'Is it really Charlotte Peel?' he said softly.

She turned round, and there was David Leigh. He was still shy and well-meaning in that essentially English way. She'd last seen him in the airport lounge. He'd been the only one of her friends who had come to see her off. He had been very upset over her resignation, and now he was standing next to her, looking embarrassed, and not quite sure whether he should be talking to her.

'Charlotte – what brings you here?' He noticed the dark rings under her eyes – she didn't look happy. Her whole body seemed to droop with exhaustion. He gave her the answer to his question. 'Are you on holiday?'

'Yes. I'm on my way to India – to Bombay. There was a chance to stop off for the night here, and I thought I'd take a last look at the city. It's still as beautiful as I remembered it. It's a long way from Suffolk.'

'Is that where you went to? I love East Anglia; the number of times I have stood looking at the Nile and thought of the Deben.'

'Is that where your home is?'

'No, not really. My parents lived in Ipswich.'

How strange to look down into the water and talk of Suffolk. Perhaps it was that David was British, and the subject was safe. He was far too well trained to mention sensitive subjects such as Charlotte's resignation from the Diplomatic Service.

'We miss you. We enjoyed your parties. Social life is not the same since you left us.'

Charlotte smiled. 'You're very kind, David. But I haven't missed the life. I love my cottage. I work in Ipswich, at a solicitor's office.' It was easy to lie to this earnest young man. It avoided awkward questions. Why didn't she say she was coming back to marry Hassan? After all, lots of people married divorced men. Now she had left the Foreign Office, she could marry whom she pleased.

'Where are you staying?' David was looking at her thoughtfully. She didn't look like someone on holiday; but then Charlotte had always been a loner, in spite of the fact that she had been one of the more socially active members of the Embassy.

'In the Hilton. I'm only there for one night. It was easy to book in there. My plane leaves tomorrow morning, but I felt I must get some air.'

It was easy to carry on lying once one had started. She wanted to avoid all mention of Hassan, but David decided to risk the subject. After all, he had been the cause of Charlotte's dismissal. It was why she had left under a cloud – in disgrace some might call it.

'Yes. It's safe, anyway.' He looked down into the water.

'I'm so glad you got rid of that Eygptian fellow, Charlotte. We've had a lot of bother with him lately. He's not exactly welcome at receptions these days. I hope you didn't hear from him again.'

Charlotte's heart missed a beat. She struggled for breath. The wall was near, fortunately, and she was able to steady herself against it.

'What's he been up to?' She forced a laugh. 'No, of course I haven't seen him again. I left all that behind when I left Egypt.'

'Thank God for that. We all thought there was something not quite above-board about him. He was too nice; too charming. Then the police came and began to ask questions. You see he was suspected of being involved in drugs – sending stuff to London. They've got no proof, but they were checking that no one had been asked to take a package to London. They know he was friendly with some of our staff. As it happened, we haven't seen much of him since you left. He just dropped out of circulation, as they say. So we weren't able to help the police.

'Then, yesterday, they were in the Chancery again. He now seems to be linked in some way with that Knightsbridge jewellery raid – I don't know if you read about it last week. Most of the stuff was smuggled out of England. But one piece, a bracelet, they seem to think may have come here. None of our staff has been to London recently, and we've no new arrivals. I say, are you feeling all right? Shall I call a taxi?'

'No thanks, I'm fine. It's just tiredness after the plane journey. I hate flying, as you know. I've also been working too hard lately. I shall be fine in a moment. Why do they suspect Hassan?'

'Oh – give a dog a bad name – that's all. He's been in prison before for some international thievery. We didn't know this, of course, otherwise we would never have allowed him to set foot inside the Embassy. The Ambassador was furious when he found out. He – that is Hassan – sounds a thoroughly bad lot. He served two years for drug-running back in the late sixties. That's where he got his money from. We'll soon know if there's any truth in these rumours, if he's left the city. They always bolt sooner or later. A good job you got rid of him, otherwise the police would be arresting you now for complicity.'

Charlotte looked at David in utter disbelief. She didn't believe a word of this story. The Ambassador must be suffering from the heat if he believed it. She'd seen Hassan the night before – he hadn't looked like a hunted man! He would come to her tonight, and they would laugh at the story. He'd never shown the remotest interest in drugs. His money was all in cotton. But she didn't want to seem too interested.

'He didn't seem like a crook,' was all she said, and dismissed the subject.

She wanted to get away from David Leigh. Her thoughts were in a turmoil. She needed to work things out alone. She had to go. Possibly, the man they were talking about, the wanted criminal, was even now trying to telephone her in the flat.

'I'm glad to leave you with these important matters. Give my regards to old Anthony. Tell him to stop finding dope-peddlers behind every curtain. I'll say goodbye, as I'm meeting someone for drinks this evening. Not Hassan,' she said with a laugh, 'someone I met on the plane who sells cars.'

'I'm glad to hear it. You worried us all with your taste for exotic men.' David turned, and made his way back to the Chancery. Charlotte watched him go. Another link with the past broken. She knew she couldn't go back to these people again. She had severed the umbilical cord. Her people were those little brown men down on the shore hauling the blocks of stone into position. They were Hassan's people, and they would soon be hers.

She walked quickly back to the flat. She had to see Hassan soon, and hear him deny those rumours. There was absolutely no proof. Even the police weren't sure. They were simply working their way through a list of suspects. Anyone connected with the business world and embassies would be investigated. Hassan was no drug-peddler. He despised junkies. It was ridiculous to think of him organizing a raid on a jeweller's shop in London.

This time the lift was waiting for her. She stepped in and pressed the button without thinking. Now her brain was in a turmoil. She didn't give the lift a second thought. Halfway to the top, a thought struck her, like a blow from a hammer. The books! The parcel she'd bought from London! She'd never looked inside it. Hassan had taken it from her as soon as she arrived, and she had forgotten about it. It was heavy – too heavy for a bracelet. Books were heavy. She knew that. Those days when she had cycled round Cambridge with a basketful of books were not so long ago. Why hadn't she opened the parcel? It had reached her too late in Suffolk. She was already on her way to the airport when the paper-boy came up with the package.

She pushed the thought out of her head. Hassan loved her. He said they were books on English architecture. Even solid James hadn't questioned the parcel. Hassan loved beautiful things — beautiful buildings — and books on western architecture were difficult and expensive to buy out here. He had promised to marry her. He was speaking to his wife this weekend. It was ridiculous to think of herself as his accomplice.

But as she walked into the empty flat, where the curtains were closed just as she had left them, she was overcome with a feeling of panic. She suddenly saw herself alone in this cruel city, unable to go near her friends because she might be accused of aiding and abetting a criminal — a thief on an international scale. Her legs felt weak. She had to sit down. She had to have air. The room suddenly felt stifling.

Charlotte opened the balcony door and looked out at the pyramids. 'Please God, let him telephone soon,' she prayed, not certain if she was invoking the Christian God or the gods of the Pharaohs. She desperately wanted Hassan to telephone there and then. She loved him wildly. She needed a sign that he was still there . . . She resisted the urge to have a drink. Drink never solved anything. Sometimes it helped her get to sleep.

She sat down on the edge of the cane chair. The muezzin had just begun the evening call to prayer. She was suddenly conscious that the city was very alien; that her ticket was only one way.

'Hallo there! Come and join me for afternoon tea. I'm sure you must be British. The British always drink tea at this time of the day. I've got cake as well.'

Startled, she looked up at a cheerful face gazing down at her from the top of the white partition wall. It was the smoker from the previous night. A shock of curly black hair, a ready smile and dancing eyes convinced her that he was a friend. He looked young, no more than twenty-two, and fun. His face was cheerful and irresponsible.

'That sounds nice. I'd love to come, but I'm expecting a telephone call.'

'That's no problem. I'll catch you as you jump over the wall, and I'll throw you back again when you hear the phone ring. Don't refuse my kind offer because of a telephone. It might even be out of order anyway. Phones usually are in this city.'

'You're right. I'll come. Wait, I'll fetch a chair.' She desperately needed company. She had to calm her imagination, and she liked the look of the face on the top of the wall. She liked his smile and his pedantic English. Like a lot of educated foreigners, he spoke her language too correctly, with a vaguely 1930s vocabulary.

She fetched a chair from the dining-room, and climbed to the top of the wall.

'Good evening. My name's Charlotte.'

'I'm Youssef, how do you do? Now, step down carefully onto my chair. I'll catch you if you fall.'

She jumped onto the young man's balcony. It was almost identical to her own.

'Now, come and have some tea. Do you take milk and sugar?'

9

He was very polite, very charming and very young – his face unmarked by experience. He lived for pleasure, and knew people liked him. He had never experienced rejection. He was now looking at Charlotte admiringly.

'I didn't realise I had such a beautiful neighbour. Usually, there are only businessmen in your flat; people who only stay for one night, and then go away. There's never been a woman there.'

'Thank you for the compliment. I'm only here for a short stay – on holiday, to see old friends. I used to work at the British Embassy, and I made a lot of friends here. What do you do?'

'I'm at the university – trying to learn medicine. I hope to cure all these people' – here he waved a hand over the city below him – 'unfortunately, in this country, medicine is linked with hygiene, which is linked with sociology, which in turn boils down to economics and finally politics. I don't really know where to start.'

Charlotte smiled. 'You'll be a student until you die if you try to understand all that lot. You'll have to take up religion too, as much of all this' – here she waved a hand over the Nile and the Corniche below her – 'is the product of Islam. How do you get rid of inertia, when the Faithful are always waiting for Allah to find the solution?'

'It's easier to leave it to Allah than stir oneself. Soon, it will get too hot to do anything. I'm sure energy and zeal are linked with climate.'

'I'm sure they are. Now I want to do nothing else except sit on my balcony and drink lemon tea. Disease and a bad water supply seem a long way away.'

'I'm so sorry, I forgot. Let me pour you some tea. I always drink it at this time of day, if possible. I'm going to your country next week, so, you see, I shall be used to your customs.'

Charlotte looked at the young man. 'Are you going there on holiday, or business?'

'Business, I suppose. I'm going to study at one of your hospitals for two years. St Thomas' in London. Have you heard of it?'

Charlotte smiled. 'Just about. It's one of our biggest. Which branch of medicine are you involved in, or aren't you old enough to specialize?'

'Nervous disorders. That's what I'm most interested in, as well as public health. The body is fascinating, but the mind is even more absorbing. I'm lucky to get a research grant to go to London. It is also my good fortune to meet a beautiful English girl who can tell me about her country.'

He poured out the tea very expertly from a very English-looking teapot. He carefully placed the sugar lumps in the cups. He handed the cup to Charlotte, who felt she was on stage in a 1930s drawing-room comedy. In fact, Youssef looked rather like a Noel Coward hero, with his English-type grey trousers, white skirt and striped tie. He ought to be making his entrance back stage centre through French windows, swinging a tennis racket.

'Is this your flat?' Charlotte looked round with interest. The furniture was the same as hers – the same light wood, the same striped upholstery. It seemed very opulent for a student.

'No, it belongs to my father. He's a surgeon in the hospital below.' He pointed to the barrack-like building she had seen last night. So it was a hospital, not a prison.

They talked for an hour or more – discussing the medical system in Egypt and endemic diseases. He was an engaging young man – very serious. His appearance and charm were misleading. He looked as if he spent his days playing polo, and his evenings in night clubs. But in fact he cared passionately about public health. His admiration for the English National Health system was boundless. Charlotte smiled at his enthusiasm, remembering the time she had had to see the local doctor in Suffolk, and had to spend most of the morning waiting her turn in a depressing waiting-room.

'That's nothing to the queues we have out here. It's quite common to arrive at the doctor's surgery at eight o'clock in the morning and stay there until lunchtime. There are far too many people, far too many diseases, far too few doctors.'

The sun was beginning to descend behind the pyramids. The evening was setting in. She had to go. Hassan might telephone at any time now. Evenings were his time. She sprang to her feet, unable to sit still any longer talking to this slim young man. She daren't talk about Hassan. The meeting with David had upset her. Although she didn't believe his story, nevertheless she didn't want any more upset. Youssef was from the same social class as Hassan. He might well have met him at some social gathering. She didn't want to risk mentioning his name. She finished her tea, and rose to go. Youssef looked genuinely sorry to see her leave.

'I would love to talk to you again. It's not often that I have the opportunity to meet such an intelligent person. You have that rare combination of intelligence and beauty. Most of the women students at our university tend to be very dedicated, very intellectual. I suppose they have been treated as men's chattels for so long that now, in these days of sexual equality, they have to prove they have brains as well as bodies. I agree with them, but they don't have to prove so hard.'

'We had the same problem back at the turn of the century. Women used to hide their sexuality. We called them "blue stockings".'

Youssef laughed. 'Yes, it's a good name. Most of our women students don't wear stockings nowadays. Blue jeans would be more appropriate. Please let me help you over the wall.'

He got up and helped Charlotte to her perch. 'I know you are on holiday, and you have several friends out here, but if you aren't doing anything special tomorrow, I am riding in the desert with some friends. We shall probably go back to the house of one of their grandparents in the evening to eat some supper, and listen to some music. I should be delighted if you would come along with us. My friends are very amusing, and the horses are very placid. The friends are all students, like me. One of them is coming to London with me, so tomorrow is really our farewell party, as we leave on Tuesday. Do come. We shall leave at about four in the afternoon, after siesta.'

Charlotte perched on the wall, and looked down on the eager face of the young Egyptian.

'Thank you. It's very kind of you to ask me. I think I am going to somebody's house tomorrow, but if nothing happens, I should love to come with you. I used to ride when I was here before, and I'm quite used to horses. I was brought up with them. It was the one useful thing about my childhood. I've got some blue jeans, by the way – will they do? You won't object?'

He grinned at her. 'They'll be fine. I'll give you a call before I set off. The desert is wonderful at this time of the year – not too hot.'

Charlotte dropped down to her balcony. She went into the sitting-room and turned on the standard lamp. The moths came in through the open window, and fluttered round the light, unable to leave its hypnotic glare. She liked Youssef. He reminded her of the young diplomats she had worked with in her previous life. There had been a young Australian she had been attracted to before Hassan had come on the scene. Why hadn't she accepted his invitations? Why had she found Hassan so overwhelmingly attractive? After all, he was nothing to look at. His figure was becoming heavy – his eyes were not the bright eyes of a young man. But she was captivated by his sensuality. Sexual pleasure had become a drug. She couldn't live without it. He understood her body very well.

It was still only early evening. The telephone didn't ring. Charlotte sat alone in her room wondering what she should do if Hassan didn't ring. Was there a telephone on the houseboat? Should she go there tomorrow or leave it for one more day? He had to come soon. After all, he had installed her in this flat, and surely he would want to use it for his own pleasure. Maybe his wife was being awkward. Perhaps he was with her at this very moment telling her all about their affair. Maybe she was creating a scene. Hassan loathed emotional scenes.

She sat there in the pool of light cast by the standard lamp, watching the moths, and listening to the sounds from the Corniche below. The blare of the car horns went on incessantly. The traffic jams were a nightmare. Why had she come here? What was she doing in this city? Why didn't she rush to David and tell him the truth – that she had come back to see Hassan and that she was now very frightened?

She went to the kitchen and made herself a tomato sandwich. Mohammed would be back tomorrow. She wanted to see his brown face again. Maybe he would know about Hassan. After all, it was only yesterday that she had been with him. It seemed like an eternity. She felt she was living in a time capsule. Soon the door would open, and she would step out into another world, another age.

Perhaps the phone was not working. She crossed the room to the machine, and lifted the receiver. The familiar hum greeted her. There was no fault there. No, she would have to be patient until Hassan had sorted out his affairs, and came to her. He had been insistent that she shouldn't come looking for him. She would have to stay here until she was summoned. She had grown used to his unpredictability when they had been lovers in the past.

There was a pile of English books and magazines on the coffee table. She smiled at the familiar cover of *Country Life*. It reminded her of her parents' sitting-rooms. They had always taken the magazine wherever they lived. These copies were out of date. She idly flipped over the pages, smiling at the photographs of English cottages, and eighteenth-century antiques. The magazine was as English as Trollope, or the choir of King's College Chapel.

She turned another page. There, looking out of the glossy page, was a photograph of the collection of jewellery which one of the aristocratic households was about to sell to a London jewellers. She glanced quickly at the article. Yes, these were the jewels that had been stolen in the Knightsbridge raid of a few weeks before. The bracelet was particularly fine – a solid gold band studded with diamonds and rubies. It dated back to the seventeenth century when one of the founding members of the family had been a favourite mistress of King Charles II. It would be very heavy, and very valuable. She thought back again to the parcel of books, and heard the words of David Leigh. What if Hassan *had* engineered the raid? What was she to do if the Embassy doors were now shut to her?

She shuddered with a sudden fear of the unknown. The idea of Hassan as an international crook was ridiculous. He had sent for her, and paid her fare. He had made love to her with tremendous passion. Of course he would come. He was speaking to his wife, that was all. Charlotte didn't even know where his wife lived. She might even be in Alexandria. Perhaps Hassan had gone there for the weekend to sort things out with her.

She felt comforted by the thought. She crossed to the balcony hoping to catch a scent of Youssef's cigarette. But all was quiet next door. There were no lights on, and the radio was silent. She wished she'd asked him to lend her the radio. She was beginning to miss her record player and guitar. She wanted music tonight. It would have soothed her and stopped her obsessive preoccupation with Hassan.

Hassan hated obsessive women. He wanted them to be always available, always beautiful, always undemanding. Perhaps children would come, she thought. She wanted Hassan's children. She had taken no precautions the other night, half-hoping that she might get pregnant. She wanted children desperately.

The nagging pain at the base of her stomach told her plainly that her hopes this time were useless. She'd forgotten her period. She'd remembered to bring a supply of Tampax, as she knew they were expensive and hard to find out here. It was a nuisance, though, especially if Hassan were to come. He hated making love to her when she had a period. He liked his women perfect, and didn't want to be reminded of their imperfections. She had always felt guilty in the past when her period came at an inconvenient time, as though it was her own fault, brought on by her own carelessness or mismanagement. He had even refused to sleep with her at those times, leaving her to her own bed, whilst he went off to the spare room.

The pain didn't go away, and by the next morning she found her period had come. Hassan would be angry, but it wouldn't stop her riding horses. She thought back to Youssef's invitation and decided that should he come for her, she would go riding with him and his friends. If only Hassan would communicate with her!

She'd been lazy in the morning, sending Mohammed out for more food, and then dismissing him around lunchtime. He'd been reluctant to go; he wanted to be useful. He thought she should be receiving friends, and wanted to put on a new gallabiya to open the door. The sight of his cheerful face on the Saturday morning had cheered her immensely. He'd wanted more money for the house-keeping though, and she made a note to cash some traveller's cheques during the following week. The few she had were very precious.

She asked Mohammed who paid his salary, thinking that perhaps Hassan did, or some landlord, or agency. She felt a trifle uneasy when he replied with a cheerful grin 'You, lady.'

'When would you like me to pay you?'

'Some time next week will do.'

She'd asked him how much he was expecting, and he named a sum which sounded reasonable, as she had paid her own servant roughly the same amount before. She knew that Embassy officials always expected higher rates than outside people; still, it was a worry. She hadn't very much money. All her capital had been spent on the cottage in Suffolk. There was very little over after the builders had been paid, and the solicitors. She hadn't expected to pay anything for this visit. Had she been in England she wouldn't have been able to afford a foreign holiday this year. A servant in a strange city would cost a lot of money, which she hadn't got.

She shrugged off the gloom. After all, it would only be for this week, and then Hassan would take over. Although she disapproved of husbands accepting all the financial responsibility, in this case, Hassan had summoned her to Egypt, with the expectation of marriage. She smiled at the thought. She was behaving like a heroine from a Jane Austen novel. Of course Hassan would pay Mohammed when she asked him. Meanwhile, she had enough to live on for a couple of weeks.

She was pleased to see the top of Youssef's curly head over the wall after lunch. He was delighted to see her.

'You're going to come with us, aren't you?' he called out. 'It's a lovely day – the desert will be at its best, and we won't be late home. Do come. My friends will all love to meet you.'

She made up her mind. She would go. The riding would be good for her. She needed the exercise, and Hassan would want her to be occupied.

'Ten minutes, and I'll be with you,' she shouted, as she rushed up the stairs to put on her jeans, and a cotton tee shirt.

The road out to the pyramids was just as she remembered it, and Youssef's black Volkswagen gaily painted with yellow stripes rattled its way along the concrete road lined with restaurants and hotels. It wasn't far. The stables were at the foot of the pyramids, and the horses would be ready, she knew.

They met the others at the stables — a flimsy building made of reeds, with a make-shift wooden roof. The friends were a likeable bunch. They reminded Charlotte so much of the days when she was a Third Secretary, with few responsibilities. There were two men about the same age as Youssef, and two girls, one beautiful and slim with the lovely name of Jasmine, and the other — one of Youssef's dedicated 'blue stockings' — with a thick figure, and a face marked by small pits — like the holes on a sponge. Her hair was unkempt and greasy, scraped back behind her ears. Large pebble glasses didn't help her appearance. She had the unlikely name of Dalilah, and obviously doted on Youssef. Charlotte remembered that the name was quite common amongst Egyptian women, like Rose or Mary in England.

Charlotte was introduced, and they all welcomed her like a band of friendly puppies. She felt out of place — too old and too experienced for this crowd of happy-go-lucky extroverts. They all had Youssef's infectious charm — his gay acceptance of life and all its pleasures. They seemed not to have a care in the world between them.

The head groom, a dashing young man in turban and gallabiya, led out a collection of fine horses for their selection. Youssef and the groom were old friends. He was a regular customer. He led a beautiful chestnut horse up to Charlotte. It looked frighteningly tall, about sixteen hands. Charlotte was used to horses, having been brought up with them in her childhood.

'What's his name?' she asked the groom who was called Zaki.

'Whatever you like, Madam,' was the reply. She laughed. These horses must have a weird collection of names between them.

'Then I shall call him Oliver, after Cromwell. He was one of our rulers.' Oliver had a cropped mane, and reminded Charlotte of a Roundhead.

'A good name, for a good horse,' shouted Zaki. 'He's very fast, but sweet-tempered.'

'I'm sure he is,' she called back. These horses knew the desert far better than the riders. They knew exactly how long they were expected to go in one direction, and woe betide the rider if he didn't change course at the right moment. The homeward journey was taken at a full gallop; food and shelter were a great incentive.

That afternoon there was nothing she liked better than to let the horse take her wherever he wanted. They were a laughing crowd of irresponsible students, with not a care in the world. Youssef led off his team at a gallop up the desert track to where the three pyramids stood looking out across the Nile to the distant Moqattam Hills. She'd forgotten how beautiful they were in the late afternoon light.

A group of tourists were painfully climbing Khephren's pryamid with its strange cap of limestone. It was a painful process, hauling the body up from one block of stone to the next. She stopped to watch a collection of American tourists in fancy hats bought at the dockside of Port Said. They were clustered round the base of the Great pyramid, like a flock of sheep gazing in bewilderment at the frantic guides and camel drivers. 'Come into my tent,' they shouted at some obese matron from the mid-west of America. It was a case of grabbing a tourist, hauling him or her onto a camel and setting off round the base of the pyramid. Each wobbling heap was treated to ten minutes' mythical history, and ten minutes' badgering for money.

Charlotte found it a sad sight, the grunts of the camels, the shouts of the tour operators, and the raucous screams of the tourists. The pyramids were not built for this.

The students found the sight amusing. Only Dalilah felt Charlotte's shame.

'Don't worry,' she said, 'they're not your people.'

'No, but mine are the same. They would turn an expedition to the pyramids into a cheap and noisy outing.'

'And why not?' Youssef had joined them. 'They don't understand why these monuments were made. They only know about the Pharaohs from what they see on the movies, or read about in novels. They want to go inside, and see a mummy rise up from its stone slab and curse them for invading its privacy. In fact it's a wonder that Zaki here hasn't thought of that. Come on Zaki, you would love to dress up as a mummy and chase these fat ladies round the death chamber.'

It was difficult to be serious with these students. They galloped away across the desert towards Sakkara, the wind blowing Charlotte's long hair straight out behind her. Oliver went well. They had been given fresh horses; hers was still enthusiastic and hadn't yet given the hint that he wanted to go home.

Dalilah rode well. Her stocky figure took on a dignity on horseback. Her short legs moulded well to the horse's side, and she held her back straight.

Jasmin was the least capable rider. Her body bumped around on the saddle like a loose sack of wood. At any moment, Charlotte thought she would fall off. But Jasmin's horse was old and wise. He knew his rider. He didn't want any trouble – merely a peaceful hour despite the painful load on his back, and then, with any luck, a speedy return to his stable and fodder. He did his best to keep Jasmin in the saddle; he didn't want any upset caused by a rider falling off his back and holding up the return journey.

As the sun moved round, the party made towards the river. There, amongst the palm trees they came to a small house. Said, Youssef's friend, had invited them back there for a meal and to meet his grandparents.

Servants took the horses. It was very mediaeval. The old couple were inside dressed in traditional clothes. Coffee was offered and the glasses of water, necessary after the ride over the sand dunes. Introductions were made, and Charlotte found herself the honoured guest, as the friend of Youssef, whom they knew very well. Said and Youssef had been friends and students for fifteen years. Outside, the sun was going down, and through the open windows Charlotte saw the outlines of the date palms, and the gleam of the irrigation canal.

Charlotte would never forget that evening. It was the end of her innocence – her last carefree evening, with friends whom she would not see again. Said was going to England with Youssef, and that night he was saying goodbye to his grandparents. Dalilah was going to lose Youssef, and Jasmin was parting company with Said. There was an air of 'fin de siècle'. No one was in the mood for laughter. 'Ichabod, Ichabod,' thought Charlotte. 'Why does the glory always have to depart?'

They ate lamb kebabs, grilled over a charcoal fire, and bowls of sweet cakes for dessert. As darkness fell the servants lit the lamps, and shadows flickered along the plaster walls.

Two figures crept quietly into the room. As the last plates were cleared away, one of the newcomers reached for his drum – a primitive instrument, a piece of skin stretched over a clay pot. Gently he began to beat out a slow rhythm. The other figure picked up a small reed instrument, and began to play the traditional melodies of Arab music – haunting music cascading through the Eastern tonal scale.

Unseen by the audience, a woman had come into the back of the room; a black-robed figure, her face hidden by the old-fashioned veil. She started to sing in a rich contralto voice. Charlotte understood the Arabic. She sang of love, and the desire for the unattainable. A lady was rich and proud, beyond the reach of the poor farmer.

The three musicians worked perfectly together – an intricate interplay of harmonies and melodies. This was music that Charlotte loved – not the sophisticated music of the Alexandrian night clubs, but the music of Arabs, full of feeling and very moving. It reminded her of the time when James had invited along to his house in Cambridge a group of Indian musicians and they had played like this. It was the outpouring of the soul. Listening to it, one understood everything – the nobility of man, his artistry and his restlessness; also his cruelty, his greed, and his lust for power.

It was a magical evening. With reluctance, they left the old couple, and went outside into the warm and velvety darkness.

'Youssef, it was a perfect evening. You will miss all this in London. We have nothing to equal it. Why do you want to go to our overcrowded island with all its vulgarity and garishness? Didn't the sight of those tourists at the Great pyramid turn you off going to London? They seem to typify the west.'

'Yes, I shall miss all this. But you must remember that Said comes from a wealthy family. Most of our people don't live in houses like this with servants to bring the meals, and singers to entertain them. Our people live mostly in appalling poverty which, with any luck, you will never see, or experience. Those Americans, for all their vulgarity have something to teach us. You too, in England, have something I must understand. Your Health system is the best in the world. People do not die of starvation in your land. You don't have to fight cholera and bilharzia . . .

'Just around the corner from this idyllic house, you will see at sunrise tomorrow, a little man sitting up to his waist in water. All day long, until the sun sets, he will turn the wheel of a shaft to raise water from the canal for Said's grandparents' date palms. He lives on a plateful of beans a day. In winter he will not be able to move his legs with arthritis, and he will cry all night with pain. His wife will not be able to afford pain relievers. He will die at fifty. *That* is why I am going to London.'

Charlotte was silent. The music had filled her with sadness. The horror of human existence was all about her.

They got on their horses, and in the darkness made their way back to the stables at Giza. There was a bright moon overhead which lit up the desert, casting shadows on the sand dunes. The horses knew the way. The looming shapes of the pryamids were impossible to miss. The party was subdued. It was the end of an era; life would not be the same after this evening. Youssef and Said would become immersed in western medicine and culture. The two women would stay behind to fight poverty and disease.

They handed the horses over to the waiting grooms. Sadly they shook hands. The others were going back to their families.

'Goodbye, Youssef. May God go with you,' said Dalilah, embracing the now-weeping Youssef. He got into the car and silently he and Charlotte drove away from the group standing waving in front of the stables. Youssef was going to his grandparents' house on the Alexandrian road, but he insisted on driving Charlotte back to the flat in Garden City. He would not come up to her flat.

'May God be with you, Charlotte,' he said as they shook hands. 'I don't know why you came to our city, but I hope everything goes well for you. It is not a good place to be alone in. Look after yourself.'

She smiled at the expression. It was one of the most poignant. She had last heard it used when she visited her grandfather in hospital. In the next bed to his, a man was dying of cancer of the bladder. His family had arrived, and their parting words were, 'Look after yourself, dad.' But there was comfort in clichés.

She watched the 'beetle' drive away. A friend had gone.

The lift was waiting for her, and she was carried back to her flat at the top of the building. 'Hassan, Hassan,' she thought, as she opened the door. 'You must ring. *You must*.'

10

On Sunday, Charlotte went back to the house-boat. She'd slept badly – her dreams demon-haunted. She was aware of her room gradually filling with light – at first a pale ghostly grey, and then a dazzling whiteness. She didn't sleep at all. She should have got up, and watched the sun rise over the Citadel, but she was frightened. Her confidence was gone. She didn't want to be reminded of man's immortality; she didn't want to hear the Call to Prayer.

She heard Mohammed arrive and the rattle of china as he left the tea tray outside her bedroom door. She didn't want to see him. When all was quiet again, she got out of bed, and picked up the tray. There was a pot of tea, and some hard western-style biscuits, like dog-biscuits. They were Mohammed's status symbols – British ladies always ate biscuits with their tea in the old days. She would have preferred the local yoghurt.

Her stomach still hurt. She glanced at herself in the mirror. Her face was white and lined with tension. Her eyes looked terrified. She could feel the tension in her shoulders and across her forehead. She had to fight a mounting panic. She lay down on the bed, drawing her legs up in the classic foetal position. She should have gone to get some aspirin, but didn't want to risk the walk to the bathroom. The womb-like position helped the pain. She leant over the side of the bed and poured out some tea, trying not to move the middle part of her body. The tea was good, and the biscuits, although as hard as rocks, were in fact just what she needed.

She thought briefly of the party of the previous day. She had liked all the students. How nice they had been to her, a complete stranger. She would miss them. They were all off to start their new lives.

She looked at her watch; it was after eleven o'clock. The day was well under way. Why hadn't he rung? She thought back to the nightmare of the night before, when she had tossed and turned in that twilight state between waking and sleeping. She had been in a pit, shaped like a lobster-pot; its sides were too steep and too slippery to allow her to escape. Again and again she had climbed up towards the light, only to fall back exhausted to the bottom. 'How real are dreams?' she thought. 'Was all this physical exhaustion the result of intense mental activity?' She remembered a lecture she'd been to years ago, where the speaker had said that the subconscious was the real part of the brain. Left to itself the brain functioned as it should and always came up with the right answers. Other mental activity was the result of man's will – what he *wanted* to think. Dreams were reality.

She shuddered. Looking up, she saw the fly that had annoyed her all night. It was still frantically trying to find a way out of her bedroom. She sat up suddenly. Where was Hassan? The thought struck her like a flash of lightning. *Where was he?* Her situation was becoming ridiculous. She couldn't stay in the flat a moment longer without knowing where he was. He had forbidden her to come to the houseboat, but that was last Thursday. It was now Sunday, and she hadn't had a word from him all that time. She had to find him, and get some sort of confirmation of her position.

Also, she thought again of her financial situation. She couldn't afford this flat. Mohammed would soon need more money for food, and she would have to give him his wages that week. She had only very limited means, as she hadn't managed to save much whilst she was in the Diplomatic Service, and the cottage had taken all her savings. She had to contact Hassan, just to know where she stood. He hadn't paid all that money to get her out of Egypt, only to desert her as soon as she arrived.

Action was needed! Charlotte jumped out of bed, ignoring the cramping pains in her inside. A warm shower helped. She put on the same blue dress she'd worn on the first day, and slipped her feet into the leather sandals. She combed out her hair, and briefly dabbed her face with powder, chiefly to stop it shining too much. She then walked out of the flat and out of the front door of the block of flats. The concierge, or 'bawwab' as they were called by the locals, called her a taxi. He was puzzled by her, but wisely asked no questions. If she was somebody's mistress, then where was the lover? If she was a working girl, then why didn't she work? Miss Peel was a mystery, and therefore someone to be treated cautiously. She could be hiding from the police. She might even be about to let the flat out to prostitutes! Whatever she was up to, he was going to keep his distance.

The taxi took her to Zamalek. She remembered the name of the road, which led along the river on the far side of the island. When they got to the part where the road petered out into a track, she dismissed the taxi driver, realising, as she paid him, that she had very little Egyptian money left. She'd have to cash some of her precious traveller's cheques that afternoon.

The house-boat was still there, tied to a bollard on the bank. Her heart began to beat wildly. She was actually frightened of seeing Hassan again. But she had to have evidence that he was still there. She would be reassured by the sight of the record player, or the purple cushions.

She walked across the gangway. She heard the sound of music and voices raised in laughter. Something, though, was not right. The music! Hassan would never have tolerated this tinny popular Arab music from an inferior radio. It was turned up very loudly. She had to beat on the door to make herself heard. The bead curtains were the same, but the fat man with his trouser buttons undone was not Hassan. This man was gross, with a heavy face, and large rubbery wet lips, startlingly red. His breath reeked of garlic.

She looked behind him into the cabin, and saw a fleshy woman lounging back on the purple cushions, her bodice gaping; one huge breast lolling out of the scarlet velvet. Her black hair tumbled round her shoulders; her skirt was drawn up round her waist showing fat pink thighs, and the tuft of pubic hair. She was very drunk, and leered at Charlotte.

'Well?' The man lurched forward towards Charlotte. 'Do you want to come and join us?' He made an obscene gesture.

The woman below laughed, and slowly and deliberately parted the thick folds of her vagina. Suggestively she rubbed her fingers over the red lips. Then, still looking at the man, she undid the rest of her bodice, and lifted out the other breast. Charlotte could see the stiff brown nipples. The man began to breathe heavily. He gazed at the woman below, with only half a glance at Charlotte. The woman's vagina began to glisten with the friction.

'Please,' said the now-desperate Charlotte. 'Does Hassan Khatib live here?'

'Who?' said the man. 'Does it look as though he does?'

'He did last Friday,' said Charlotte; she felt mounting panic which threatened to overwhelm her. The scene in front of her began to sway and recede. She had to hang onto the doorpost to stop herself falling. 'These cushions are his. That bed is his.'

'Then come along and try it after I've finished with this one,' roared the man. 'I've lived here for six months. I've never heard of Hassan Khatib. Go away and leave us alone.'

He was groping desperately inside the front of his trousers, his eyes on the woman below. With a quick motion, he released the huge swollen penis, and almost fell down the steps onto the sprawling woman.

Charlotte felt sick, not so much by the scene in front of her – she knew the realities of sex – but by what the man had said. Where was Hassan? This was his boat. These were his chairs, his kitchen, his bed. Where was the man? She turned and ran away from the nightmare scene. She reached the side of the road and was violently sick. She rested her head against the palm tree, and tried to think collectedly. From the houseboat she heard the coarse laugh of the man and the drunken shout of the whore. This was not a nightmare; this was reality.

She stood up and looked round. She counted the number of house-boats moored along the bank. There were only four on this part of the river. This was the first in the row. She couldn't have made a mistake. She went to the next one, but that was deserted. The one after had a dog on board, tied to the end of a long chain. He meant business; guard dogs in the Middle East usually did, and he would have torn her to pieces had she put one foot on the deck.

The last boat was inhabited by a pale young man with an unkempt beard, who seemed to be in a hashish-induced paradise. The smell filled the boat. The young man was only just articulate. No, he had never heard of Hassan. Yes, the fat man had lived on the boat for six months. No, he had never seen anyone answering Ahmed's description.

Charlotte was stunned. She was actually in a state of shock. The boat was Hassan's but the grotesque couple on board had nothing to do with him. Where was he? Why had he not communicated with her?

She'd dismissed the taxi. There was a long walk ahead of her. She had to get back to the bridge and go to the main square in the tourist quarter to cash her cheques. At least she had a flat to go to.

She walked along the bank of the Nile, blind and deaf to the sights and sounds of the river. She went back towards the July the Twenty-Sixth Bridge, and her vague plan was to get to El Tahrir Square where she could get some money. Her brain was numb. She walked like someone in a trance along the tree-lined streets of Zamalek's residential quarter. At any other time she would have enjoyed seeing once again the white villas of the English senior diplomatic staff, with their smooth green lawns, freshly-watered by the gardeners. But that afternoon there was only one thought in her head – *where is Hassan*? It went on repeatedly, like a refrain from a litany.

At the bridge, she stopped, exhausted. The walk had calmed her. Hassan had rented the flat for her – therefore he expected her to stay in Cairo. He'd probably gone to Alexandria, or wherever he kept his wife, and had given up the house-boat. After all, he had told her not to go back to the house-boat again. She had disobeyed his orders and had a fright, that was all. She'd got what she deserved. She had to go back to the flat and wait there as she'd been told. As soon as Hassan had sorted out his personal affairs, he would come to her.

She stopped at the bank and cashed her cheques. She had very few left. She ought to see about earning some money by teaching English. She had a good flat, and her students could come to her there.

The Embassy doors were closed to her now. Hassan's name had been connected with a crime, and she was connected with Hassan. If that parcel of books had enclosed the bracelet, then she was in real trouble. She didn't want people to ask questions. She wanted to hide and wait. She believed her rescuer was far away. Her hideaway was very comfortable. Perhaps she would start to write something. She had often thought that she would like to write a novel, but had never had the time or the urge to do so. Now that she had time on her hands, she could make a start.

Charlotte stopped at a stall, and bought a cheap biro and an exercise book. The paper was of poor quality, and the pages were ruled with thin red lines. But it would do. Tomorrow, she would think of a plot and begin. Perhaps she could start by writing down her experiences, and her thoughts about Egypt. The desert expedition had given her lots of ideas.

She walked back to her flat – the exercise stopped her thinking, and eased her stomach pain. She reached the flat, which already she thought of as 'home', and Mohammed was just winding his turban round his head, in preparation for his journey home. He wore a round skullcap when he was working around the flat. The turban was his travelling headgear.

He was pleased to see her. 'Good evening, lady. Have you had a good walk?' He insisted on speaking to her in English, although, by now, he knew she spoke excellent Arabic.

'Yes. I walked too far, I'm a bit tired.'

He noted her white face, and the shadows under her eyes. 'You must take it easy, Miss Charlotte. You are not yet used to this climate. Rest on your balcony. Have you seen your friends?'

'Oh yes,' she lied. 'I've been over to Zamalek for lunch. I am having a wonderful time.'

He smiled at her. 'Good. There is much to be enjoyed in this city. Tomorrow, I'll need some more house-keeping, as there is not a lot of food left in the fridge. Could I have my wages too? Monday would be a good day to pay me. It is usual.'

'Of course. I'll pay you when you come tomorrow.'

He turned to go. Just then a thought occurred to her. 'Mohammed, does Hassan Khatib employ you?'

He looked puzzled. 'Hassan Khatib? No lady – I've never heard of him. I work for Mr Doss.'

'Mr Doss?'

'Mr Doss who collects the rent. He's the landlord.'

'So Hassan rents the flat off a Mr Doss,' thought Charlotte. 'That's why I pay Mohammed. Hassan only rents the bricks and mortar.'

Mohammed left. Charlotte sat down and gazed out towards the pyramids. Already the sun was moving round to its late afternoon position. The muezzin in the nearby mosque was starting up the evening call to prayer – an unearthly sound. 'In the name of Allah the Compassionate, the Merciful', the phrases rolled out. 'There is no god but Allah, and Mohammed is the Messenger of Allah.' She wished she could believe this.

The Call to Prayer was recorded on a tape, and broadcast over the city through a loudspeaker. Tonight, the tape was showing signs of wear. There was a painful whine as the machine revved up, and at the end, the beautiful prayer ended with a loud thud. At any other time, Charlotte would have found the effect funny, but tonight, in her highly emotional state, it sounded mocking and callous, laughing at man's gullibility. If messages were to be divine, then the machines used to convey them ought also to be divine. Otherwise the prayer was diabolic. The demons were tormenting her again.

She shut out the noise by putting her hands over her ears. Her nerves overstretched. She thought of the whisky bottle in the sideboard, and drank a large tumblerful, with a little tepid water from the kitchen. She was too numb to go in search of ice-cubes. The whisky calmed her. A second glass stopped her thinking, and with the third, she passed out altogether. Slumped forward on the sofa, her hair falling over her face,

Charlotte was asleep before she had time to put her glass down. The remains of the whisky dribbled down onto the carpet, staining the cream satin upholstery of the sofa.

11

It was dark when she woke up. She had been asleep for about six hours. She lay there on the sofa wondering where she was. The smell of the spilt whisky jerked her back to reality. The shock, the long walk, the strong drink had made her pass out.

Charlotte got slowly to her feet. Her dress was crumpled and damp with sweat; her hair hung over her face in strands. The pain in her head was matched by the pain in her stomach. She felt sick. As soon as she stood upright, she knew she had made a mistake. The room was spinning round, her head throbbed, and she knew she was going to be sick. Gasping for air, she rushed upstairs, the sudden activity making her feel worse than ever. In the bathroom, she fell on her knees in front of the lavatory and was violently sick. She stayed there, clasping the plastic seat as if in prayer, until her stomach was completely empty. Then she ran a scalding hot shower and stood under it for a long time, letting the water pour over her hair. It was as if she wanted to wash away the memories of that hideous afternoon.

She could wash her body, but her mind was in turmoil. Where was Hassan? And who were the obscene couple on the house-boat? Because it *was* his house-boat – she was sure of that. She remembered all the details of the furniture. She was blessed with an almost photographic memory for places and people. She trusted it completely. Her brain was out of control. Fear and loneliness had numbed her reasoning powers. She was rapidly getting into a state of terror which left her body paralysed. She was like a caged animal, removed from its natural surroundings and suffering from shock. She took comfort from routine activity.

She dried her hair briskly. She put on her dressing-gown. She was thirsty, and went down to the fridge for a bottle of tonic water. She carried it to the balcony at the back of the apartment. The city, spread out below, was quiet. A few lights glowed in the darkness. It was a beautiful night – the sky overhead was studded with stars. The moon had vanished. She felt alone – terrifyingly alone. It was as if the whole city had been wiped out by a plague, and she alone had survived.

The night was warm. She wondered whether she should bring her bed out there – but the paralysis had her in its grip and she could not make the effort. Even small decisions were beyond her at this stage.

A scream shattered the silence, followed by another and the crash of pottery. Charlotte leapt to her feet, feeling the hairs stir at the nape of her neck. Her heart pounded. She went to the side of the balcony, and looked over the wall. Two cats, with backs arched and claws extended, were facing each other on the edge of the balcony wall. One had knocked over a pot of geraniums as he flew at his rival. The two shapes, with their arched backs and tails straight up in the air, were fiendish. These were not the quiet Suffolk cats she was used to. They weren't fat and comfortable, asleep in front of the fire, these were lithe and deadly. They were the fighters of the night, desperately hungry and jealous of their territory. They lived out of dustbins – whatever was left over after the humans and dogs had been there ...

Charlotte shivered, and clapped her hands. The two shadows slunk out of sight. They had never been petted or stroked; they knew only curses and blows. They had never known affection, and humans were shunned. The fat cats of the wealthy Cairenes were shut away securely at night. These demons would have ripped them to shreds, and then eaten them.

She was overwhelmed with loneliness. The sky was too vast, the distant city, way below, too remote. She turned and went inside, back to her bedroom, and lay down on her bed, curled up in the womb-like position. Thank God she had a good flat and a servant, although she would have to get rid of him soon if Hassan didn't appear.

She thought of the Embassy, just a stone's throw away. Could she not go to the Consul and throw herself on his mercy – as thousands of British holidaymakers did every year? But at the back of her mind there was the thought that if Hassan *had* been the instigator of the Knightsbridge robbery, then she would have been his accomplice. She had already left the Embassy in disgrace. She had been dismissed from the Foreign Office. She was now only a private citizen in real trouble. She couldn't go back to her old Head of Chancery to say that she had come back to Cairo to marry the man she had been warned about, and who they were all looking for at that moment.

Charlotte thought again of the whisky bottle. It was a quick way to oblivion. But she pushed aside the thought. It only made her sick. She would lie there until morning, and then decide what to do . . .

Dawn came at last. She couldn't actually see the sun rise from her bedroom, but the room was undoubtedly getting lighter. Another night was over. A new week was beginning. How much longer did she have to wait?

At eight o'clock Mohammed brought up the tea. She heard him place the tray quietly outside the door. She had to see him today – he wanted paying, and instructions for the shopping. She ought to get to grips with her domestic situation. She thought briefly of her financial situation. There was no money in her English bank account. She had made no arrangements for overdrafts. Her cottage was her only capital, and she had left no instructions to anyone for selling it. Once again she felt her heart beat wildly in panic. She had to keep control. Today she would pay Mohammed, and wait for Hassan to contact her. At least the flat was hers.

Mohammed was in the sitting-room polishing the furniture with the strong smelling paste which all the suffragis used as furniture polish. He looked at her with concern.

'All right, lady?'

'Yes, thank you. I had a rough night.' She saw the whisky stain on the upholstery, and hoped he didn't know what it was.

'You don't look very well. Have you had bad news?' He had lapsed into Arabic.

'No; all is well. I drank too much, that's all.' As a devout Moslem he was probably shocked. But he was used to the ways of the westerners.

He shook his head. 'It's very bad for the health. You will be very ill if you drink too much, Miss Charlotte, particularly as the weather gets hotter.'

She carried her tray into the kitchen, and made herself a frugal breakfast out of the contents of the fridge. She was hungry as she hadn't eaten anything much since the kebabs at the desert party.

'Mohammed, after you've cleaned I would like you to do some shopping for me. I'd like a chicken and some fresh fish if you can find some. I also need rice and salad and some beer and lemons for tea.'

'Yes, lady. I would also like my wages, if possible. I have to pay my rent tomorrow.' He put down his duster.

'Of course. How much do you expect?'

He named a figure which amounted to roughly thirty pounds a week in English money. It was on the high side, but he came six days a week, and he did anything she wanted. It compared roughly with what she had paid her previous suffragi. Still it was a worry, if Hassan didn't come soon. The house-keeping wasn't cheap either, as Mohammed shopped at the westernized shops for most of the expensive food. The markets were good enough for vegetables and salads. It was all too worrying.

She sat on the front balcony, and tried to appear normal. Mohammed was in the kitchen changing into his shopping robe. He had several gallabiyas – a white one for cleaning, a blue and white cotton one for shopping, and a blue silk one for best.

He was away about an hour; an hour in which Charlotte read and re-read an article on Arundel Castle, and the history of the Dukes of Norfolk. She had to keep her mind occupied. She wasn't taking in any information, but merely using the reading process to stop her mind from thinking about her predicament. One pause in her concentration, and the demons swept in.

Mohammed returned with the shopping. He was beaming with pleasure. He had found a large ugly fish in the market and was looking forward to cooking it for her and her 'friends' that evening.

He was to be disappointed. 'I think tonight I shall eat alone, and go to bed early. I had a big party last night, and it doesn't do to have too many late nights.'

'No, lady. I shall cook you the fish, and you will see how well I can cook. Perhaps you will ask your friends later in the week?'

She paid him his wages, and listened to the clang of the lift-door as he went out. He'd be back later to cook the evening meal.

Charlotte tried to relax in the sun. Her balcony was just the right size and there was plenty of room to stretch out on her cane chair. After all, she had this marvellous view, she had paid Mohammed, and there was plenty of food in the fridge. She was all right for a week, and anything could happen in that time.

At four o'clock there was a knock on the door. She jumped up, her lethargy forgotten. It had to be Hassan. Pride was forgotten. She would hurl herself into his arms. She felt sick with relief. The nightmare was over. She would go anywhere with him; she didn't care if he was an international jewel thief. She would leave this flat instantly.

She reached for a comb, and quickly put her hair in order, thanking her luck that she had washed it that morning. She tied the belt of her robe tightly around her waist. She knew Hassan hated sloppiness. Her bikini would please him, but she couldn't open the door in a half-naked state.

The knocking on the door became more persistent. 'I'm coming!' she called out as she put her feet in her slippers. She ran to the door and opened it, her face alight with anticipation. A little man stood there, round, dressed in a western grey suit. He wore dark glasses. There was a file under his arm, and in one hand he held a briefcase. He looked official, like someone coming to read the electricity meter.

'Good evening, madam. My name is Michael Doss. May I come in?'

It took a few moments for Charlotte to control her disappointment. She didn't want to see this little fat man with dark glasses. But the name rang a bell. Of course – he was Mohammed's employer. He probably wanted to know if she was satisfied with the suffragi and the apartment.

Mr Doss looked Charlotte up and down, and she was glad she had put on her bathrobe. He spoke perfect English, and she judged from his name that he wasn't Arab. His skin was pale, not white like a European, but more olive, like the skin of a Greek. He was almost certainly a Copt. She spoke first.

'Excuse my dress, but I have been sunbathing.' He dismissed her apology with a wave of his hand.

'Don't worry; I am used to seeing half my customers in fewer clothes than you have on.' He didn't quite leer, but she sensed he would become familiar if she gave him the slightest chance.

She didn't know whether she should offer him a chair. Should she offer him a drink? There was just enough whisky left, and as he wasn't Arab, he would probably accept one. She remembered she had beer in the fridge. That was always popular.

Mr Doss sat down on the sofa, thus removing the necessity of asking the question. Charlotte decided to offer him a beer. To her surprise he accepted as though it was his right. When she came back with two bottles and the two glasses, he had opened his file and was getting a biro out of his jacket pocket. He took the glass.

'Cheers,' he said, with a very English accent.

She smiled. 'Do you have many English customers?'

'A few. Mostly American. Mostly businessmen.'

'Do you have many from my Embassy?'

'No – none from the Embassies. The diplomats have their own arrangements. This apartment would also be too expensive for them. The senior staff live in villas, and this would be beyond the rent allowance of the junior staff.' He drank his beer, and took out a small cigar.

'Do you mind?' He waved the cigar in her direction.

'Not at all; please go ahead.'

They sat in silence for a few moments. Charlotte wished Mohammed would come back and start cooking the fish. She was touched that this man was concerned with her welfare. She would tell him she was pleased with his suffragi and his apartment. She had no complaints. He smoked his cigar; it was all very relaxing. She waited for him to speak.

'Are you satisfied with your apartment?' he said.

'Thank you – it's very comfortable.'

'Is there anything you'd like? I could find you another table, or perhaps another rug to go here.' He pointed with his foot to the place in front of the coffee table.

'Thank you – I like it as it is. I don't want anything at all – maybe Mohammed has some ideas for the kitchen.'

He waved the suggestion aside. Suffragis weren't supposed to have ideas.

'You're happy with him? He's willing?'

'Thank you; we get on very well.'

Mr Doss nodded. He then picked up his biro, and looked round the room.

'I shall have to have an inventory of all the furniture. Not now. I don't want to disturb your evening. Can my man come tomorrow?'

'That will be fine. I don't know how long I shall be staying here. I have friends who might put me up.'

Mr Doss nodded. 'That's up to you. You can stay with whomever you choose. The apartment is usually taken for a month at a time, but we could arrange a shorter let if necessary. I shall need a month's rent in advance, though. Do you want to pay now? I don't need all of that amount this evening, but I must have a deposit. Most of my customers pay a month in advance.'

12

For a moment she didn't take in what the man had said. When she understood, the room began to recede in front of her. Terror made her speechless. She felt herself gripping the sides of the chair to stop herself falling.

'I don't know what you mean,' she said eventually, trying to keep the panic out of her voice. 'I don't owe you any rent. Mr Khatib is paying for this apartment.'

Mr Doss consulted his file. 'I don't know of a Mr Khatib. This place was booked last week by a Mr Andopoulos from Alexandria. He has supplied us with tenants before, although I don't know where he lives. He usually phones from the Cecil. It was a bit unusual this time, because he normally pays in advance. It's our rule, you know. We are business people.'

'How much *is* the rent?' she asked. Her voice came out as a whisper; she had to clear her throat to make herself heard.

'For this flat, eighty pounds a week. Then there's extra for the service charge. That means that the lift works, and the stairs and corridors are cleaned every day.' It was still difficult for Charlotte to take all this in.

'Mr Doss, there's been a mistake. I haven't got that amount of money. I was expecting the rent to be paid by a Mr Khatib. I haven't got a month's rent on me. I shall have to cash some cheques tomorrow.'

Mr Doss' manner changed. He sensed trouble. A strange woman with no money was to be got rid of quickly. His face looked long-suffering. This was going to be tedious.

'What do you propose to do? You can't stay here without paying rent. I have a waiting list for this apartment.'

She thought desperately. 'Let me have it for one week, until I find somewhere else to live. I can pay the week's rent now. I can't stay here for longer than that.'

Mr Doss looked at her curiously. He was not used to strange

young girls living alone without money. They usually had protectors – firms or Embassies, or pimps.

'Haven't you any friends who can help you out?' he asked.

'Not yet; I haven't been out here long enough. I thought my employer was going to pay. I'll take it up with him tomorrow.'

He shrugged his shoulders. 'It always pays to get these things sorted out before you start work,' he said in a paternal way. 'Why don't you leave this until you've spoken to your employer tomorrow?'

'Let me pay one week's rent now. If he sorts things out, I'll let you know.' This way she could get rid of this loathsome man, and give herself time to think.

Mr Doss stood up. 'Very well. I'll take a week's rent now. Mind you – that will only take you up to Thursday night. Then I shall need more.'

She paid him the money, and watched him write out the receipt. She couldn't wait to get rid of him. Finally he left, and she sat down in despair. Not even the apartment had been paid for! She now had to leave the place, and wait for Hassan to come and find her. She would have to find a small room somewhere. She couldn't afford a hotel.

For the first time ever, she felt a surge of anger towards Hassan, who had landed her in this mess. Because it *was* a mess. There was no way out for her. Ordinary citizens could go and see the Consul – receive a lecture on how to manage their affairs better, and probably get a loan for the boat-fare home. But she wasn't an ordinary person. She couldn't go near the Embassy. To start with, she had lied to David Leigh, who now thought she was in India. She was involved with an undesirable local. She had disobeyed her friends. She had disregarded the advice of her ex-Head of Chancery. She might even be in trouble with the police, because she still had that nagging anxiety at the back of her mind about the parcel of books.

Charlotte had no doubt that Hassan had simply overlooked the small matter of the rent and Mohammed's wages. Money had never worried him. He had always lavished the best things on her. He probably thought she was rich. Diplomats had that reputation. Hers was a glamorous image. Hassan had only ever seen her at cocktail parties – he hadn't seen her planting potatoes in Suffolk. He might even be prepared to give the rent back to her when they next met. If not in actual Egyptian pounds, then in kind – a ring, or diamond bracelet. After all, she was to be his wife.

Somehow she would have to hang on until he came. Or at least, until she knew for certain what was going on. Pride stopped her going to the Ambassador. A stiff-backed pride which she had inherited from her Calvinist grandparents. How could she ask for help? To go crawling back to her old life? To watch them look at her with exasperation; to treat her like a foolish child. How could she go through all that when there was still a strong probability that Hassan would come? No, she had to stay on in his city and see this affair through. She would have to find a room somewhere. Leave her address with Mohammed, and teach English. It was always possible to find people wanting to learn a language that was indispensable for success in the commercial world. This was the challenge she needed. She would not leave this city until she heard what had happened to Hassan. She knew he would come soon. He could not have deserted her. He had made love to her – and she was sure it *was* love; and he had talked about marriage. After all, he had paid for her air-fare. He couldn't have done that simply to abandon her to her fate. Where was her commonsense? Where was her courage? She had never before lacked either.

The key turning in the lock pulled her together. Mohammed was coming back to cook supper. She would have to behave like the 'memsahib' for that evening at least. She picked up the same copy of *Country Life* which she was beginning to know by heart.

'Good evening, lady. I won't be long with dinner. Is everything all right?'

She forced a smile, determined to act out the charade. 'Yes, thank you, Mohammed. I am looking forward to your cooking.' He disappeared into the kitchen. Soon the smell of boiling fish began to fill the apartment. Her stomach heaved at the smell. She'd have to eat it. It was Mohammed's first proper meal.

At half-past seven, he laid the grand table, designed to seat eight people, and now with only one place setting. He'd put on his best gallabiya and white turban. This was to be an occasion.

'Ready, lady,' he said in English. It was the right language for the occasion.

Glad that she had changed into a dress, Charlotte took her place at the head of the table, feeling like Queen Victoria, or some eccentric colonial lady, left behind when the British left India. Reality had receded. He had even lit the candle in the centre of the table.

Mohammed reverently handed her a dish on which a pale grey fish reclined in a sea of yellow sauce. Once again the room swayed. Was she going mad? The whole situation was getting like a surrealist film.

Charlotte took a helping, and mercifully Mohammed left her to eat it by herself. One didn't stay to watch ladies eating. It was his place to serve. She took a mouthful. The fish was rubbery and tasteless — the sauce rich with a strong-tasting butter. It was probably made from the water buffalo's milk. She felt her stomach heave. Silently she pushed back the chair and tipped the grey plateful over the balcony. She hoped it would disintegrate in the air. Eleven floors was a long way to fall. The cats would like it, though. She didn't hear it land.

When Mohammed came back she was just scraping the few remaining pieces onto her fork.

'Was it good, lady?' he asked.

'Excellent.' He looked pleased.

He'd made a salad of lettuce and cucumbers. That was better. With the hard bread it was quite a good meal. The dessert was strawberries and cream, bought that morning at great expense from the market. They were the first of the season. Mohammed beamed with pride as he put the dish in front of her. She liked strawberries, and thinking that this was going to be the last proper meal she would get for some time, she ate the whole plateful, wincing slightly at the cream which tasted as strongly as the sauce. It was very British; very colonial. Mohammed was in his element.

The moths were coming in – attracted by the light. She got up to close the windows, and then changed her mind, and asked for the coffee to be brought to her outside on the balcony. Waiting for the coffee, she began to think rationally. She was an intelligent lady – not known to panic readily. She had to take action. She couldn't sit around in limbo forever. She went over the arguments, as though she were writing an office report for Anthony. She had always prided herself on logical thought.

She had no money for her fare home. Besides, she wanted to be sure that Hassan wasn't coming back. She couldn't afford Mohammed. She had this flat for a few more days only. She couldn't go near the Embassy. She might even be arrested. She had no friends. If she was to stay on in Cairo, she would have to earn money quickly. She could give English lessons; then she would have enough money to pay her fare home, especially if she went by cargo boat from Alexandria to Venice, and then across Europe by train.

Mohammed! *He* was the answer. She'd ask him for help. She'd lose face by it. Mohammed would be deeply shocked, but she would have to take that risk. After all, she was an Arabist. That made her less of a 'memsahib' in his eyes.

He came into the sitting-room to clear away the place mat, and polish the grand table. He had changed into his home clothes, and there was a smile of satisfaction on his face. He was pleased with the evening; he was doing what generations of suffragis had been doing for a century. Miss Charlotte was a proper British lady. She called him: 'Mohammed – I need your help!'

'Yes, lady. What can I do for you?' He beamed with pleasure.

'Mr Khatib hasn't turned up. I shall have to move from here to a cheaper place. My friends cannot lend me much money. I can manage if I teach English and French. Do you know where I can rent a cheap room for a few weeks?'

Mohammed's face fell. Charlotte felt as though she had fallen from grace. She had let him down. British ladies never admitted to not having any money.

'Miss Charlotte, you cannot live in too cheap a place. It would not be proper. How much can you pay?'

'Not more than ten pounds a week,' she said. It was the truth. It was all she could afford at that moment, and not for too long. She had to have something for food.

He looked concerned. 'Miss Charlotte, there is nothing for that sum. My small apartment in Bulac costs twenty pounds a week, and my wife and sons all work to pay for it.'

'I don't need a whole apartment. One room would do.'

Mohammed looked very upset. 'I can see my brother. He works in Al Qalaa – near the Khan el Khalili. He might know of a room. But it's not the place for an English lady,' he said, looking very worried. The British only lived in Garden City and Zamalek.

Charlotte knew the area around the Khan el Khalili. It was in the old city built by the Fatimid rulers of the tenth century. It was an area of bazaars and small alleys. The tourists went there to buy jewellery and leather goods. She could live there very cheaply – teach English and wait for Hassan.

'That will suit me very well until my friend comes, and I earn some money. When can you see him?'

He thought for a moment. 'If you could make your own tea tomorrow, Miss Charlotte, then I can see him on my way into work. The tram stops near his shop. He's a barber – for men. He might know of a room, but it's not easy for a lady to live on her own in the Khan el Khalili. They will think you are not respectable.'

'I have no alternative. I should be most grateful if you would see your brother tomorrow.'

He went off to collect the coffee cup. He looked depressed and disappointed, and once again Charlotte felt she had not only let him down, but also her countrymen. She wasn't behaving properly. She waited for the 'Goodnight, lady,' smiled reassuringly at him, and settled down with *Country Life*. At least that made him look relieved: he knew the magazine.

There was no more she could do that night. Tomorrow she would sort out the new room. She'd leave her address with the bawwab and Mohammed would also know where she was living. She would survive. In a small room, she would not be too worried about money. She'd soon get enough to pay her fare home, if Hassan did not turn up. That idea, though, was still unthinkable. Somewhere he had got delayed. Probably his wife was being difficult. She'd heard that wives didn't always do as they were told. They could be very awkward. It would do Hassan good to know that he was marrying a survivor.

Charlotte felt suddenly exhausted. Having made the decision she felt drained of nervous energy. But at least she was making some effort to put her life in order – anything was better than this eternal waiting. She closed the balcony doors and went up to her room. She couldn't be bothered to take off her dress. Kicking off her sandals, she collapsed on the bed and tried to sleep. She must have dozed off, because it was several hours later before she woke up. Her head was aching, and there was a sharp pain in her abdomen. It couldn't be her period, which although heavy, was no longer painful. This was different. Waves of cramp engulfed her. She broke out in a heavy sweat. Her dress was soon soaked, and her hair stuck to her face. Another wave of pain made her gasp out loud. 'What is it?' she whispered. Suddenly, she realised. The dinner! Either the fish, or the salad, or most likely the strawberries and cream had been contaminated. She was in the throes of what the British called 'gippy tummy'.

Charlotte had to get out of bed. Standing up was agony, and she groped her way to the bathroom stooping like an old woman. Once again, she fell on her knees in front of the lavatory, and spent the rest of the night there, embracing the bowl. The vomiting came first, and then the diarrhoea. All night long, her body threw out all traces of that supper. Her muscles began to ache with the exertion of retching on an empty stomach.

At last Charlotte's body was satisfied that all traces of bacteria had been expelled. The waves of nausea subsided. Slowly she got off her knees, and cleaned her teeth. She ran a hot shower and stood under it for several minutes trying to wash away the memory of those hours. She was extremely weak, and very thirsty. It was an effort to dry herself and crawl down to the kitchen for tonic water. She daren't risk the tap water, although she had been told that it was safe. Then she painfully climbed the stairs to bed and fell asleep.

Mohammed found her there at ten o'clock. He had come in late as he had called off to see his brother, as promised. He saw that she hadn't made any tea. He knew something was wrong. Going upstairs he saw the bedroom door was open. In spite of his training he decided to go in. She was lying there fast asleep, her body half on the bed and half on the floor. Her hair was still damp from the shower. It hung over her face like a veil.

Mohammed ran forward and lifted her onto the bed. She was so light. There seemed to be no substance to her. She woke up with the movement, and to his relief, smiled at him.

'Oh Mohammed, I've been so ill. I've been sick all night. It's over now.'

He fussed around like an old hen. He disapproved of her. Women shouldn't live on their own. She should either be at home with her mother, or with a husband protecting her. It wasn't his place to tuck her up in bed, but remembering his two daughters at home, he forgot his principles, and made her comfortable. He was a naturally kindly man.

He also knew all about gastro-enteritis. He made lemon tea, and brought her up a bowl of yoghurt. She remembered how a doctor friend had told her that yoghurt was bacteria free, and she felt safe eating it. Mohammed heaped brown sugar on it, and gradually she felt her strength returning.

'Now Miss Charlotte, you must stay here for the rest of the day, and you will be well by tomorrow. I'll go out and buy a chicken to make soup. It will do you good with rice. Sleep now.'

As he turned to go, she asked him whether he'd seen his brother.

'Yes, he was in his shop. He knows of a room that will suit you. But at the price you are prepared to pay, it's not very comfortable. But it's in the bazaar, and you'll be near people. But rest now. Tomorrow, I'll give you the address.'

Relieved, Charlotte turned over to go to sleep. The movement strained her overworked muscles. She heard him go to the bathroom, and clear up the mess. She heard the clank of metal bucket and smelt the tang of disinfectant. The familiar sounds calmed her. She slept at last, mentally and physically exhausted.

13

The room was over a coppersmith's shop. The taxi took her to the Bab Zuwayla on the Thursday afternoon. She stepped out of her cab into a different age. Her past receded. She was starting her new life in the Middle Ages.

There was no one about at that time of the day. Cairo enjoyed a long siesta. Only a beggar sat sightless in the gateway. A spindly dog, without substance, flitted out of the shadows like a soul shunning the daylight.

Charlotte looked round. A cobbled street, shuttered shops. Above the buildings, the great southern gateway from the mosque of Al Muayyad. One of those shuttered windows was hers. The houses belonged mostly to well-to-do artisans. They were substantial two or three-storeyed buildings. She was holding the piece of paper which Mohammed had given her, with an address on it, and she now went up to the small figure of a man sitting dozing in the entrance-way of his shop. He was slumped forward over his goods, hoping for a hardy tourist to brave the heat of the day.

Charlotte was thankful she could speak Arabic. 'Good afternoon,' she said. She waited. The man, expecting a customer looked up, blinking in the sunlight.

'Good afternoon. What can I do for you?'

She showed him the piece of paper. He pointed upwards. 'It's up there. Go along up. My brother will be along soon for the rent. Meanwhile he is sleeping.' He implied that all civilized people were resting at that time of the day.

She went in through the wooden door, heavily carved with Islamic patterns. The copper nails looked as though they had been there for centuries.

Slowly, she climbed the stairs, worn smooth by countless generations of bare feet. There was the door, with the number 15 riveted on it in copper. An iron key was in the lock.

She went in. Inside, she was pleasantly surprised. It was

bare, as were most Egyptian rooms. She was pleased to find that the window looked out onto the street. By turning her head slightly to the left, she could see the stone arch of the gateway. Her wooden shutters were elegantly carved. They were the traditional shutters, or *mashrabiya*, of mediaeval Cairo. The window projected over the street, and she could sit there in the evenings and enjoy the show below. There was no glass in the frame – just the wooden shutters to keep out the heat and the flies.

There was a low bed, with a rug thrown over it, and a round copper tray placed on a stool in the centre of the room, to serve as a dinner-table. The fire was a brass burner standing against the wall. In winter one bought charcoal and lit one's own fire. Then there was a stool, and a water pot, and that was all. She would have to fetch her own water from the pump outside in the street, and use a communal lavatory somewhere at the back of the house. She could use the burner for cooking, if she had to. Maybe the landlord would let her have a pot, although food in this area would be cheap to buy. She could eat at one of the hundreds of small cafés that cooked the fried meat balls, and the dish of fava beans, which the locals called 'fool'. It was the dish of the poor, and only cost a few piastres.

There was a cupboard behind the door, and Charlotte hung up her few clothes. She then sank down on the bed, and looked around. She liked the room. It was clean, and there wasn't much furniture. She hated ornaments, and other people's clutter. It was hot, though. The sun beat down remorselessly from midday onwards. She got up to close the shutters, but that only made the heat worse. She would just have to get used to it.

Gradually, as the afternoon wore on, the street outside came to life. First, she heard the metallic clanking of the water-seller's cups. He was there at the gateway offering water, and a liquorice-flavoured drink to the shoppers. Then, the squeaking of bicycle wheels. This was the universal form of transport in the Old City. It was every tradesman's ambition to own one. They wove their way through the throng with breathtaking skill. She never saw one hit anybody.

She went to the window and looked out at the scene below –

like the first act of an opera when the curtain goes up. There was the old coppersmith. He'd woken up from his siesta, and had started hammering away at his pots. Today he was making coffee pots. Turkish coffee was drunk everywhere in Cairo. It was offered to anyone who looked mildly interested in the goods on the stalls. It was always offered with a glass of water.

The bakers' apprentices went by – huge baskets of flat unleavened bread balanced on their heads. Skilfully, they wove their way through the crowd, never spilling one loaf. Some of the apprentices were on foot, shouting for a clear passage through the crowd. Bells were a luxury, but everyone could use his voice.

Now the whole quarter was awake – people swarming through the gateway dressed in the long robes of the merchants and apprentices. Children fought and wrestled in the sun. Dogs darted in the alleyways between the shops on their eternal hunt for food. The beggar had woken up, and added his pathetic cry to the general din.

The noise was deafening – the cries of the street sellers, the shouts of the children and the endless tap-tapping of the coppersmith. She would come to know all these sounds by heart. Later, lying on her bed, she would see the scene outside. She would recognise the smell of the Egyptian cigarette as the coppersmith's 'brother' joined him at four o'clock for coffee and a gossip. The chatter from the café next door, where news was exchanged, and the affairs of the world were sorted out. She felt as though she was living in the middle of a stage. Her bed was the centre of that entertainment.

Charlotte hadn't closed the door of her room. It opened slowly. She lay there quietly, raising her head slightly to see who was coming in. She wasn't frightened of robbers. She had nothing to steal. She had brought very little with her from England. She supposed her bracelets and rings might be worth something.

The door stayed open. No one came in. She sat up. There in the entrance were two little girls – about nine and ten she guessed. Both wore long dresses, ragged at the hems. Their feet were bare; one had beads round the ankle. Their hair hadn't seen a brush or comb for weeks. It hung round their faces in dark strands.

The eldest came forward and looked at Charlotte. She had curious brown eyes, and an enamel hand of Fatima round her neck, the Moslem good luck charm.

'Hallo,' said Charlotte, in English. The little girl shot backwards to where her sister was standing. Both now stared at Charlotte.

'What are your names?' Charlotte asked, this time in Arabic. 'Don't be frightened.'

The eldest came forward, her eyes fixed on Charlotte.

'I'm Fatima. This is Dalilah.'

Charlotte smiled at the name. 'Do you live here?'

'Yes.' Silence. Then they decided they'd had enough of this strange lady. They backed away out of sight. Charlotte could hear them whispering.

A few minutes later they reappeared, this time with a small neat man, dressed in European clothes, but with an old-fashioned fez on his head. Charlotte hadn't seen this headgear for a long time. It was associated with Farouk and the old régime of Pashas. Nasser had put an end to colonial clothes, just as Peter the Great had cut the hair and beards of the Russian *boyas*.

He was brisk and cheerful, and spoke in broken English.

'Good evening, Miss Peel. My brother said you wanted to take this room. I hope it pleases you.'

'Thank you. I shall be very comfortable.' The two children were edging forward. 'Are they your children?' she asked.

'Praise God, yes. I hope they don't bother you.'

'I shall be pleased to see them. Perhaps they would like to learn some English.'

The man was delighted. He was called Ahmed, and was related to Charlotte's suffragi, Mohammed. She was to learn that many of the Cairenes were related. 'Brother' merely meant 'from the same family'. Cousin or uncle, would be the English equivalent.

The room was only eight pounds a week. She was relieved. She could live here for five weeks without too much hardship. Food would be a problem, though. Ahmed came forward with an idea.

'Miss Peel, if you would like to teach Fatima some English, and French if there is time, I could send you up some of our evening meal. It won't be much. We live very simply; some fool mudhammas, or falafel is the usual. It might help until you find your friends.'

So that was the story; she was searching for friends. It would do very well.

She smiled her thanks. 'That's very kind. I should be delighted. If Fatima comes along tomorrow, we can begin. I am most grateful to you.'

The man bowed his acknowledgment. 'She will come tomorrow. I will tell my wife to send up some supper when we have ours.'

Charlotte paid him a week's rent in advance. He looked pleased. He asked her if there was anything she needed. She mentioned a coffee pot and a plate and fork. He said they would all arrive with the evening meal. Charlotte began to relax. For the moment she was safe.

True to his word, the supper appeared shortly after the Imam had called the Faithful to prayer from the Al Muayyad mosque. She had forgotten how near it was. Morning and evening she would be deafened by the prayer. She didn't dislike it. It came round with a reassuring regularity. Later, when she would spend much of the day in bed, she was able to tell the time of day by the sound.

Tonight, Dalilah brought up the food – peasant food – fool mudhammas, cooked with spices and tomatoes. There was a small carafe of olive oil to add to the dish, and a piece of the unleavened bread. A dish of yoghurt called leban zabadi completed the meal. It was delicious. The fool, too, was unexpectedly tasty. She scooped it up with the thick bread, and could have eaten more. She was very hungry after the upset of the previous night. Dalilah stood there watching every mouthful. She sat cross-legged on the mat, a graceful figure despite the dirty hair and the calloused feet. Charlotte hoped she wasn't eating the child's meal. She offered a piece of the bread to Fatima, but the child shook her head.

'I have eaten,' she said.

After the meal, Charlotte went downstairs to thank the

family. They were all there, in one room. Ahmed's wife was cooking at the primitive oil stove. Four children sat around the low table. Ahmed had already been served. He waved Charlotte towards his family. Coffee was offered, but tonight, Charlotte declined. She didn't want to intrude. She thought she would go out into the cool evening air, and explore the area.

A maze of alleys led off the main street. It was like stepping out of a time capsule into the Middle Ages. All Ahmed's family were coppersmiths. She watched the 'brother' at work. He was not a talkative man. He tapped away with his hammer long after she had gone to bed, and it was the first sound she heard in the morning. He looked her up and down with interest, noting the dirty blue dress and her pale face. He thought she might be a junkie. Certainly they all thought she had been jilted by a lover. They all wondered how she was to survive in such an area.

As Charlotte walked on, the man looked up from his hammering. 'If you are going to walk, don't go far. This is not an area for ladies on their own; not at night. You can go with Ahmed some time, but do not go on your own. There is a good café the other side of the gate, if you want coffee. The man is all right. He is my brother.'

Another friend. She took his advice. The café was in the next street under the gateway. The tables were out on the pavement – the lighting, a naked electric bulb. But the radio was playing Arab music, and the locals were gathering for their evening entertainment.

Charlotte was the only woman present, but the owner of the café had heard of her. He came forward, bowing. She ordered her coffee, 'mazboota' or medium sweet, and decided to spend a few piastres on some tahina, served with the round Egyptian bread called 'aiysh' by the locals.

She was obvioulsy a curiosity as she spoke Arabic. The customers wanted to ask what she was doing in such a place; ladies like her usually arrived in that area by taxi, made their purchases, and left.

That evening, Charlotte was almost happy. Away from Garden City, she wasn't continually reminded of Hassan.

She'd left her address with the bawwab and Mohammed, so he could find her if he wanted to. As long as she had not received any instructions to go away, she would stay in the city. The anger was still there. He had put her in a terrible predicament by not explaining the financial conditions of the apartment in Garden City. She had been embarrassed, and lost face with her servant. For the first time she let her mind contemplate the idea that he might not want her back. That she had in some way displeased him, or that his wife was being difficult. If that was so, he should have told her. She would then have borrowed her fare and gone home. But this silence was worrying. Why had he disappeared?

The problem was too difficult to solve. Meanwhile she sipped her coffee, and was grateful to have a roof over her head, and kind people around her. She would start English lessons tomorrow. She was assured of a plateful of food a day. Life was interesting; she had much to be thankful for. She was going to survive, and was going to find out why Hassan had abandoned her, after paying her air fare. That was the mystery. He couldn't have tired of her in one night!

The beggar by the gate came shuffling towards her – a repulsive sight in a torn robe with both hands in bandages. His eyes had disappeared; there were only two sockets filled with yellow pus. The flies swarmed around his head, as if he was already dead, and the corpse was being devoured by maggots.

In spite of the fact that he couldn't see, the beggar made straight for Charlotte. She sat there, stiff with terror and repulsion. Physical deformity of all kinds filled her with horror. She couldn't believe that such a creature could still be living. She didn't know whether she should give him money. She had always been told that it was fatal to give baksheesh. It would only encourage others, who would arrive in swarms. She couldn't get used to the beggars in Cairo. Her friends had told her that most of the deformities were faked, like the rogues in Alexandre Dumas' *Court of Miracles*, but this man's eyes were real. They were deep pools of yellow pus. They were *real*.

Ahmed's brother came up and spoke to the man. Disappointed, he turned away. Charlotte couldn't bear to think that he was starving. He had so little to live for. She got up from the table and went over to the café owner.

'Here, give him this. He could at least buy some coffee. Tell him I'm not a tourist; I haven't much money.' The man shrugged his shoulders, but went up to the beggar as he left, and thrust a few piastres into the ragged pocket of the man's robe. The beggar turned, and bowed towards Charlotte.

It became her habit to give the man a little each day. He sat there by the gate so patiently. He always recognized her step, and her voice. He was part of the street scene, crouching by the gate in his dirty robe and turban, a stick at the ready to beat off the dogs and the cruel children. She didn't know where he went at night.

Around her, men were talking and laughing. They lit their hubble-bubble pipes, or 'nargili' as they were called, and got out the backgammon boards. This was the real Cairo. She should have lived here when she was working for the Foreign Office. Diplomats shouldn't be hidden away in westernized apartments. Sitting here, drinking coffee and listening, they would learn more in one evening than several weeks in the cocktail circuit.

The men looked at her curiously, but the owner of the café had passed the word around, and no one bothered her. Some even nodded to her when she made a move to leave. Some looked her up and down, not with desire, but with curiosity.

Charlotte was conscious of her filthy dress. She'd worn it for a week now. She had to find a cheap laundry. Maybe Ahmed's wife would wash it for her, and she could hang it across the road, as most people did in this poor quarter. Meanwhile, she would buy herself a cheap skirt – long, so that she wouldn't look too conspicuous. She went off down one of the side streets, noting that the café owner watched which direction she took. They were keeping an eye on her. She decided to play safe, and not to roam too far.

She plunged off into a maze of tiny streets, dark alleys filled with small shops. The smell of spices was overwhelming. All the smells of the East were there – cloves, cinnamon, garlic, aniseed, and the ever-present stench of the open sewer, which flowed down the middle of the road in true mediaeval fashion.

Charlotte found a stall selling cheap cotton skirts. She chose one in a muslin-type of material with blue and green stripes. She hoped it wouldn't be too transparent, but it would be cool. She didn't want to attract any male attention. She bought a cotton blouse to go with it, and a broad band to go round her head. She felt her long hair an embarrassment. Men looked at it. It probably wasn't proper for young women to walk around with their hair unbound – not in these parts of the city. Charlotte might even have to cover her hair with a scarf. Long hair was sometimes seen as an advertisement for sexual availability.

The clothes were very cheap – the price of a plateful of falafel. Outside the European quarters prices were very low for a westerner. Charlotte was beginning to measure everything by the price of food. If she could earn just a small amount of money, she could live for some time.

The roads were narrow and evil-smelling. She ought to go out only in the daytime. She turned round and made her way back to the main street, conscious that hundreds of eyes were watching her. Whether they were human or animal, she didn't know, but it was unnerving. Behind every shutter there seemed to be faces watching her – faces that withdrew quickly as she looked at them. The whole area would soon know about her. She ought to stick to the places which Ahmed had recommended. His friends would look after her, but here she was in hostile territory.

She got back to the coppersmith's shop. He was still working. His brother had joined him, smoking his nargili. They looked up as she approached.

'Goodnight, Miss Charlotte. Keep your shutters fastened tonight. The wind has turned. It's coming from the desert. Can't you feel the heat? The Khamsin is on its way!'

14

The sun disappeared the next day. A veil of sand had come between it and the earth. It was like a Biblical visitation; frogs or snakes would rain down at any moment.

She'd forgotten the Khamsin – the time of the year when the natural order of things was turned upside down. The north wind which always blew over Egypt was suddenly swept aside by a warm blast from the Sahara, bringing with it blinding clouds of choking dust. The desert had come to the city.

She woke up that morning to find the air suffocatingly hot. It was almost tangible. The light which filtered through the closed shutters was a sultry yellow. The end of the world seemed to be at hand. It needed only a mad prophet to stand at the gateway urging repentance, to complete the impression. But there was no mad prophet – just an ominous silence. The world had gone inside to await the cataclysm. She got up to open the shutters, but the air that oozed in was repulsive – soup-thick with sand and redolent of drains. She shut it quickly. Better the stifling heat than that stench.

She put on the same blue dress and went outside to fill her water jug. The effort made her stream with sweat. She had found the communal lavatory last night. It was outside, at the back of the shop, a wooden edifice built over a bottomless pit. She had prayed that it would not give way: it would be an unspeakable way to die.

Water was brought up by an ancient hand-pump. Charlotte had been told that the water was drinkable, and she would have to risk it. She couldn't afford the bottled variety. She worked the iron handle and filled her jug. Then, on impulse, she continued to pump water over her hair and shoulders soaking her dress, but feeling the lethargy going.

The café next door was open. There were few customers. No one was speaking. There were no signs of backgammon, and the men seemed too tired to light up their hubble-bubbles. It was as if they were all preserving their energy for the ordeal ahead. The owner recognized her, and nodded in her direction as she sat down. Very conscious of her wet dress and hair, she ordered coffee and a piece of flat bread.

Charlotte ate without tasting. She knew she had to eat. Survival was becoming a predominant factor now. She was pushing the thought of Hassan out of her mind. Anger had given way to a determination to get on with her own life. She would not be defeated by an unscrupulous man.

Wearily she climbed up to her room. The door was open and there was the ragged figure of Fatima. She said nothing but looked expectantly at Charlotte. Of course, she had come for her lesson. The lesson meant food that night – she would survive another day. She remembered the cheap notebook she'd bought the other afternoon when she had cashed her traveller's cheques. She went to get it and smiled at the child. If she was going to teach English, then Fatima could be her first pupil.

She wondered whether the child could read and write in her own language. She called her over and sat down on the bed, patting the space beside her.

'Do you go to school?'
'Sometimes.'
'What does this mean?' She wrote the child's name.
'Fatima.' The child laughed.
'Now write down all the names of your family.' The child did this without hesitating. She wrote neatly and clearly. It wouldn't be too difficult to teach her the western alphabet. But she would find the different script difficult. It would be better to start by teaching her verbally – pointing to different pieces of furniture, repeating the names until the child had the sounds off by heart, as one would teach a baby.

She was fascinated, watching the child struggle to pronounce the English words. A different part of the throat was needed to get round the sounds. Charlotte and Fatima spent an hour learning basic vocabulary, like Shakespeare's Henry V and Katherine de Valois. Gradually sounds emerged that were recognisably English. The parts of the body, as Shakespeare found, were a useful and highly entertaining start to learning the language.

The door opened and unnoticed by pupil and teacher, the other child came in. For a time she stood there, taking in the scene. Soon she became bored and began to explore the room. She found Charlotte's shoes; she'd brought only two pairs with her, but one of them was a pair of white high-heeled shoes she'd bought that spring in Cambridge. Dalilah climbed into them, and in the manner of all little girls, tried to walk round the room. But unlike most little girls, she didn't make a sound. It was several minutes after she'd come into the room that Charlotte noticed her. Then she burst out laughing at the sight.

Dalilah, like her Biblical namesake, was enchanting. She was the prettier of the two, and her father's favourite. Fatima was the more serious and the better scholar. Dalilah found concentrating very difficult. After repeating two words she began to play with Charlotte's bead necklace, or start to comb her hair with Charlotte's comb. In fact the brush and comb fascinated both girls. After a few days they would both arrive, and solemnly brush each other's hair. Fatima loved playing with Charlotte's. She would brush it for hours, and then plait it into two long braids, Red-Indian-fashion.

Charlotte enjoyed both children. She practised her colloquial Arabic and found out a lot about the Quarter she was now living in. Fatima and Dalilah were essentially children of the Quarter. The family had lived there for generations; other parts of Cairo which Charlotte mentioned were unknown. They had never crossed the river, and had never seen the pryamids close to. The father hardly ever took time off. He worked all days of the week, except for a few hours on Friday when he went to the local mosque to pray. There were no regulations limiting his work. Work was money. He had a family to keep and grandparents, who were now infirm, so money had to be earnt, because they were his responsibility.

The little girls went to the local school occasionally, and played around the streets and alleys. They came to no harm, because the Quarter looked after its own, as Charlotte had discovered on that first night when she had explored the stalls in the nearby street.

Fatima brought her the bowl of fool at midday. There was water in the jug. She ate the food mechanically, as it was now so hot that breathing was difficult. The air was full of fine grit that got into clothes and under bed-covering. She scratched her head continuously, even though she had washed her hair that morning. She lay down on her bed feeling lethargic and unwell.

She must have dropped off to sleep because when she woke up, the empty bowl had been taken away, but no one had disturbed her. Atmospheric tension had now reached a level where something had to give way. She understood now why the crime-rate soared at this time of the year.

Suddenly, the shutter rattled. The wind had started; not the usual brisk breeze which pushed the feluccas along towards Upper Egypt, but a howling blast of sand-laden air. It struck the window with full force, bursting open the shutters and filling the room with dust and grit.

She ran to shut the window, forcing her way across the room. Outside it was almost dark. The road was a swirling inferno of sand and rubbish. The Bab Zuwayla gate was invisible. Two men were standing with their backs to the wall, their faces covered with scarves. It was dangerous to breathe in this air, particularly if one's lungs were weak.

Charlotte forced the shutters together, using all her strength. The catch wasn't very strong, so she used a leather strap to tie the frames together. Then she groped her way back to bed, listening to the howling wind and staring at the ceiling. It was still suffocatingly hot, despite the wind which was like a blast from an oven. She was lying in a pool of perspiration where her back touched the cover. Her eyes were streaming, and she saw that the room was covered in sand.

This was the Khamsin at its worst. Before, when she had been with the Embassy, it had been merely an irritation. Then there had been air-conditioning, and glass windows to keep the sand out. They had all hated the 'canned air', but it was preferable to this tepid pea-soup.

She was trapped – the nightmare of the lobster-pot was now a reality. She would have to stay in that room until the wind eased off. It could blow for days. No one but fools and beggars went out when it was at its height. But there was nowhere for her to go. Her life was here – teaching English and trying to survive in an alien culture. She had been tipped here by a man who had deserted her.

Charlotte was now very angry. Her body trembled with rage and despair. Why had he brought her all this way, only to leave her? Why did he spend all that money on the air fare, only to see her for a few hours and then leave her? These were the questions she couldn't answer. Again she thought of the parcel of books, and the article in *Country Life*. Was Hassan a crook? The Embassy thought so. Had she been an accomplice? Had she been exploited by an unscrupulous charmer – someone who knew her emotional make-up and her frustrated sexuality? She couldn't face it. She turned her face to the wall and cried desperately. She wished she could wail, or beat her head against a wall like the Egyptians, and so drive out the pain.

That evening, there was no sign of Fatima. The Call to Prayer reminded Charlotte that the day was coming to a close. She felt appallingly lonely – deserted by everyone. She took the jug and went down to the pump in the street. It was still deserted. As she opened the street door, the hot blast of air nearly knocked her off her feet. She leant against the wall and tried to tie a scarf over her hair which streamed round her eyes like a banner. But she had to take it off, and tie it round her mouth and nostrils. She fought her way to the pump, and with an enormous effort filled the jug. Then she took off her scarf and for a few blissful minutes let the water cascade over her shoulders. Had she been alone she would have loved to have taken off her dress and let the water wash the sweat off her body. As it was, she saw the streaks on her arms and legs where the water had cleaved a way through the dust. She let the water run over her legs and feet, then picked up her jug and battled her way back to her room. There was still no sign of life. Even the dogs had slunk away into their holes and corners, and the beggar hadn't come to the gate. The café was empty.

Back in her room, Charlotte stood the jug by her bed. The evening was drawing in. She wasn't tired, but her body was lethargic. She was coming to the end of her resources. She didn't know what to do, or where to turn. All doors seemed closed to her. The Embassy was out of the question. She thought of James in Cambridge, but he was in the States, or she thought he was. She was entirely on her own.

Somehow she dropped off to sleep, waking up frequently and feeling very ill. Her head throbbed when she moved, and once again she was feeling sick. She wanted to go to the lavatory, but couldn't face the effort needed to get up and go out of the house. She was extremely thirsty, but the pump seemed a long way away. She had soon finished the water in her jug. When morning came she would have to make the effort to go to the pump.

Morning came at last — recognizable by the gradual emergence of the furniture out of the darkness. Once again the Call to Prayer announced the omnipotence of God. She didn't want to face the new day. She was in the grip of despair. She felt herself succumbing to the fatalism of Islam. She could survive by lying on that bed, and filling her water jug once a day.

She was saved by Fatima. She didn't notice the door open and the little girl come in. Suddenly she opened her eyes and the girl was there.

'Hallo, Fatima. What time is it?' she said.

'It's ten o'clock. Can I have my lesson?'

She had to get up to see to the child, who seemed impervious to the Khamsin. She was eager to start the lesson. She'd brought her own pen and paper — a new notebook which her mother had bought for her in the bazaar.

'Wait whilst I fill my water jug.' Charlotte needed to wash away the dust and the sweat of the previous night before she could teach the child. She would get some coffee from the café.

When she got back the child was brushing her hair. She was a serious girl — even whilst brushing her hair she didn't smile. Dalilah was all charm and allure. She would have practised her attractiveness on Charlotte, whilst using the brush. She would have been dancing round in the high-heeled shoes. Fatima concentrated on getting rid of the tangles, and smoothing out the strands of matted hair. The dust from the Khamsin was caked round her eyes and mouth, but the child seemed impervious. This was the way to survive — ignore the wind, and try to carry on as normal.

She started the lesson. Instinctively she knew this was how she would win. She could only survive through her own effort.

The child had shown her the way.

The next days passed slowly for Charlotte. The family liked her; the children learnt quickly. Fatima was the most intelligent and learnt the English letters quickly. It took Charlotte a good part of the day to prepare the next lesson. There was a real risk that Fatima would get ahead of her!

Dalilah was different. She was essentially frivolous – born to be admired. She loved to dress up in Charlotte's clothes, even in the middle of a lesson. Especially she liked to put on western make-up. Charlotte didn't use much, but it fascinated the child. She looked extraordinarily attractive when she painted her lips and pencilled round her eyes.

'You ought to be locked up,' Charlotte thought, remembering that she would in fact be kept indoors until a husband was found for her. Liberation had come to Egyptian women, but not to this social class. Girls were adored by their fathers, but kept away from other men until the husband took over. If Dalilah had been a village child she would have worn a veil at the onset of puberty, but here in Cairo, the veil had almost disappeared.

April passed into May, and the Khamsin gradually blew itself out. She was not unhappy, though she wasn't making any money. Her small capital paid the rent, and her English lessons provided her with food. The coppersmith spoke to her whenever they met, and they talked about politics – the plight of the Palestinians and the rising cost of living. No one asked her why she had come to live in that part of the city. They were too polite to enquire why she had no friends, and little money. She seldom saw Ahmed's wife. She seemed to spend most of her time in the kitchen or gossiping to the other women in the Quarter. She wore a veil in the street. In the kitchen she showed her face – a pleasant placid face that had once been beautiful.

Charlotte shared the meals – simple food. Sometimes there was fried meat. Once she ate roast pigeon. Nearly every day there was a plateful of fool which the family ate with olive oil. She mopped up the plate with her piece of bread, eating the last crumbs, as did the rest of the family. She now realised that food was precious.

But money was now an urgent problem. One day she spoke to Ahmed.

'I have to earn some money to try to save my fare back to my own country. Can you find me any more pupils? I won't charge much for lessons, but I must now start saving.'

He nodded. 'I'll do my best. I have a brother who is a shoemaker and a leather-worker. His son Mahmoud is a bright boy. It would be useful if someone in that family could speak English. Mahmoud could go to England to sell his father's shoes. He gets a lot of orders from England, and is always looking for someone to translate his letters. I'll speak to him about it.'

Charlotte looked forward to having a new pupil. It could be the start of proper classes. She had enough money left for four weeks' rent, then she would sell her jewellery. It was time to think of going home. Hassan she had thrust out of her mind. To survive, she had to forget what had happened on that house-boat in April. It was enough to get up in the morning, to nod to the café owner and Ahmed's brother, and eat her beans and bread. The two girls came for lessons every day, and were soon speaking simple sentences, much to their father's delight.

One morning in June, Charlotte woke up feeling very ill. Her head ached violently and she couldn't bear to look at the light coming in through the shutters. She felt sick and her stomach hurt. This time she knew it was serious. When she looked at herself in her little hand mirror, her skin had turned a bright yellow, as though she had been painted in the night.

When she sat up, she vomited. There was a bowl by the side of the bed, and when she looked, she saw that the liquid was bright yellow. She lay back, too weak to get up. This wasn't the old gippy tummy, or the Khamsin malaise. This was serious.

Fatima appeared as usual, and stood by the side of Charlotte's bed. She stroked her face, obviously puzzled by the dramatic colour. Charlotte was too weak to speak, although she forced a smile. The child disappeared. Then she came back with her mother. This was unusual. Never before had the mother set foot in Charlotte's room. There was the sound of voices outside the door; then silence.

Charlotte lost all count of time. She was aware, later in the day, that a strange man was at her beside, dressed in a grey suit, and the old-fashioned fez on his bird-like head. Small and sparrow-like, he had half-rimmed glasses perched on his nose. She remembered those glasses. He peered at Charlotte, looked at her tongue, and examined the whites of her eyes which were now bright yellow. She vomited again, and the little man darted forward to examine the yellow liquid.

'She has hepatitis,' he said. 'A bad attack. She must stay in bed and drink only water. It must be boiled, or if possible bottled. When she keeps that down, then she can have a little bread and yoghurt. Later, some soup, but no fat. Fool is safe, but no olive oil. But best of all is yoghurt. It's the only safe food for westerners. It will take a long time for her to get over this attack, and it could recur. Europeans seem particularly susceptible to this virus. They don't have our immunity. Maybe it's our food, maybe our water – we don't know. But she's in a very low state of health. There's not much you can do for her, but keep an eye on her, and don't give her anything to eat until she can keep down water. Where does she come from? Why is she here? She ought to go home after this attack. She'll be very weak, and she's too thin. She needs looking after.'

He left the bedside, and she could hear the voices murmuring outside in the corridor. She didn't care what they were saying. She had the basin if she wanted to be sick – that was all she needed at the moment, and to be left alone.

She gave up. The following days were spent in a twilight state of pain and nausea. She drank the water which Fatima offered her, and was aware from time to time of someone standing by her bed. She recognised Dalilah, who gently combed her hair and washed her face, and the little man in the fez stood looking at her from time to time. Most of the time she was left alone to endure the headache and watch a fly sail round the room in a hopeless manner. She watched it beat its wings against the closed shutters, but she was too weak to get up and let it out.

The heat grew in intensity. She felt she was swimming in her own perspiration. The shutters remained closed. She wouldn't have been able to tolerate the sunshine if anyone had thought of opening them. Cairo moved into its hottest season.

There were days when she thought she would die. There were days when she didn't care if she did. Then she thought of Hassan and the suffering he had caused. Then the mental pain became worse than the physical, and she groaned aloud. But there was no one to hear her.

15

She was back on the house-boat – only this time as a spectator. The two performers were Hassan and the grotesque woman she'd seen on that second visit. Helplessly she watched him make love to her. She was forced to watch all the lurid details, to hear the words of love, and to shudder at the revolting laughter. She writhed in pain, calling out to him to stop, but the laughter went on, torturing her with its mockery.

For days she lay in bed, passing from periods of lucidity to delirium. Sometimes, she was conscious that dim shapes stood by her bedside giving her water, and combing her hair. The little man with the fez appeared from time to time and gave her pills and more water. She could remember being sick and it was a long time before she could tolerate any food. The bowl stood by her bed, and she gave herself up to bouts of retching as though she was trying to rid her body of every drop of moisture. Someone came in to empty the bowl, and brought her more water. Someone combed her hair and wiped a damp cloth over her face. Someone made her bed, moving her onto the floor whilst they straightened the rug.

After a week, the bouts of vomiting became less frequent. The hammers in her head stopped their persistent clamour. She was beginning to surface again. The shapes by the bed disappeared, and only came back to bring her bowls of fool and yoghurt. She got back her health on yoghurt. It was the one food that was quite safe to eat anywhere in the Middle East. At first she could only manage small quantities, but by the second week, she could go on small expeditions to the pump and the lavatory. Her strength was gradually coming back but mentally, she was at a very low ebb.

One morning she sat up in bed and reached for the little hand mirror which had so delighted Dalilah. The face that looked back at her was a stranger's – a death's head, with yellow parchment skin stretched out over prominent bones.

Her hair looked thin and out of condition. It was matted and there were touches of grey at the temples. She had aged over the last ten days. Her body was like an anorexic's. She prodded her shoulder-blades, and felt her ribcage. She looked like a famine victim from the Third World. Charlotte shuddered and put the mirror away. She remembered how debilitating hepatitis could be. It took almost longer to get over the effects of the attack than the attack itself. She doubted whether her liver would ever be the same again.

There was a knock on the door, and the little sparrow-man came in, his fez moulded to his head as though he'd been born in it.

'I'm glad to see you sitting up. You've been very ill.' He came forward and peered at her. 'My name's Dr Abu Afia.' He stretched out his hand with a smile. Charlotte took it gratefully. Her hand looked as small as a child's.

'Thank you for your help. I don't remember much about the attack. I have never had hepatitis.'

'You've had a bad attack and you're going to be very weak for a long time yet. Your landlord and his wife have looked after you. There wasn't much for me to do. You have good friends. It's now largely a matter of rest and diet. The little girl Fatima kept you supplied with water. The wife boiled it for you specially, in spite of all her other work. The child says you're teaching her English.'

'Yes. I shall have to start again soon. I must earn some money. I owe a lot of rent. And how much do I owe you?' she asked, suddenly remembering that the Embassy wasn't paying her bills now.

He waved aside the question. 'Please don't worry. Ahmed settled that. When you have recovered, and are earning money, then you can pay him back. He will be pleased that you are better.'

'What caused the attack? Is it infectious?'

'You were very infectious, but we kept you away from the rest of the household whilst the attack was at its height. The disease is caused by a virus – that's all. You picked it up somewhere; either from food or water, or from the lavatory. We have an immunity to it, but it's very common amongst

Europeans. It's one of the diseases of Africa. I'm afraid you will not be able to drink alcohol, and coffee might make you sick to start with. Ahmed will see that you have some good soup and bread, and we'll try to put some flesh back on these arms.' He picked up her arm which was as thin as a matchstick. He shook his head with disapproval.

'We must get you back to your own people as soon as you are strong. Is there anything to keep you in Cairo, now? Your friends didn't come near you when you were ill, so I shouldn't rely on them for friendship, if I were you. Is there anyone in particular whom you would like to see? Does anyone keep you here?'

She thought for only a few seconds. 'No,' she said. 'There's nobody.' She felt nothing. Just emptiness. Hassan had been exorcised by her illness. The pain had gone. She felt emotionally drained.

The doctor looked at her keenly. 'Good. I'm glad there's no one. No one is worth the suffering you've been through. You talked a lot when you were delirious,' he said by way of explanation. 'I'm sorry you've had a bad experience from one of my people. We're not all like that,' he added.

She felt herself redden with embarrassment. Had she mentioned any names? How much did the family know? But she was too tired to care. They had all been unbelievably kind. It was her job now to get better, and pay them back somehow.

'Get back to sleep now. Fatima will bring you your soup. Eat all you can, and rest. The Khamsin is over; the weather in early summer is wonderful. Tomorrow you can take your class out into the sun.' He shook her hand again, and was gone. It was the last she saw of the little doctor. He had been very kind.

But she was left with depression – partly due to her illness, partly due to her feeling of incompetence. Her life was in ruins. She had been both blind and stupid, and deaf to commonsense. It was up to her now to retrieve what she could from the wreckage.

Charlotte tried to prepare a lesson, but her fingers were too feeble to hold the pencil. Fatima came and sat by her bed, and she told the child stories, about Hansel and Gretel and the Little Mermaid. It was strange to tell these stories from Grimm and Hans Andersen to this child who had never seen pine forests, or the rushing streams where trolls lived. She had never seen a cave or a mountain, a snow-field or an icicle. But she knew all about trolls and fairies. Egyptian folklore had legions of spirits called 'afrites' and djinns. She believed implicitly in the world of the supernatural. It was a bad djinn who was responsible for Charlotte's illness.

The family were very kind to Charlotte. The child came twice a day with food, and one day, Ahmed himself appeared and helped Charlotte out into the street. There, tucked out of sight of the strollers, he'd put an ancient velvet armchair. The red material was frayed and stained, but it was comfortable, and Charlotte would curl up like a cat in the sunshine, and watch the world.

The apprentices nodded to her; she became the family mascot – their good luck charm. She wanted no more. She had reached the stage where she was happy to be looked after. She couldn't think of responsibilities, or making money. It was enough to get her bowl of food, and sit in the sun watching the world of Cairo go by. She felt a sympathy with the beggar who shuffled to his place by the gate in the early morning. Both of them were resigned to their lot.

One evening as the sun went down, she got up from her chair as usual to go inside and sit with the family. Suddenly she changed her mind. It was a marvellous night – warm and fresh. She thought she would walk to one of the streets near the mosque of El-Azhar. She suddenly needed exercise. A short walk would lead her to the spice bazaar.

Calling out to Ahmed, she set off towards the narrow alleys of the spice stalls. The Souk of El-Attarin was one of the most attractive streets in mediaeval Cairo. There was no need to ask the way. You literally followed your nose. Sacks of saffron, cinnamon and ginger filled the air with their scent. On all sides were stalls piled high with dried fruits and flowers to be crushed and turned into perfumes and oils. She was fascinated. Here was a Cairo she had never seen before, nor ever knew existed. As darkness fell, thousands of lights were lit – mostly strings of electric light bulbs, but also the occasional copper gleam of an old-fashioned oil lamp.

Nobody took any notice of her. Since her illness she had become insignificant. In her long skirt, with a cotton headscarf knotted round her hair, she looked like a western hippy, a derelict washed up in this city, probably living there for the cheap heroin.

Charlotte stopped at the coffee shop 'Kirsha's' in the Midaq Alley; a famous place built on the sight of an ancient pharmacy. Tonight there were chairs and tables outside on the road. The hubble-bubble pipes were lit, and people were settling down for a long night of gossip and entertainment. It was not a night to go to bed early.

She sat down at one of the corner tables. She still had a little money left. Tomorrow, she'd cash her last traveller's cheque, and pay what she could to Ahmed. But tonight, she thought she'd try the coffee. Her illness was receding. She'd tried the local coffee yesterday, with no ill effects. With the drink, she ordered a plateful of *kanafa*, a very sweet pudding made of some sort of cereal and covered with syrup and chopped nuts. She felt in need of sugar. The coppersmith's food was good, but monotonous.

Suddenly, she was conscious of a man staring at her from the opposite side of the café. She felt a ripple of fear. She didn't want any male attention at that moment. So she ignored him, and got out her exercise book and pencil and settled down to describe the scene. The thought had come to her that morning, that she ought to try and write about her experiences. After all, she had been through a lot in her life. She couldn't yet write about the affair with Hassan – not yet, but she could start by writing about the two girls, and life in the bazaar quarter of Old Cairo.

She paused over the first sentence. How to begin? She looked at the group of backgammon players next to her – middle-aged, heavily-built, dressed in trousers and shirts. There were no ties to be seen. They were the off-duty shopkeepers. They wouldn't wear the gallabiyas of the fellahin or suffragi class. They owned the spice shops and the perfume stalls that line the Midaq Alley. They'd left the shops to the assistants and had come to relax with friends in this famous coffee shop.

The man opposite continued to look at her. He had a notebook in front of him, and as she looked at him surreptitiously she saw he was sketching her with a piece of charcoal. She began to be intrigued. Who was he? He was obviously interested in her face, because he didn't realise he was staring at her, which in any culture would have been rude.

He was alone, concentrating on his drawing. She shrugged her shoulders and let him draw what he wanted. If he propositioned her later on, she could always get rid of him.

Her *kanafa* was good, sticky-sweet and filling. Suddenly she craved food. After weeks of starvation she longed for all the sweet food she could get – not meat, but sweet sticky food. She scribbled away busily, now describing the waiters. This was their busy time. Several of them seemed to be foreign. They weren't Arab, but called to each other in a language which Charlotte understood to be Greek. It was going to be a busy evening. The Khamsin was over, and the hot Cairo nights were beginning.

'Hello. Are you a writer?' She looked up. The man was standing at her table. He was only a little man, shorter than she was, about five feet four, she guessed. He had the broad shoulders and slim waist of an athlete of some kind. He could have been a boxer or a wrestler. She looked into black eyes twinkling in a friendly manner. His hair was thick and black, receding in front, and grey at the sides. She thought he looked about forty-five. He spoke excellent English, with a foreign accent that wasn't Arab. His manner was straightforward and friendly; there was no hint of lechery in the way he was looking at her. Just interest.

'May I sit down?' He waited for her to answer.

'Please do, but I'm not for hire.'

He looked puzzled, and then laughed. 'I didn't think you were. You wouldn't be here if that's what you were looking for.'

Thinking he meant that she looked so dreadful that it was beyond belief she could have been taken for a prostitute, she said,

'What do you mean?'

'That you don't know the district. You can't have lived here long. There are other cafés and places where I would go if I needed to "hire" a lady.'

Was he laughing at her? He didn't seem to take anything seriously. She decided to answer his first question. 'Am I a writer? The answer is maybe. I'm just a beginner. Are you an artist?'

He tipped back his chair and laughed. 'Maybe. I draw the odd face; I paint lurid pictures for American tourists. There's nothing like a good sunset to pull in the customers. It gives them a hint of Rudolph Valentino. I have thought of including a sheik or two, but there's not many of them left, and they won't stand still long enough for me to draw them.'

Charlotte laughed for the first time in weeks. The little man was delightfully modest. She wanted to see the drawing he'd made of her.

He went on. 'It's not a very noble way to earn a living, but it's honest. It's easy to starve in this city. Thousands do. But it's also quite easy to earn money. It's a question of seeing what people want, and then giving them the product. People on holiday always spend money. Paintings are more cultural than photographs. I only give them what they want to see. I hoped you were going to buy your picture.'

He produced the sketch he'd been making of Charlotte. She stared at it in fascination. Huge brown eyes, heavily outlined in charcoal gazed out of the sheet of paper. He had drawn a caricature – all eyes, and a great mane of hair. The rest of her was just indicated.

'Is that me?'

'I'm afraid so. I think you need feeding up. You need lots of that – ' he indicated the empty plate of kanafa.

'I've been ill. That's why I'm thin.'

He nodded. 'You look ill. Have you friends?'

'Of course. I live by the gateway, by the Mosque. I teach English.'

'So you're local. I live near here, just off the Street of the Spices. I suppose I could call myself an artist, but I'm also a bit of a musician. Sometimes Abdullah here lets me play my pipe and drums. Sometimes he doesn't; then I draw his customers.'

'I'd like to hear you play.' It was a long time since she'd

heard any music. She was beginning to like the look of this man. He was obviously poor, but he was cheerful and intelligent. She also thought the sketch of herself, although unflattering, was good.

'I haven't any money; not much anyway. Can I buy you a coffee in return for the drawing?' She liked to be in control of the situation. Never again would she expose herself and risk rejection.

'I should be delighted to accept. It's the first time a lady has bought me a cup of coffee. Are you what they call a liberated lady in the western world?'

'No, but I believe in sharing.'

'Good, so do I. You won't find many people here who will share your views! Most people believe in holding on to what's theirs, and keeping others off their pitch.'

'I've found great kindness here, and compassion. I can never hope to repay their hospitality, particularly when I was ill.'

'It's part of their religion – in the name of Allah, the Compassionate, the Merciful. It's what Christians are supposed to believe, but I'm afraid western society hasn't much room for the compassionate.'

'You're not a Moslem then?' she asked.

'No. I'm not really a Christian, either. I don't believe in any God up there. Life is cruel, a jungle. We look after those we love, or those we think may benefit us in some way. The rest we kick out into the street. I suppose I should be Christian. I was born in Greece, and my family had me christened. That makes me a Christian, I suppose.' He smiled broadly at her, as though the whole subject was a joke. 'What about you? I suppose you were born in Kingston-upon-Thames?'

She laughed. 'How do you know that place? Have you ever been to England?'

'Oh yes. I know your Home Counties well. You speak with their accent. I shall have to look out for hundreds of small Arabs talking like your Queen, if you teach them English.'

'Why were you living in the Home Counties?'

'Years ago, I studied art at the Slade. I had digs at Kingston-upon-Thames. Very beautiful, but very difficult to get there.'

'How long ago was that?'

'Ages ago; when I was young. Now have some more of that pudding on me. It's like Shredded Wheat with treacle, don't you think?'

She liked talking to him. He was not disturbingly sexual. Yet his body was fit and muscular, and he was not unattractive. She could feel his energy. He was bursting with vigorous life. She felt pale and unhealthy in contrast.

She ate a second plateful of the sickly sweet. The food was nectar after her long fast. Her body was craving for sugar and it was pleasant to sit here with this engaging man and let him entertain her. For once she let herself relax.

He turned out to be a Greek from the Piraeus, and his name was Andreas Andreas Angelopoulos. He was well-known in the restaurant. Halfway through her second plateful of the pudding, he left her, and walked over to a group of men sitting in the corner of the restaurant. They made a space for him at their table, greeting him with smiles and inviting him to sit down and play backgammon with them.

Charlotte watched him intently. He was of them, but not one of them. His Greekness set him apart. But she liked his merry laugh, and his broad shoulders. What had brought him to this city? Why should a man who could sketch as well as he could be forced to make his living painting cheap pictures of sunsets over pyramids?

She finished her food and got up to go. She would have liked to thank the man for his generosity, but she didn't want to disturb the game. She looked at him as she left the café. He felt her glance and looked up. He waved. He was far too absorbed in the game to get up and speak to her.

She walked back along the Street of the Spices, breathing the heavily-scented air, and stopping to watch the shopkeepers weighing out the spices in tiny silver scales. Spices were still very precious.

Back at the coppersmith's shop, she saw Ahmed standing there looking worried.

'I'm back,' she called out. 'I've not been far, but I've eaten some food in a café. I'm beginning to feel better. Tomorrow, we'll get on with the English lessons, and Mahmoud can start whenever he likes. I am not going to be ill ever again. From now on, I shall take care of myself, and your family. You have been so kind to me. You are my friends.'

Ahmed bowed at the compliment. He was delighted to see her smiling again. It was time she got her strength back, earned some money for her fare, and went back to her own people. They would miss her, but this wasn't her home. Women should not live on their own.

16

It was several days before she saw him again. The English class took up a lot of her time. Mahmoud turned up the next day. He was a solemn ten year old – curly hair round a smiling face; the skullcap on top of the curls, white teeth and striped gallabiya. He was charming and full of fun. He also took his lessons very seriously. He was in his element in a street game of football, where he would outrun all the other boys. But in the classroom he was aware that his family's honour was at stake. As the son of a shoemaker, he wanted to do well. He knew that English would be very useful to his family.

He was also respectful towards Charlotte. There was none of the cheerful irreverence of the English child towards his teacher. These children had been trained to respect learning. They were used to sitting in silence, to listen, to write down the things to be memorized and to learn them by heart. Nothing was learnt unless it was committed to memory. Even the theological students at El-Azhar learnt the Koranic texts by heart.

Charlotte didn't question the system, but she did take the class into the street. She sat in her velvet armchair, with the children squatting on the stone cobbles beside her, in the manner of all teachers and pupils throughout the world.

At first, she merely pointed to objects, and the children repeated the word, until the sound became recognizable. They all learnt quickly. Fatima, as expected, held the lead. Charlotte had no textbooks, and the children wouldn't have been able to buy any, had they been available. But for the time being, she made her own. She wrote out the Grimm's stories in simple English, and drew little illustrations in the margins. These stories she would read to the children, gain their interest, and then ask them to draw the letters.

They enjoyed this. She prepared the stories in the afternoons, when it was too hot to go outside. Sometimes one of the children would come quietly up to her room, and look over her shoulder as she worked. Fatima was soon able to pick out the words she already knew, and make a fair job of tackling a new story. But it was a long time before any of the children could build up a new word phonetically.

Charlotte was almost happy with her days. The mornings she spent in teaching the children; the afternoons, in preparing the next day's lessons. She found herself keeping a 'progress sheet', for each child, in the manner of an English school-teacher, and she made a list of all the words she was certain were familiar to each child.

Charlotte was now respected in the neighbourhood, in the way that a wise woman is respected in any culture. People on their way to the bazaar would stop to watch her with the children. Her velvet chair became a well-known sight. Long after she'd gone, the chair was still placed there each day. Had she lived in a less sophisticated society, she felt the chair would have been venerated, like David Livingstone's in Central Africa. The velvet armchair would always be known as 'the English teacher's chair'.

She also began a small sideline in translating English letters into Arabic. The bazaar owners, in particular, would receive letters from tourists, back in their own countries wanting goods for their friends at home. The leather-worker used to get a spate of letters at the end of the tourist season, asking for camel saddles, and slippers. He'd send letters in the mornings through Mahmoud, and Charlotte would write the quick translation for the child to take home at dinner-time. In return, they would bring her fruit, or platefuls of sweet sticky cakes. One man brought her some perfume – heavy and sweet with the scent of roses.

But she was not making any money. Ahmed didn't bother to ask for his rent now that his daughters were progressing in English and he could see a future for them in translating his friends' letters. She ate the same food as the coppersmith and his family, and relied on gifts for extras. Sometimes she felt like a Buddhist priest outside his temple. Her old blue dress and cotton skirt were like a uniform, the assortment of gifts placed by the chair like a row of begging bowls. She felt an affinity with the beggar in the gateway, except he couldn't see, and spent his days counting the coins with his withered fingers.

In the evenings, Charlotte began to write. She started by writing up the account of the day's teaching, in the manner of a student teacher filling in his report sheet. Then she found herself expanding on the children – Mahmoud's steady plodding, Fatima's quick memory, Dalilah's inability to concentrate for more than two minutes at a time. She wrote about her meals, her conversations with the coppersmith, the people she saw going into the Mosque. Then she wrote down her impressions of the other Cairo she'd seen in her first few days – the peasant boys with the gamoose, the women unloading stones, the man at the water wheel. She quickly ran out of paper, and one of her main expenses was buying cheap notebooks, which she found in a small dark shop in the next street. She saw she would spend her few remaining piastres on these books. She needed them for teaching, for writing out the fairy stories and for her own thoughts. She was soon getting through three a week. She only bought the cheapest paper, wafer-thin and ruled with irregular red lines, but at least she could record her ideas.

By the middle of June, Charlotte was down to her last ten pounds. Soon she would be destitute. It wasn't enough to teach three children for just the rent and food, unless she decided to stay in that room and that street for the rest of her life. She had adapted quite well. Her clothes were shabby, her hair now braided into two plaits, which Dalilah brushed out every evening, only to re-plait in the morning. Like the locals, she went round in bare feet, and the soles of her feet became hard and calloused on the cobbles. If she went to the local café, then she slipped on a pair of old brown leather sandals. Once she caught the leather-worker looking at these ancient shoes, bought in Cambridge light years ago. One day, he could restrain himself no longer.

'Miss Charlotte, let me have your shoes tonight, and I will make you a new pair out of some odd pieces of leather.'

'That's very kind; but I can't afford any. These will do for a bit longer. Look, they still keep my feet off the stones.' She lifted her foot to show the sole of the sandal, which was indeed free from holes.

'They are very good shoes; but I would like to make you a new pair. You teach my son. Soon, he will be making money by talking to my English and American tourists. I should be pleased to make you a new pair.'

Charlotte smiled at the thought of Mahmoud as an export manager for his father. So she gave him the shoes, and sure enough Mahmoud arrived the next day with a fine pair of Egyptian sandals, modelled on her old pair, but made in new soft leather. He had left a strap which went over her big toe, and there was lacing to go up her leg, like a mediaeval shoe. They were very comfortable.

The children watched whilst she put them on, and broke into spontaneous clapping when she'd finished. Mahmoud, whose family had provided this comfort for the teacher, beamed with pleasure. He was particularly attentive that day.

To celebrate her new shoes, Charlotte went back to the Kirsha café in the spice alley. It was just the same – the same group playing backgammon. The waiter nodded to her as she ordered her coffee. He remembered her, for by now her 'fame' had spread to most of the Old City. They knew she wasn't a beggar, or a drug addict. They regarded her with a sort of benevolent affection, as one would a weird old lady who was kind and harmless, in an English village. There was some talk of a love affair, some talk of being robbed. But she spoke their language, and lived peacefully amongst them, so they had come to accept her.

Tonight, the waiter served her coffee, and wouldn't take any money. She felt even more like a holy woman, being fed by the community. As she thanked the man, she felt she was bestowing a blessing. He bowed and smiled as he walked away. Perhaps there was something magical about being able to speak foreign languages!

Andreas arrived soon after she'd been served with her coffee. He glanced round as he came in; perhaps he was looking for her, she thought. She wasn't sure, but he was certainly pleased to see her.

'Hallo again. So you've come back to our "local".'

She laughed. 'It's not quite like Kingston-upon-Thames.'

They were straight away back where they had left off. It was as if they had never been apart.

'May I join you?' he said. She nodded. She liked the way he asked permission. He never presumed that he was welcome. Andreas was shy. But he wanted to be accepted. He still had his sketch pad under his arm.

'Are you working tonight?' she asked.

'I work all the time. I'm always looking for new things. The western tourists will soon be leaving. They're the ones who pay out money for sketches of themselves. We'll soon be getting the Saudis — the Gulf people. They come here for shopping and often buy the odd sunset or Sphinx as souvenirs. They like their colours good and strong, though — egg-yellow sunsets, mixed with liberal splashes of blood red. None of your English watercolours.'

Charlotte smiled. 'I can't quite see a sunset in Egypt painted like a Turner landscape.' She thought for a second of the misty light over a Suffolk river, and the outlines of the cormorants against the grey sky.

Andreas sat down and put his elbows on the table and looked at her quizzically. He was a strange mixture of the Arab and the Greek; but his manners were English. Sometimes the conversation was as polite as if they had met in a pub in Reigate. Even his clean cotton shirt and cotton trousers would not have caused comment in an English café. But his eyes were not English; black like pools of liquorice, with golden dancing flecks. A mouth that was red and expressive. Hands that were large for his frame, and used continually to express his thoughts and emotions.

She wanted to ask him if he had a wife or family, but there was something about him that didn't encourage personal questions. Neither did he ask what an obviously educated English lady was doing in an Arab quarter of Cairo with calloused feet, and no money. Where were her friends? Where was her family? What kept her here? All that he would have to ask later. It was enough that she enjoyed his company, and the wariness had gone from her expression. She was a long way from trusting him; she was like a wild creature that has been hurt by a human and so mistrusts everyone. But like a wild creature that has known domestic comfort, she was timidly returning to the kitchen door asking for scraps. The first clumsy move on his part, and she would be off.

At the end of the evening, or rather when she began to tire, he asked if he could walk home with her. She jumped with alarm. She had indeed been hurt. Would she ever trust anyone again?

'Don't worry,' he said gently. 'I'm only coming to keep an eye on you. The alleys are full of thieves and rogues. I won't harm you.'

Looking into his sympathetic face and those mournful eyes, she felt she could trust him. Again she nodded. 'It's not far. Just by the Bab Zuwayla gate.'

He got up to leave; she had the feeling he already knew where she lived. Probably the whole quarter knew the wise woman's room!

She had nothing to fear; Andreas walked by her side, and she felt safe, even when a beggar lurched past, his face a mass of sores, his arm a stump wrapped in a dirty bandage. Almost certainly he would have pestered her for bakshish had she been on her own. She was terrified of these beggars. Although most of them were blind, they had an uncanny knack of knowing exactly where she was going. It was almost impossible to throw them off the track. To give a coin was a disaster. Almost immediately she could be surrounded by a mob of women with emaciated children, their eyes liquid with flies, all thrusting hands in her face. As long as she stayed in her own quarter she was safe. But to step outside the boundaries was to court disaster. She could no longer afford taxis.

The little man trotted along beside her. She was taller than him by about five inches. But he bounced along on the balls of his feet like an athlete. He had a tireless stride. She was still feeling the lethargy which was a legacy of the hepatitis, and was quite breathless by the time they came to the familiar outline of the Mosque by the gateway.

'You should walk more. These lovely June evenings are just right for a stroll. Why don't you come with me one evening when I go to a restaurant and draw the customers? You could pass the bowl round for the money, if you like. If you untied your hair, and wore that long skirt, you would be quite an attraction. You could pose as my sister. There'd be a share in the takings, if you like. Enough to go towards your rent.'

She hesitated. He understood. 'Don't worry, I'll not try to seduce you. I'm past all that. I left that behind when I moved here from Florence. You would be useful – an attraction. Why not come?'

Still she was wary. 'Thank you, I'll think about it. Will I see you again at the café?'

'For the next few days, then I go to Alexandria. At the end of August, I'm back in the cafés by the pyramids. My friends and I play to the crowds in the summer months. I join up with two others, and we tumble and juggle, and entertain the diners at the smart resorts. Have you ever seen a "gully gully" man? They are marvellous jugglers – magicians really. Why not come and pass the hat round for us? It would free one of us to carry on with the act. Do you play an instrument?'

She thought quickly. 'Yes, I play the guitar – a little. But I have never played Arab music. I could play traditional western melodies, though. The tourists might like that. I sometimes used to play and sing back home.' She thought briefly of James' elegant house in Trumpington Street, and the cultured guests listening to her singing the Elizabethan songs.

'Well, it would be different. They might like that, and you certainly look the part. We could dress you up a little – a Crusader's lady, or a female troubadour. There might even be some extra money in this,' he said with a smile. 'Don't worry about my friends. You will be my "sister" and they will look after you. Let me know soon, if you would like to come and join us. I'll see if I can find a guitar. I play a small hand drum, and my friends play a variety of Arab instruments. A guitar will make a difference.'

He turned and walked quickly away, still with those short springy steps. She liked Andreas. He took her mind away from her troubles, and she was beginning to trust him. As she climbed the stairs to her room, she thought she would go to Kirsha's tomorrow, and see him again. It might be a chance to make some money. She remembered once hearing about a student friend of hers, who had spent one summer 'busking' in Geneva. He'd played a guitar and a penny whistle, and had made a hundred pounds a week playing traditional Irish airs. He'd wanted her to go with him, to 'bottle' was his expression.

    That night she went to sleep quickly, thinking of jugglers and buskers, and the little man with the springing walk and the twinkling black eyes.

17

The afternoon sun beat down on the rows of glistening bodies stretched out under the umbrellas. Seal-like, they clustered together in colonies, huddled in the small patches of shade; the occasional arm raised to cuff a restless child, like the flipper of an elderly bull seal, disturbed in his sleep.

It was too hot to move. Despite the onshore breeze, the heat was intense. The sand was too hot to walk on in bare feet. There was no sound; even the ice-cream seller, and the water carrier were curled up in the shade of the wall that shielded the beach from the Corniche. They would only stir themselves around four o'clock when the herd would begin to wake up and demand instant attention.

Sidi Bishr was one of the smarter beaches in Alexandria. These bodies were all well-fed. By day they lay basking on the beach; by night they swarmed into the restaurants and casinos in search of pleasure. The day was spent in recuperation. Whereas the fellahin covered themselves up against the heat, these wealthy bourgeois took their clothes off, hired an umbrella, and lounged the summer away.

In front of them stretched the Bay of Alexandria, one of the most spectacular coastlines in North Africa. The sweep of the Corniche, the white sand, and the incredible blue of the Mediterranean made this beach one of the most beautiful in the world.

Not far from the herd of basking seals, a girl was sitting with her back propped up against the wall. She looked like a western 'hippy', one of those strange creatures which haunt Alexandria and Venice – anywhere the sun shines, and the living is cheap. She squatted like a native, her cheap cotton skirt tucked round her brown bare legs. A beaded scarf covered her head to shield it from the sun. She was engrossed in her writing. A cheap exercise book was propped up on her knees, and she wrote rapidly with a biro, the sort one can buy anywhere for a few piastres.

A few feet away, a man was lounging against the wall, a cheap straw hat covering his face from the heat. He too was preoccupied with his work. He was sketching the girl – rapidly, with short, decisive strokes of his charcoal. It was almost as if he was frightened of running out of time. Soon, the magic of the moment would disappear; the herd would heave themselves towards the cafés, and the girl would lay down her pen and stand up. He rarely caught her in such a pose.

Occasionally, she would look out to sea, as if for inspiration; sometimes she would impatiently cross out a word. This was the danger signal. Too many crossings out, and she would throw down the pen and jump to her feet. But this afternoon it was too hot to jump anywhere. It was almost too hot to write – the sweat streaming down her arms made the pen slippery to hold.

Near the man and the girl, with them, but apart from them, were two other men, sprawled out asleep. They had turned to face the wall, their backs shielded from the sun by a piece of straw matting. They couldn't afford even the few piastres needed to hire one of the umbrellas. But the straw shield was adequate, and they were used to heat. It was better than relying on newspapers and a park bench in a northern city.

Charlotte, because it was Charlotte, came to the end of the exercise book. She went on writing on the back cover in small, neat handwriting, the lines closely spaced to save paper. When the book could take no more words, she threw down her biro, and looked across at Andreas, who was frantically finishing the sketch before she moved.

'That's another book finished; I'll have to try to buy a new one tomorrow. The pen's about to run out as well,' she whispered across to him. There was something about the hot still atmosphere that made talking a sacrilege. Tonight, the seals would be laughing and shouting, and the night air of the city would throb with all types of music; but during the sleeping time, the effort needed to project the voice across the shimmering heated air was too great.

Andreas put down his charcoal, and moved nearer to Charlotte. He dragged himself over the hot sand like one of the beggars one saw in the alleys at night, pushing their legless torsos along with their hands; their trunks strapped to a platform on wheels. Andreas flopped down beside her – the exertion had made the sweat stream down his face.

'I shall need paper, too. I've got enough for today, when these wake up.' He waved his hand at the slumbering bodies.

'Why don't you draw them now; whilst they're still asleep?' smiled Charlotte.

'What – and get cursed at, instead of paid! The wealthy don't like realism.'

'No, but people who love real art would pay you lots of money for true pictures. Look at me here' – she picked up the paper with her sketch – 'it's the most unflattering portrait I've ever seen. You make me look like a famine victim crouching over her dead baby. I wouldn't pay you a piastre for that, if I were one of these, but in fact I think it's very good; one of the best you've done. If I lived in Rome or Venice and saw you painting that in the street, I would give you ten pounds for it, gladly, and think I'd got a bargain.'

'But we're in Alexandria. These fat, complacent people are our customers. They don't want the truth, they want flattery. We've got to eat – today at least, and they pay more money for flattery. How could I draw that mountain of flesh over there – or the woman next to him? I presume it's his wife. As a matter of fact, he does present an interesting angle.'

The man's head was towards the Corniche; his feet to the sea. From where they were sitting, they had a fine view straight down the mountain of his body. Only his big toe was visible from behind the enormous belly. His wife lay next to him, her flesh squeezed into a tiny scarlet bikini, designed for a young girl. Her breasts and his belly rose and fell in unison. Both were the same length; both the same width. Both had gleaming black hair, and shaggy tufts of pubic hair curled out of the woman's red bikini bottom. Nothing was visible of the man's lower region, as the mountain-range of his stomach obscured everything, except his big toes.

Andreas drew quickly and decisively, before the couple woke up. He liked working in charcoal, particularly when he was trying to translate bodies into a series of symmetrical shapes which was what he was doing that afternoon. Charlotte watched him, his face absorbed in his work. He was good. He undoubtedly had talent. Again she thought that he was wasting himself in this life. He could draw sunsets without thinking. He deserved better things than to sit in cafés amusing tourists.

The ice-cream seller had seen her move. Had it been anyone else, he would have been on his feet to serve her. It was nearly time for the herd to start the ritual scratching and spitting which preceded waking up. But she was not of the spending class. She was at his level. She was waiting for the beach to wake up and pay her money. She had none to spend on his ice-cream. But she might be able to afford water; and sure enough, she beckoned the old water-seller over, and asked for a cupful. Charlotte had become immune to water-borne germs. She could drink practically anything, now; in fact, in July, one had to drink from anywhere, from sheer necessity. She still wouldn't touch the pools and canals, but most villages had stand-pipes and the water had not harmed her.

She gave the man a coin and drank the water gratefully. She offered some to Andreas; he shook his head. They were used to sharing a cupful of water. The two figures under the straw matting didn't move. They would stay there as long as they were allowed to. There was not much point in waking them up before four. There was a long night ahead of them. One was a musician, and one a juggler – but both could double up as tumblers if called upon. Their turn would come later.

Some of the corpses were stirring. A trembling ripple was disturbing the regular summit of the belly in front of Charlotte. He snorted, and turned over, thus putting an end to Andreas' work. He wasn't comfortable in that position, and turned to face his wife, helping his stomach over as he moved. The movement disturbed her; she scratched her gleaming breasts, now streaming with sweat. She turned away from her husband, her belly flopping onto the sand; her breasts oozing out from the thin piece of material which tried in vain to restrain them. Andreas began to sketch frantically. If only he could get the rough outline, he could fill in the details later. He was engrossed; he couldn't even stop for a drink of water, otherwise the couple might move again.

All around them people were waking up, scratching and sighing. Soon they would stagger to their feet and stand under the beach showers. Some would lurch towards the sea and roll in the surf. Some would start to throw a beachball at friends, languidly at first, but later with mounting enthusiasm. This was the moment when Charlotte went to pick up her guitar, hidden away from the sun under a shelter of straw matting which they had built on the beach to protect their instruments.

Gently she stroked the strings of the old instrument that Andreas had found for her. She watched the reactions of the bodies around her; if they snorted and glared, she stopped. But if they sighed and smiled, then she played on. She played the music of the Renaissance – Monteverdi madrigals which she had adapted for the guitar. French chansons she sang herself. In that hot still atmosphere her voice carried well. She had a beautiful, clear, alto voice, and she sang the songs unfalteringly. She was very popular with the smart Alexandrians who thought her playing 'cultured'. It was certainly different from the usual form of street entertainment – a fire-eater, or a performing baboon pathetically going through a boring ritual of gestures, taught him by whips and blows.

They liked her singing in English. Most of the well-to-do Alexandrians spoke it quite well. It was the language of the commercial world, whilst French was spoken in polite society. She would place her headscarf on the floor in front of her, and during the course of the evening it would soon be covered in coins. Her audience was intrigued by her sad beauty. She seldom smiled. Her singing transported her away to distant Cambridge, where she had sung to James' guests. Now, sitting on the sand in this fashionable resort, she could, for a few moments, think of the world she'd lost.

Andreas loved her like this. He had sketched her so often as she played her guitar – her face withdrawn from the world, like a nun's. He wanted her so much to smile – to laugh spontaneously. He couldn't understand what had made her so self-contained, so resigned in her sadness, as if this was all she expected of life. One day she would be happy, he was certain.

The husband and wife were awake. They heaved themselves

to a sitting position and called over the ice-cream seller. He was busy now. Everyone was wanting ice-creams. He circulated from umbrella to umbrella handing out the coloured sticks. The water-seller, too, was in demand. He moved off down the beach, his mugs clanking. This was the time when the whole herd needed watering.

The fruit-seller came next, his tray laden with slices of red water melon, apricots and nectarines. He was instantly busy. A slice of water melon was delicious after a sleep in the sun. Andreas called him over, and bought a slice for himself and Charlotte. He waited for her to finish her song, but couldn't resist biting into his slice – the pink water running down his chin. He spat the black seeds out onto the sand. Soon the beach would be covered with black specks. Soon, the ants would come, greedy for the sweet liquid.

Then the jasmin-seller appeared – a string of the heavily-scented flowers around his neck. That afternoon, the fat man in front of Charlotte summoned him over, and bought one for her. He had been listening to her singing with interest, and was fascinated by her withdrawn beauty. She smiled her thanks but didn't stop her song – a gentle air of John Dowland's. She felt like an opera singer who had been tossed a bouquet at the end of her performance. He hung the wreath of flowers round her neck, she bowed to receive the garland, but didn't stop her song.

With the food-sellers came the beggars. They only had a few minutes to glean their piastres. They brought with them a reminder of all the sorrows of the world – like a minor chord in the middle of a Beethoven symphony. They seemed to say: 'Rejoice whilst you can. Tomorrow you could be like us. This is what all flesh comes to.'

Charlotte cringed from the sight of the twisted bodies and stunted limbs. They didn't bother her, though. They saw she was a receiver of money, not a spender. But they had seen the fat man buy the garland. It was enough. They could spot generosity a hundred yards away. In a few seconds he was surrounded by the sad mob – deformed children, legless men dragging themselves over the hot sand and blind women, their faces crawling with flies. She bowed her head at the sight, but went on playing. The fat man was philosophical. He threw the crowd a handful of baksheesh, and watched them squabble and scream over the few coins, like gulls on a pile of garbage. In a matter of moments the beach bawwabs arrived — tall figures in gallabiyas, armed with sticks. They fell on the crowd of unfortunates, and in moments they had shuffled away, the legless man crawling sideways towards the Corniche like a hermit crab going in the wrong direction.

Now the beach had woken up. The showers were in full swing, the balls were flying about, and people were making for the sea. The two men under the wall were prodded awake by Andreas. It was their time. People needed to release energy, or watch other people release energy before dinner. Yawning, they stood up, and shook the sand off their bodies. They were Greeks and like Andreas came from the same area of Piraeus. Both were young men — Alexander, the taller and thinner, was half Andreas' age. Demetrios was nearer Charlotte's. She had often wondered whether they were gay, or if either of them was in love with Andreas, but they had never shown any particular affection for anyone. After eating, they liked to sleep, anywhere they could, and at any time of the day. When they were asked to perform, they did so, recognizing Andreas as the business manager.

They were good companions. At first, they had been suspicious of Charlotte, thinking she was Andreas' mistress, and therefore a liability. But after she had shared their food, and collected the money, and later on played the guitar, they accepted her as an equal. She was flattered by their trust, and had become fond of them. She knew nothing about either of them, or why they were here in Egypt, or where they would go in winter.

They ran down to the sea, and splashed each other like children. There was no need of towels. A few minutes in that temperature and they were completely dry.

Andreas put away his paper and charcoal. He took off his shirt, and stood there in his coloured shorts. Charlotte looked up and saw his lithe, muscular body and smiled. He was very strong. He gave the signal, and the three men went into their tumbling act, an incredibly fast routine of leapfrog and handstands. Andreas seemed to be made of rubber. He was pushed over, but he bounced up. He jumped over Alexander, he jumped over Demetrios, and then he jumped over them both. The act finished with a human pyramid, with Andreas at the top.

The crowd began to gather, then to cheer. The three men didn't stop, leaping, wrestling, rolling over and over, like rubber balls. Their energy was limitless. After a while, Charlotte put away her guitar, and went towards the crowd to collect money. She had stopped being frightened of the mob. Once she had cringed from asking for money, but now, when she knew they would all want their supper, she fearlessly went forward.

The Alexandrians were generous. They had taken to this sad girl and her three companions. It helped that the men were Greek. The Alexandrians liked Greeks. A woman singer was also a novelty. So that afternoon they gave generously, and Charlotte began to plan the supper.

The three wrestlers had come to a halt. They lay on the sand exhausted. Laughing, the crowd dispersed, and the three struggled to get their breath back.

Charlotte went up to them and said gently, 'That was well done. We've made three pounds. Tonight we can eat dolma and falafel. I'll get it, and we can eat it here on the beach. Why don't we give the casinos a rest tonight?'

Alexander gave her a look of gratitude. They were all getting tired. The season was well-advanced, and they had performed three times a day for several weeks now.

Andreas stood up, his body covered with sand. He was by far the most energetic of the three; small and tough, he was made for tumbling. 'Why not? Let's have our own party tonight. But first we ought to play outside a couple of restaurants just as an apéritif! That will get our appetites going. I'd like to try and draw you by moonlight – it's a full moon tonight.'

The crowds were dispersing. There was a steady trek up to the Corniche. Soon the cafés would be full – the charcoal burners would be lit, and the air would be full of the smells of grilled prawns and pigeons. Then the Alexandrians would want to be entertained – first with music, then with juggling, and later on with dancing. Not until the early hours of the morning would the town become silent. People went to bed late. As the sun rose, the town would be deserted. Only the odd beggar would be rummaging amongst the heaps of garbage, and the sweepers would hose down the Corniche ready for the next day's pageant.

18

The restaurant was full that evening. It was a perfect night, and for once the Alexandrians decided to risk sitting outside to eat their evening meal. Usually they liked to sit inside, shielded from the Mediterranean breezes, real or imaginary, by glass walls. But this hotel on the outskirts of Al Agami had a restaurant actually on the beach. A wall, a garden, some palm trees, separated it from the surrounding sweep of sand.

Tonight, the terrace was overflowing with wealthy holiday-makers, brown and fit from the long days in the sun; the women elaborately coiffeured and expensively dressed. The beach ovens were glowing with heat – the air filled with the smell of grilling prawns and kebabs. The waiters were rushed off their feet, serving four tables at once and watching out for new arrivals with that sixth sense which that profession seems to possess. Voices were subdued, plates full, and glasses filled with the local Egyptian wines which Moslems on holiday drink with remarkable lack of inhibition, as if Allah had given a special dispensation for the month of August.

Many of the Alexandrians weren't Moslem. That was why the group of musicians at the far end of the restaurant were playing and singing Greek music. It was a large cosmopolitan gathering, not a gallabiya in sight. The men all wore suits; probably the ties were obligatory. The women's silk dresses were from the fashion houses of Venice and Athens. Diamond rings flashed in the moonlight; pearls glowed on the full white throats of the middle-aged matrons. Every man had his solid gold signet ring. This was the occasion to display one's wealth. This was where the shopkeepers of Cairo, the lawyers and bank managers could impress their rivals and their customers. The women were possessions to be shown off.

The groups were mostly families, coming together to enjoy the summer season on the Mediterranean. Daughters were displayed with pride, like a carnation in a buttonhole. The season in Alexandria was of their 'coming out' parties. The well-brushed hair gleamed in the moonlight. Mothers had spent as much on their daughters' outfits as they had on their own. They had been told to sit up straight – to be nice to their father's colleagues, to push out their chests, and to display their legs. But the young girls had minds of their own. Mothers could control their posture, but no one could control their eyes. Nowhere in the world can a pair of eyes be better displayed than in Egypt. From the time of the Pharaohs to the present day, Egyptian women have been expert in the art of cosmetics. The heavily-outlined eyes of the dancers on the tomb wall paintings were copied by every woman in that restaurant. With one look from those dark pools, fringed with long lashes, a man could become a slave. The mothers might arrange the introductions, but the daughters made the choice, and under the spell of those eyes the men were helpless.

Andreas, Alexander and Demetrios were on the raised platform at one end of the restaurant. Andreas had perched his bottom on a stool, and was playing his small drum. The other two were on either side; Demetrios slightly forward to reach the small microphone which the manager had provided. He sang the songs of Greece. When pressed, he could sing in Arabic, but tonight, the crowds wanted Greek music. Alexander played from a selection of reed pipes, picking up first one and then the other when the music changed in style. Charlotte sat apart from them. Later she would wander around the wealthy diners and collect the money. This was all the payment they received, but on a night like this, they would do well. Sometimes, if the manager thought she would go down well, she was asked to play her guitar. Her music was essentially western. She would have been better received in Venice or Marseilles, but sometimes she was asked to play for the novelty effect. But on the whole this audience preferred the music they understood.

Tonight Andreas and his friends were doing well. Andreas could also play the bouzouki. He had learnt as a child in the back streets of Piraeus. The hot night air throbbed with the passionate music of the Greeks. A different audience, not so polite as this one would have been on its feet joining in the dance by now. These people went on eating, flirting, bargaining, preening. They applauded politely, but paid well when Charlotte collected their money.

The evening ended with a belly dancer – not now as common as in the past. The new prudishness which has invaded Islam had trickled through to Cairo and Alexandria. Since the time of Nasser, the belly dancers had been told to cover up their navels. But in holiday places in high summer they were a very popular 'turn', and dancers were not too difficult to find. Tonight, the woman who stood up from the shadows when Andreas changed his drum to the clay instrument of the fellahin, wasn't young. She was in her forties; her figure heavy. But she was dressed in the traditional costume of the dancers, and even displayed her midriff with abandon, defying the regulations. The audience fell silent. The woman was well-known and well-loved. She was paid by the manager, and well paid. Women as good as she was could name their own price. Not for her the passing round of the headscarf or copper pot.

Andreas loved to accompany these dancers. For once he forgot his native land and entered wholeheartedly into the soul of Islam. The beat became slow and seductive. Alexander began to play the Arab pipes. He played the music of the Bedouin – the timeless music of the desert people. A string of liquid semitones, at first hesitant like the first sexual overture, then faster and more confident as the dance proceeded. The night air was filled with the throb of the drum and the haunting wail of the pipes – an unearthly sound, as old as the Pharaohs.

The audience was spellbound. The dancer was motionless at first, just the flick of a hand and a rustle of the beaded skirt. Then the body began to gyrate, slowly at first, then faster and faster, the stomach muscles rotating in time with the drum. Her hands stroked her breasts, also rotating with a strange eroticism. She offered them both to the imaginary lover. She stroked his back, caressed his hair, received his embrace. Now her hips were thrust forward, and the muscles of the lower part of her body went into a state of frenzy. The back arched to receive the man. The breasts swayed to his caress. Her mouth was open to receive his kisses, and her tongue flicked like a snake's over the full lips.

No one moved. The men were bewitched. Even the women put aside thier knives and forks and watched breathlessly until the climax came. The dancer sank to the floor in a trance of ecstasy – her hips raised to the man, her muscles thrusting rhythmically in time to his imaginary penis. At last she subsided – her face distorted with pleasure. The last drumbeat died away. The audience relaxed. One universal sigh released the tension. The men turned to their neighbours. The women picked up the forgotten knives and forks; the young began to clap.

The applause was tremendous. The glory of human sexuality had been laid before them. The dancer's full body reminded them what life was all about. There had been nothing offensive in the act; it was not the blatant coarseness of the nightclub stripper. It was a re-creation of the sexual act through dance and music – it was a tribute to man's immortality. The woman was a true artist, and this traditional dance of Islam was a true art form, in spite of the puritans.

The musicians gathered up their instruments. It was after midnight; the manager was pleased with them. The audience was happy; the sales had been high. He gave them a handful of prawns – giant ones taken out of the sea that morning. As an afterthought, he added two bottles of Rubis d'Égypte, a rose-coloured local wine. The cook let them have bread and dolma – the food of Greece, vine leaves wrapped round spiced meat. He even added a large portion of the local cheese which Andreas called 'feta'. They carried it down to the beach in a large fig-leaf which Charlotte picked from the tree by the musicians' platform.

On the beach, they turned away from the hotel where the lights were gradually being extinguished one by one. Above them the sky was an expanse of velvet, studded with gems. The perfect circle of the moon gave them more than enough light to see by. Charlotte found time recede. This was the goddess Isis of the Pharaohs – always depicted as a remote, unfriendly figure. The music, the dancer, had affected her in a strange way. She had watched the woman spellbound, memories of

Hassan flooding back, but this time without pain, just a terrible longing.

The three men were in high spirits. Demetrios made a small fire out of some dry wood he seemed to carry round with him. He liked his comforts. The prawns were speared on thin sticks and roasted over the flames. He'd even wheedled some tahina from the cook; the oily, garlic-flavoured paste went well with the prawns. Soon the air was filled with the pungent smell of the food which Demetrios was guarding with loving care. Andreas turned to Charlotte. He sensed her sadness.

'Come; your turn I think. A love song from France, whilst Demetrios cooks.'

The mood changed. To accompany the high spirits of the men she played the enchanting songs of the mediaeval troubadours. She sang in French about love and despair and seduction. The men applauded.

'Time for you to learn to become a belly dancer,' said Alexander. 'Then our fortunes would be made. We could all retire and eat like this all the time.'

The thought of Charlotte rotating in a beaded skirt made them all laugh. Charlotte's body was completely straight – her hips boyish and her breasts almost nonexistent. Her illness had left her emaciated and all of Andreas' good food could not alter this. They passed round the bottle, the prawns were ready and the four settled down to the meal

It was a night she would never forget; it was the last time that all four would be together. It seemed to be the last night of irresponsible friendship. From that night on, life would never be the same. It was the watershed of that particular group.

Demetrios was restless. He'd eaten well – every scrap finished up. Andreas lay back on the sand and was obviously content. But the music, the food, the moonlight, and the dancer had affected the Greek.

He jumped up. 'Come on, Alexander. We've money to spare. We've eaten well. The dancer has reminded me of things I would rather forget. It's ages since I've had a woman. I haven't even smelt one for weeks. This slave-driver here keeps us all working. Put away your pipes and let's go. I want a young woman with flesh on her, and who knows her job. The women of Alexandria are famous for their beauty, and their expertise.'

'And other things as well. There's not enough money for your medical bills,' said Andreas raising his head from the sand.

But the two men were inflamed. There was no holding them. Once the thought had entered their minds, they were eager to be off. Already Demetrios was heading back along the beach towards the hotel. He was the only one who had a car – an old black Volkswagen which the team used to get them to these places outside Alexandria.

'We'll stay here tonight,' shouted Andreas to the retreating figures. 'But come back for us tomorrow. Leave the ladies alone in the Main Square. They'll rob you of everything – even your trousers.'

But they didn't hear him. They were off at a run towards the hotel. 'There they go – to their doom. They'll be fit for nothing tomorrow. Let's hope they keep out of trouble. They don't often break loose like this. But a Greek with money in his pocket and wine in his belly can be a devil.'

'Where did you find them?' asked Charlotte, who had often been intrigued by this trio. Andreas produced another bottle of wine which he'd kept hidden from the others. Now, sitting cross-legged on the sand, the bottle between his knees, he looked like a satyr or a Bacchus. With one jerk he pulled out the cork and handed the bottle to Charlotte. She drank sparingly. Her illness had weakened her tolerance for alcohol. But the Egyptian rosé was harmless – weak and refreshing She took a long drink and passed the bottle back to Andreas.

'Here, you take it. I've had enough.'

'I found those two in Cairo – at the restaurant near the pyramids. They were both hungry, both Greek, and both good musicians. We've been together now for over a year. We were in Alexandria last summer, and then in the winter months we entertain the western tourists in Cairo. It's a good life, but we'll never be rich. I suppose one day they'll go back to Greece. Alexander, you know, was a law student in Athens. He dropped out a couple of years ago to see the world. His father is a rich man in the Piraeus – in marine insurance. He was furious when Alexander gave up his career. But he could take it up again at any time.'

'And Demetrios? What was his past?' He was the older of the two – nearer Charlotte's age.

'He worked at the port – what you'd call a docker. He hated the life. There was not much money; he married a local girl, and I believe they've got a child. He liked to sing and play in the restaurants. He liked the easy life. Too much drink, too little money. The usual thing. Then one day he got on a boat and came over here. He's been here ever since. I don't think he'll ever go back to Greece.'

'What about the wife and child?'

Andreas shrugged his shoulders. 'They went back home to her parents, I suppose. That's what most people do when they're deserted by their man.'

He settled himself down in the sand. There was not a breath of wind. He'd hollowed out a place in the sand to fit his body, and he would sleep there that night. Charlotte lay down beside him. She trusted him. He had protected and entertained her. Ever since she had said 'goodbye' to the family of the coppersmith, he had been her guardian. She couldn't have been given a better one.

Tonight, he took her hand. He turned it over and looked at the palm – the outlines of the veins standing out clearly in the strong moonlight.

'And you, Charlotte? What brought you to the Bab Zuwayla? I know nothing of you except that you've come from Kingston-upon-Thames, and that you play the guitar. Your hand tells me that you will live a long life, and you have a good brain. You've been in one of the learned professions, and you have loved too much, and unwisely. That's all. Who was he?'

It was a night for confidences. Charlotte moved nearer to the little man. She held his hand tightly. Then she told him everything – her job, her love for Hassan, her return to England, her journey back to Cairo. When it came to the recent experiences – her desertion, her fears about the robbery, and her illness, she broke down and sobbed. Andreas took her in his arms, and waited for the storm to subside. In those tears all her grief was exorcised. Never again would the pain be so acute.

When she was quiet, Andreas still held her tightly. He felt her thin shoulders through the material of her blouse. She had suffered too much. She deserved to be happy.

'What's the bastard's name?' he asked after a while. 'If he lived in Zamalek I might know him.'

She told him Hassan's name. It didn't ring a bell.

'When we go back to Cairo, I'll make enquiries. I do remember hearing about the jewel raid. I believe they traced the thieves out here. But I can't remember reading the rest of the story. It sounds as though he was into drugs and robbery – both, in fact. But what will you do? You must go back to your own people. Together we'll raise the fare. Then you must contact your friends at home. I'll miss you, though.' He held her close.

She looked up at the strange little man with the liquorice eyes which were now beaming with tenderness. 'Yes; I shall miss you. We have been good friends.'

His mood changed. He laughed. 'Yes, I've been your servant – your manservant. And you, My Lady Fair – the unattainable of the old romances. I'm your pet dwarf, your tumbler. I'm only a clown, you know. My grandfather was a clown, and his father before him. I come from a long line of clowns and jugglers. That's where I get these shoulders from, and my short tough legs, and height. I'm only a clown.' He turned away from her.

She moved nearer, and stroked his back. 'You have been the best friend I've ever had. No one has been kinder; no one has made me laugh as you have done. You may be a tumbler and a clown, but you are the best friend anyone could ever have.'

He turned to face her, and she laid her dark head on his chest. There was no substance to her. Andreas held her closely to him. He gently stroked her hair and caressed her hand.

'My poor Charlotte. We shall always be friends. I shall always look after you. Wherever you go, I shall go. We need one another. Come back to Cairo with me. Finish your book. I'll earn money, and perhaps we can go to Venice. Later when you marry, I shall stay with you as your manservant. Never again shall anyone hurt you.'

She raised her head from the little man's chest. It was a firm pillow.

'I'll come back to Cairo with you, but you'll not be my manservant, because you're going to work – to paint. I should like to share your room; I'll go back and see my friends the coppersmiths. I'll teach the children, and write my book, and help you with your busking act. But in the daytime you're going to paint. We'll save money, not for my return ticket, but for paper and paints for you. You are a gifted artist, and it will be my job to make you paint seriously. Has no one ever told you that you are a talented artist – one who could make a living through your pictures? Have you never had advice?'

Andreas carried on stroking her hair. It was soothing, and she felt herself dropping off to sleep. 'Go to sleep now; it will soon be morning. Over breakfast, before the others come back, I'll tell you my story. This has been a magic night. It must be the influence of the goddess up there.'

That night, they slept in each other's arms – two children who had found one another. The little man was the last one to drop off to sleep. He thought back to his former life – images of people and places prevented sleep. Looking down at Charlotte, her body relaxed, her face softened into beauty, he knew that here he had found his inspiration, and his future. He had come home.

19

Morning came. The sun rose in all its splendour over the Bay of Alexandria. The two figures were still in each other's arms, clinging together for security, like the Babes in the Wood.

Andreas was the first to open his eyes. For a moment he couldn't remember where he was. Then he looked down at the face of his companion, and the memories came flooding back. There was no sign of the others, but he didn't expect to see them before midday. Charlotte lay curled up against his shoulder. His arm had been around her all night. It was going to be difficult to move without disturbing her. He looked at her sleeping face tenderly. Her body was like a child's. The brown hair tumbled round her face, overflowing onto his chest – like a peat-rich Highland torrent. The sun would soon wake her. He decided to risk moving. He could go up to the hotel and buy bread, and get water. Perhaps they would lend him a pot. The group always carried their own coffee. Milk was no problem in the country districts. He'd already noted the gamoose tied up behind the restaurant. If he got there now, he'd get the best of the morning's flow.

Gently he moved away from Charlotte. He lifted his arm over her body, and eased her into his sand-pit. She sighed and turned over, just like a wife who moves over into the husband's part of the bed when he has to get up. The sand had made a wonderful couch – warm and firm. It was better than the collection of ancient mattresses which had been their resting places throughout that summer.

He got up; Charlotte slept on. He went down to the sea, and took a quiet swim to wash the sand off his body. Then he went under the beach shower to complete his toilette. He was a fussy man. Like many people who are used to living rough, he liked to have a good wash every day, sometimes he would take two baths. His motto was 'When there's clean water, wash in it and drink it. You never know where the next supply will come from.' Looking back at the tiny hump in the sand, he set off along the beach to the hotel.

Sure enough, there were signs of life. The cook was about, sorting eggs and yawning. The kitchen boy was lighting the fire. The guests were all sound asleep, but there were the servants to feed first, and then the odd guest who liked to get up early and swim or jog along the sand. These people were a nuisance, because they expected perfect service and a long menu, before the rest of the hotel was awake.

The cook greeted Andreas. They were friends. He showed him where the pump was — lent him two pots; one for water, and one for the gamoose, who was contentedly chewing her breakfast and obligingly giving milk. Andreas bought a loaf of white bread. The cook gave him some butter, and some of the local cheese which the hotel made itself, for the use of the staff. The guests would expect French and Italian cheeses.

Charlotte opened her eyes to the sight of Andreas crouching over the fire, and the smell of coffee and cheese. She looked across at him and smiled. 'Hallo. How long have you been up?'

'Oh, a long time. Some people sleep too long. The best of the day's gone.'

She laughed. 'It must be all of seven o'clock. Bring your coffee over here and get back to bed.'

He grinned. 'Not a bad idea. Why don't you get up and have a shower over there, whilst I make the bed like a good servant. Breakfast will be in ten minutes.'

She got out of her pit, and ran down to the sea. The sun was already gaining in strength. They would soon have to leave the beach and make for the shade. The water was warm. She liked swimming, and lay on her back in the clear green water looking up at the cloudless sky and realised that for the first time in months she was happy — not just contented, but *happy*. She felt like singing.

Under the shower, she gyrated and sang — washing away the sand, the salt and the unhappiness of the previous months. She had a good friend in Andreas. The little man, despite his teasing, was her devoted friend. Together they could make something of their lives.

Andreas had extended the pit. He had made up a double

bed, with cushions of sand behind their backs. Sitting there, their toes rubbing against each other, they were both happy. They could have sat there all day, had not the sun increased its power minute by minute.

'One hour, and we shall have to find shelter. But we can come back here tonight, if it's as calm as this. It's a perfect bed,' said Andreas.

'Have you slept on beaches before?' asked Charlotte.

'Not often. I like a bed, and a roof over my head. It's only in these remote places far from the towns that it's safe to stay out all night. Even here, one could have one's throat cut, and not know what was happening. You can't risk sleeping out here alone. Fortunately, this place is only known by a few. But the hotel is no protection. They don't hear any screams in the night. They don't want to see if you've been robbed. You are not their responsibility.

'You've had a hard life. You must be a survivor. What's your secret? I've lived for a shorter time than you, but haven't managed very well. I've helped a criminal, I've been ill and miserable – I've rejected those who loved me. Here I am at thirty-five, sitting on a sand-bed twelve miles west of Alexandria with a clown and a tumbler for a companion.' She was smiling.

'Are you happy, now?' he asked.

'Yes – for the first time in years. I feel safe and well-fed. Your coffee's marvellous.'

'That's one thing I've learnt in my long life – how to make good coffee, wherever I find myself. And I have been in some strange situations. None as strange as this – lying here, propped up on a sand pillow with a lady who is all bones and no flesh, and comes from Kingston-upon-Thames.'

'I've never set foot in the place. You were the one who had digs there.'

'Digs. I like that word. I haven't heard it for years. All the students at the Slade had 'digs'. In the Mediterranean countries we always have an apartment.'

'How did you get to the Slade? Did you get a scholarship from Athens? Why did you leave?'

'Because I was bored. And because, in my youthful arrogance, I thought they could teach me nothing. I had complete confidence in myself as an artist. I wanted immediate success. I was to be disappointed, but at least I learned to speak English.'

'When did you come to Egypt? Have you ever held an exhibition here? Do people know about your sketches?'

'I have also got a lot of oil paintings. I don't only sketch. Some of my lurid sunsets I sell. But the rural scenes – the fellahin at work – the gamoose having its bath – the fishing boats coming into the harbour in the morning – are all in oils. I only stop when I come to the end of my paints, and my paper. I would like to try water colours, like your English painters, but this is not the country for soft, misty views. It's dramatic, operatic country. There is no place for the madrigal here.'

'You must carry on. *I'll* help you to buy paints. I could go back to teaching by the Bab Zuwayla. They know me there and would find me more pupils. I expect I could even have my old room back.'

'That's not allowed. Now you have acquired a manservant, he must look after you. I can put a mattress in my room in Cairo. Come and share my life. We can look after each other – that's all. One of the basic laws of survival is that sometimes it's not practical to go it alone. Help me with my painting. I'll cook for you and bully you to finish that book. Perhaps when I reach my fifties I can make something of my life. It's about time.'

'What have you done up till now?'

'Oh, drank, and bummed, and womanised, and starved. Now I know I can jog along in a country like this, where the climate is good, and there are enough rich people to toss me a few piastres occasionally.'

'Why did you start painting? Did you learn art at school?'

'I didn't go to school – not regularly, anyway. My father was a porter at the docks in Piraeus. I was one of eight. My mother took in washing when she wasn't having babies, or getting over miscarriages. I never knew her in good health. There was always a baby at the breast – one on the way, and no money. She had eight children, and six miscarriages.'

He fell silent. Charlotte waited for him to continue. She handed him some more cheese. She put her scarf over her head as the sun was getting hot, but didn't want to disturb Andreas. It was the first time he'd talked seriously about his childhood.

'My mother was always ill; my father always drunk. Ouzo is the curse of the poor in Greece, rather like gin in the eighteenth century in your country. You can get drunk for a few piastres in one of those drinking dens along the waterside in Piraeus. I was left alone – to bring myself up. I wasn't the youngest, nor the eldest, somewhere in the middle. But I was tough, although small. These shoulders I inherited from my grandfather who had worked in a circus. He was a cross between a clown and a tumbler. I only saw him once. He killed himself with drink, but I inherited his physique. I learnt to fight, and to punch hard, and I suppose I could have made my living as a boxer had I wanted to.

'I went to school on and off; and I suppose I was quite clever. Certainly I never remember learning to read and write. It always came easily. The teachers were interested in me – I took the usual amount of bullying because of my size and my poverty. I never wore shoes to school. But the other kids soon learnt to fear my fists. I knew how to punch, and I soon learnt to joke about my size. They liked to watch me tumbling and I learnt to be a clown to stop them hitting me.

'One teacher in particular was interested in me, and I was flattered. He used to ask me to his house, where he lived alone. He showed me paints and paper, and with him I started to draw. He was a good artist, but I soon found out that he liked small boys, and my body fascinated him. I was always broad-shouldered and slim-waisted. I might be small, but I'm in proportion. One day he wanted me to pose as Cupid. I was to be dressed in garlands of roses, and curl up on a sort of couch he'd got ready for me. He was to retire behind his easel and paint me. He was going to do several pictures and sell them to tourists. They always like Greek mythology.

'I took my clothes off, and put all those stupid garlands over my head. I must have been about twelve. I know I was developing, because I wondered what he was going to do about the hairs on my chest. I strutted about for a bit in my floral decorations, and the next moment I felt him behind me. He was breathing very hard. He was a big man, and attacked me from the rear. I was thrown on the couch and he raped me. Homosexual rape is just as unpleasant as female rape. I was totally innocent; the pain was excruciating, and no one believed my story when I went home. My father was drunk; my mother in bed. Neither wanted any trouble. Besides, sex with small boys is not quite frowned upon in my country. I do believe my father wouldn't have been at all disgusted if I had sold myself to the sailors along the docks.

'I never saw the teacher again. I left school, lied about my age, and my father found me a job with him down at the port. I took messages and made tea, and later took a porter's job. That made me strong. But I never grew very tall. I continually had to fight off men. I had all the attractions of looking like a boy, but with the strength of a man.'

He paused and finished his coffee. There was still more in the pot, and Charlotte filled up the metal cup which they always carried with them. Tears were in her eyes as she listened to his story. At least she had a warm and privileged childhood. Although her parents had travelled continuously, she had spent her adolescence in a boarding school, where she was sheltered from the evils of the world. Her fault was that she had been too trusting, too naïve. Andreas' youth had instilled in him a total distrust of his fellow men that he would never overcome. He hid behind his clown's mask.

'You still haven't told me how you got to England?' Charlotte said, as Andreas had withdrawn from her. He sat there staring blankly out to sea – lost in introspection.

Her question jolted him back to the present.

'Oh that! I used to paint or sketch whenever I had a few spare moments. On Sundays I used to go down to the port and paint the boats and the passengers and the fishermen. One day I was aware that I was being watched by a tall Englishman. This time I was ready for him. When he came up I flew at him ready to kick and bite. He was totally bewildered, as so many of those really nice cultured Englishmen are. Instead of propositioning me, he asked where I lived, and whether he could speak to my parents. He spoke Greek, and there was something about him that I liked.

'Well, he came home; my mother had just given birth. She'd

had a bad time and was still bleeding. She had no strength left. For once my father wasn't drunk. Mr Taylor, Patrick Taylor, that was his name, sat down at a filthy table in a kitchen still reeking of childbirth and unwashed bed linen, and asked permission to take me to England to study art. I was eighteen and still small. There were no prospects before me in Piraeus. My parents were delighted. They didn't really worry whether I would ever come home again. They would miss my contribution to the family income, though. Patrick gave them money. I was sold to him, I suppose. He said he wouldn't want repaying: I was to be his investment. I left home the following week, and I've never been back since. I don't even know if my parents are alive. I don't think so. None of my family have made old bones.

'I stayed in England until my early twenties. Patrick paid for everything. I didn't often see him – just once or twice a week. I learnt English quickly, and your customs, but I hated art school, and the boredom of your English winters. I didn't seem to be getting anywhere with my painting, either. I ran away – for a few years to Paris, living as a waiter in restaurants and hotels. Because of my experience as a boy, I was determined to prove myself a man, and spent my money on women. I couldn't stay with any of them. They never stayed with me for very long. I forgot my art – I was miserable, underpaid and overworked.

'Then I ended up in Florence – working in a hotel, but also tumbling and playing the drums in the evenings. I settled down with an American art student. She never knew I could paint. I was too ashamed to tell her. She tried to paint mostly copies of the Old Masters. She wasn't very good, but I liked her and she was fond of me. We lived together for six years, and then she left me for an Italian, who owned the local garage in Florence. They actually married. She became a Roman Catholic, and I think they had a child. I was very cut up. She was giving me the stability which I needed, but the attractions of a steady income and a husband and children were too strong. I couldn't compete.

'When she left me, I gave up – gradually drifted east, and came to this country six years ago. I like it here. I've earned my living, sort of. The funny thing is, I have gone back to painting. When we go back to Cairo I must show my work to you. Perhaps you will inspire me to paint again. You will take over where Mr Taylor left off.' He was laughing at her now. She looked so earnest.

'One day, we shall meet Patrick Taylor, wherever he is and tell him that the money he invested in you wasn't wasted. He'll be proud of you.'

'He'll be a good age now. He was in his forties when he picked me up out of the gutter.'

'Was he married?'

'No; he lived alone in Chelsea. Do you know, I think he fell in love with me. His instincts were the same as the schoolteacher's but he never gave me any reason to distrust him. Just sometimes I saw him looking at me – that was all.'

They were both silent. The joy of the morning had evaporated. The sun was now a ball of fire overhead. They had to move into the shade. The holidaymakers were drifting down from the hotel. The servants were putting out the umbrellas, and the well-fed guests were rubbing their flesh with sun-oil. Some were making for the sea. Some were throwing the bright beachballs in a desultory manner. There was a steady trek to the sea by young men with sail boards over their shoulders. It was the start of play-time.

Across the sand, they saw a figure coming towards them. He was walking very slowly. One leg seemed to be wrapped in bandages from the knee downwards. He was waving his arms; once he fell over. At first they took no notice. Then Andreas started up.

'My God, it's Demetrios! He's been hurt! Where's Alexander?'

Leaving Charlotte to pack away the breakfast, he ran across the sand to the staggering figure. She saw him stop and put his arms round the man. Then the two of them made their way towards her, Andreas still supporting the other.

It was Demetrios, but a pale and shattered shadow of himself. Demetrios the strong, the sure, had gone. He sat down on the sand, oblivious of the sun. He put his head in his hands and sobbed.

'What is it?' she whispered to Andreas. 'Where's Alexander?'

'He's in hospital,' said Demetrios. 'He's been stabbed in the chest — six times, by some devil of a Turk. He wanted the girl which Alexander fancied, some tart from the back-street gutters — worthless, but you know what a fool Alexander can be with women. I was more than satisfied with some dancer, but Alexander was slow. When he finally made up his mind to ask this girl, it was late, we were in a bar somewhere in the port area, and she turned out to be this Turk's woman for the night. It was her fault. She tipped the wink at Alexander, but you know what women are. The Turk attacked. Like all Turks, he didn't fight fair. He had a knife, and before Alexander could defend himself he'd been stabbed in the arm. Then he made the mistake of trying to defend himself with his bare hands — the Turk stabbed again and again. I tried to help, but got this —' he pointed to his leg.

'Then the police arrived. Alexander was taken to hospital and I passed out. When I came round I was in hospital too, my leg in bandages. Alexander is in a bad way. He wants you, Andreas.'

'How bad?' said Andreas.

'Very. The priest is with him. He's in the Greek hospital near the port. I've got the car. We must go at once.'

The three figures went back to the hotel, and to the car. The idyll was over. Always at the happiest moments, life delivers the worst blows. Andreas was sobbing with rage and despair, clenching and unclenching his hands to ease the pain. Charlotte was beside him. She reached out and took one of those tortured hands. To her relief, he gripped her hand tightly, like a small boy who wants the reassurance of human contact. She would not be alone again.

20

The Greek hospital was near the port, a small white-washed building set back from the road. A cobbled courtyard with tubs of rosemary and laurel bushes; over the door, a crucifix. Bougainvilia cascaded over the front of the building, hiding the tiny windows, and softening the barrack-like austerity of the exterior. As they arrived, two Orthodox priests were leaving. They politely held open the mediaeval entrance gate, and Charlotte watched them climb into the front seats. The heat was intense; the courtyard silent, except for the persistent chatter of the cicadas. But even that sound was subdued in the heat of the morning.

Inside the building, it was cool and silent. The receptionist was a young girl, who spoke to them in Greek. She knew about Alexander. She pointed down the passage to the room at the far end of the corridor. They looked back, and she nodded. Alexander was behind that door.

Charlotte felt her heart pounding with anxiety. She wasn't prepared for the scene in that room. Andreas pushed open the door, and they stepped inside. A tableau from a mediaeval Mystery play lay spread before them. The room was bare and white-washed, like a monk's cell. The window, a tiny grating was high up, near the top of the wall. It was unbearably hot. No sound, except the muttering of the priest who sat by the bed, and the laboured breathing of the young man. There was a wooden table, with an enamel bowl on it, and an ikon of Christ in Resurrection. The high iron bedstead, with the crucifix at its head; the priest in the chair, his prayer book open on his knee, and Alexander . . . Charlotte would never forget that scene. The twentieth century was a long way away.

Alexander's eyes were open – dazed with pain and bewilderment. His eyes were ringed by deep purple shadows. His face was ashen. Pain and exhaustion had drained him of all vitality. It was the face of the Christ, crucified. Only the Crown of

Thorns was lacking. The sheet was drawn up to that face to conceal the rest of his body. But they could all see the blood-soaked bandages wrapped around his body like a winding sheet. Tybalt in the charnel house.

Alexander had lost five pints of blood, and still they couldn't check the haemorrhage. It would not be long before he died. The life blood was literally draining away from him, inside that limp body. He was connected to a drip in a vain attempt to replace the blood, but the Turk's knife had penetrated his liver and his stomach again and again. He had paid dearly for that night of pleasure.

Andreas went forward and flung himself down on his knees by the side of his friend. He was openly crying. He took one of Alexander's white hands and held it against his own chest, as if to will life into his friend's body. Demetrios took the other hand. The priest motioned Charlotte to a seat at the foot of the bed. They hadn't long to wait. Already Alexander's breathing was fast and shallow, like an athlete's at the end of a race. Each breath was agony. The knife had sliced through a lung.

A doctor came in quietly. The white coat, the stethoscope, indicated a western training. He looked down at the young Greek for several minutes, then beckoned Charlotte to one side, out of the others' hearing.

'He hasn't got long now; less than an hour. He's losing blood rapidly inside. Nothing can check the flow. His vital organs were ruptured by that knife. A bad attack. These damn Greeks and Turks. When will they learn to control their hatred?' The man was Egyptian; he spoke in Arabic.

'Have they caught the Turk?' Charlotte asked.

'Oh yes, he's in prison – he's unrepentant. His only regret is that he didn't finish him off.'

'And the girl?'

The doctor shrugged. 'Who knows? Who cares? She'll be off with someone else tonight; someone who'll buy her a glass of ouzo. A terrible waste. I understand the young man is a musician?'

'Yes, a good one. And a law student from Athens. He had everything ahead of him. His parents will have to be told. He came to Egypt against their will. They'll be heartbroken.'

He nodded. 'The price of folly. Tell your friends to see me before they go. There will have to be arrangements.'

Charlotte nodded. She understood. A terrible end to the partnership. An agonising death over a worthless woman. Alexander didn't even know her name.

The end came suddenly. There was no deathbed speech. Alexander was in too much agony to draw any breath from his tortured lungs. One last look at his friends, one last struggle to fight off the inevitable, and then a look at the seated priest. The man understood. Motioning the two men to one side, the priest took over. The doctors could do no more. Now it was the duty of the Church to ease the man into the next world.

They stood whilst the priest read the prayers for the dying. Charlotte didn't understand the language, but the resonant voice held her enthralled. The man in the bed, hardly recognizable as the boy she'd seen laughing and tumbling on the beach the day before, seemed to become calmer. The look of terror left his face. The priest made the sign of the cross over the dying man – he looked at Andreas, tried to say something, and then closed his eyes. He sighed softly. Charlotte remembered the Biblical expression 'He gave up the ghost'.

The priest finished the prayers, then closed the book. Death was no mystery to him. It was as much a part of life as giving birth or taking Communion. Charlotte went forward and touched Andreas.

'It's over. The doctor must see you. He died peacefully.'

Her voice seemed to break the spell. Both men got up and wiped their eyes with the back of their hands.

'Alexander, Alexander. To die like this – what waste.'

Demetrios thanked the priest who nodded and left the room. He was attached to the hospital, and this was all part of his daily round. A Greek musician that morning, a Greek sailor that evening brought in from the drinking dens and brothels of the port. Sin, wickedness, death were all familiar to him. It was his duty to give the sinners the comfort of a Christian death. He'd see them again at the funeral in the hospital grounds.

They gave money for the funeral. The hospital waived the medical expenses. They had been minimal. Alexander was

183

almost dead when he had been brought to them. The three friends left the hospital stunned. Their life together was shattered.

The morning was over. They left the hospital in the blazing heat of the afternoon sun. They made their way to a small café near the quay.

Demetrios spoke first. 'I must go to his parents. He will be buried here, but his parents must know. He was their only son. It wouldn't be right for them to hear the news from the authorities first. I shall go back to Greece, and tell them that their son brought us all great happiness. It was his tragedy to die by the hands of a Turk.'

'You said you'd never go back,' said Andreas. But something had happened to the happy-go-lucky Demetrios. The death of his friend, the priest, the prayers for the dying had all affected him deeply. It had touched his essential 'Greekness'. He wanted to go home.

'Now I shall. I'm ready. I'm the one to tell his parents. I was his friend.'

Charlotte turned to Andreas. 'And you – will you go with Demetrios?'

The man shook his head. 'Not yet. I am not ready to go. It will be enough if Demetrios goes back. When I looked down at Alexander fighting for his life, when I saw the waste, the terrible waste, I vowed that I was going to do something with my life before I die. Who knows when that's going to be? You nearly died in June. We must make something of our lives before we go – we owe it to our parents, our teachers, our friends. Perhaps we even owe it to God – to thank Him for the gift of life. Demetrios is going to start again in Greece. I am going to start again in Cairo and you are coming with me. Together we might make something of our lives – you with your writing, and me with my painting. Strangely enough, I thought of Patrick Taylor – the man who rescued me from the slums of Piraeus, when I looked at Alexander in there. I owe it to him to try to paint something worthwhile. I ran away from him; I couldn't face the discipline and the hard work, and I was frightened of failure. He must be over seventy now; but I should like to thank him for giving me the chance to prove myself. It's not too late to start.'

He bowed his head and sobbed quietly. Demetrios put an arm round his friend's shoulders, and they sat there until the sun began to drop towards the sea. It was time to go. Demetrios was the first to move.

'Tonight, I'll stay with Alexander. I'll be at the funeral. It might be tomorrow as there is no police work involved. There might only be a few photographs. They have more than enough evidence to convict the Turk. Then I'll leave for Athens. Now, I'll go down to the docks and find a boat to take me home. I won't be back tonight – I'll be with Alexander.'

This was a new Demetrios. He'd lost his laziness, his indecisiveness. He hugged Andreas, and kissed Charlotte on her cheek, then was off, striding towards the port and the waiting ships.

The other two went back to the bare room they had rented off the Twenty-Sixth July Street. It was down a small alley off that noisy thoroughfare. Andreas and Charlotte slept on either side of the small room; their beds were just mattresses placed on the floor. Andreas flung himself down on his, and turned his face to the wall. For a long time he lay there mourning his friend. Charlotte sat behind him, cross-legged on the floor. She put her hand on his back for comfort, and together they sat there until darkness fell. She broke the silence first.

'Andreas, we must eat. Let's go out and buy some food. Then let's go down to the beach and sleep there as we did last night. We can mourn Alexander in the open air, but we must eat something. Then tomorrow we'll see about the funeral and then go back to Cairo. I am coming with you.'

Andreas turned and looked at her, his face streaked with tears. 'It's time we went. Demetrios is right. We must go on. There's enough money for some bread and cheese, and a bottle of wine. After the funeral we'll start in earnest to make money. There are now two things I want to do. One is to make some money as a painter – perhaps I can sell some pictures in the cafés near the pyramids. The other is to find out what happened to that bastard who gave you so much unhappiness. I hope he's dead.'

She shuddered. 'Leave him alone. Find out if he left Cairo by all means, but let it end there. There's no use wasting more time in revenge. Let him be.'

They bought some food at a stall in the bazaar. It was a wonderful night. The sea was warm and still – the moon a huge lantern above them. They took the bread and the wine, and the parcel of dolma down to the water's edge and looked out to sea.

'If we make enough money, maybe we can go across to Venice. They love painters there. Maybe you could set up an easel in St Mark's Square and I could write my book.' She remembered the artist she'd seen before when she had stayed in Venice for a few days on her way home. St Mark's Square was full of artists of all nationalities. There was one American who painted portraits incredibly quickly. He seemed to earn a lot of money. The tourists were actually queuing for his pictures.

'Yes, we could try; but first we must make some money for the fare. If you stay with me, we can do anything.'

They walked to the furthest end of the beach. Then they sat on the warm sand, and ate their food. Neither was hungry.

Charlotte had brought her guitar. She knew that Alexander would have wanted her to play that night. Whilst Andreas lay back on the sand and mourned his friend, she played the music of Monteverdi and Dowland. It was a fitting memorial service.

Eventually they became tired, and Andreas hollowed out a bed in the sand. As on the previous night they slept in each other's arms, clinging together for comfort. Alexander had brought them together, and from that night onwards they were not to be parted.

21

Alexander was buried in the small cemetery by the side of the Greek hospital. The same priest who had read the Service for the Dying now read the Service for the Burial of the Dead. It was soon over, and the three left the hospital in silence. It was the end of the old life.

Demetrios was leaving that day for the Piraeus, and Charlotte and Andreas went with him to the docks. Later, that afternoon they waved him off from the quay. The rusty ship with its cargo of rice pulled away from the jetty. Demetrios, the only passenger, leant over the rail, waving goodbye.

He had given them the Volkswagen, as he couldn't afford to ship it over to Greece. When Andreas had protested, Demetrios had merely shrugged his shoulders, saying rather illogically, 'I can always get another car; we can't get another Alexander.'

Charlotte had driven to Cairo that evening. Strangely, Andreas had never learnt to drive. It was odd to sit behind a driving wheel again. It was also different from driving in Egypt. The road across the Delta was straight, but the number of camels and donkeys which also used the road made the journey seem endless. It was the women who led the donkeys – black-draped figures, many with gold coins stitched to their veils, showing the world their value. Both beasts *and* humans were under their control. One hand held a child's hand; the other prodded along a reluctant donkey. Charlotte marvelled at their stamina. They scarcely gave her a glance as she drove past.

The Cairo traffic terrified her. Andreas had almost to force her through it; she felt like one of the donkeys beaten along with a stick. In fact the donkeys seemed to make faster progress!

They had made for Andreas' room near the mosque of El-Azhar. Nothing had been said, but both had presumed that

Charlotte would move in with Andreas. She would have to go back to the coppersmith's shop and explain what had happened. But she wouldn't be far away, and could resume the lessons at any time.

Andreas rented two rooms off the main El-Azhar street, near the Midaq Alley and the spice bazaars where she had first met him. The building was old, with peeling plaster-work and a huge, heavily-carved entrance door with a wrought iron ring in the middle of it, like the door to a fortress. There was a beautiful latticework window projecting over the street in traditional style, and it was the room behind this window which Andreas rented from a Greek merchant. Inside, the room was dark and cool. Light was provided by an oil lamp which Andreas lit as soon as they arrived as it was getting dark. There were faded rugs on the floor, a copper table on wooden legs, and a trestle bed under the window. At the back of the house was a tiny kitchen with a chipped sink, and a battered cooker connected to a cylinder of gas. Charlotte had never seen a mains gas supply in Cairo.

Andreas went to a large cupboard in the corner of the room and dragged out another mattress. 'You can take your pick,' he laughed. 'If you want the mattress, then you can put it where you like. Bedrooms are portable in Egypt. I can even offer you the roof if it gets too hot in here.'

But Charlotte wasn't listening. She had seen the glow of colour inside the cupboard, and had gone forward to investigate. Before he could stop her, she had dragged out a large oil painting. It was a beautiful painting of the Mosque of El-Azhar painted at sunset. The delicate minarets had been drawn with enormous care; the intricate carving standing out clearly against the darkening sky. He had captured the peace of the great courtyard where a group of students were talking together, their books under their arms. She hadn't known that he had such a good eye for architectural detail, and looking into the back of the cupboard she saw other paintings of mosques and minarets, as well as pyramids and ancient monuments of Pharaonic times.

'Andreas, these are good,' she cried. 'I thought you said you only painted lurid sunsets for American tourists. These are beautiful. You shouldn't hide them away.'

He came forward and took the paintings out of her hands.

'I did them a long time ago. They're not good – just picture-postcard views. I've gone on to sketching lately. I like charcoal and it's cheaper. I might take these down to the Mena Hotel, and see if some rich American will buy them. Let me put them away. I'll make you some lemon tea.'

He shut the cupboard door, and made her sit down on the truckle bed whilst he prepared the tea. She sat there thinking what a strange man he was, and how right Patrick Taylor had been when he saw in that young man of eighteen a skilled artist of the future.

Charlotte had moved in with Andreas at the end of August. Their lives soon settled down to a pattern. Andreas still insisted he was her servant. He cooked the meals, and cleaned the apartment. They both worked very hard, often travelling long distances to the places where the tourists congregated.

Andreas' sketches sold well. Charlotte continued to give English lessons by the Bab Zuwayla Gate, and by September she had several students, not only children, but grown merchants and shop assistants who saw the usefulness of talking to tourists in their own language. There was also a useful line in writing letters in English, so that the shopkeepers could send orders to Europe and America.

She bought herself an old typewriter, the sort of machine one finds in junk shops in England, and in her spare time began to type up the neatly-written exercise books. She was beginning to plan a book on Egypt. It would be a series of essays on all subjects – art, architecture, religion and the social life of the people of all classes. She wrote well; she hoped like Freya Stark. Her plan was to persuade Andreas to do some illustrations for her. Then she might see if she could find someone to turn it into a small book which the tourists would like to buy. She could sell it with Andreas's sketches.

Demetrios' car had proved invaluable. They were able to go further afield to sell the sketches. They went to Sakkara and sold a dozen pictures to a group of tourists who all liked being drawn with Zoser's Step pyramid behind them. It was more personal than a photograph. Sometimes the other photographers would hurl abuse at them as they thought they were taking away their trade, but there was room for them all. Andreas could produce a sketch amazingly quickly. He could catch an expression with one or two strokes of the charcoal. He would even draw caricatures of people and then sell them. Charlotte used to smile at the sight of a large Texan balanced on a small donkey with a pasha's fez on his head. Andreas would whip out a notebook and charcoal, and draw a quick sketch. Nearly always, the man was delighted with the drawing.

Sometimes, when they had been doing particularly well, she would persuade Andreas to take time off and go sketching for her. They'd take the car to some well-known tourist place – the Cairo Museum was one of their favourites, and he would draw tourists and guides, and beggars waiting to dive forward for baksheesh before the police beat them away. She'd persuade him to draw mosques and bits of buildings she wanted to write about. He was even asked to draw the wooden *mashrabiya* of his own room. She wanted a sketch of that intricate latticework, so typical of the old houses in this mediaeval part of the city.

One day, in October, they went to the City of the Dead. She wanted some sketches of the tombs. She had never been there before, but remembered someone had been there in her Embassy days, and had been very impressed. They drove out at dusk. It was to the east of the city, not far from the El-Azhar area where they lived. Charlotte didn't want detailed drawings of the architecture, but simple sketches to catch the mood of the place. Andreas grumbled that he didn't have a set of water colours. The soft evening light, the flickering fires in the tombs – which in this overcrowded city were also the homes of the living – would have been perfectly captured in water colours. Instead he sketched quickly, intending to transfer the impressions onto a larger canvas later.

The evening was already turning cold as they arrived at the burial ground of the Mameluke Sultans. They parked at the side of the dirt track and wandered through the piles of rubbish and the flickering fires. It was a lunar landscape scattered with domes like abandoned space-craft. For a place of the dead, it was teeming with life.

The poor of Cairo had always made their homes there, giving birth and dying amidst the tombs of their ancestors. It was not a sad place. Relatives of the dead and the living would go there on feast days, or simply when they felt like a day out and picnic amongst the tombs. The dead and the living joined forces to celebrate the pleasures of life.

It was these people as much as the famous tombs of Qaytbay and Barquq that Charlotte wanted to see. It was as if groups of squatters had moved into Highgate Cemetery and had made their homes among the headstones and the carved angels. No one bothered them as they walked along the unmade roads. Evening meals were being prepared; babies washed in copper baths. Dogs snapped at their heels, but Andreas sketched away unperturbed, while Charlotte thought how to describe the place. Why was there no fear of desecration? She remembered a notice she'd once seen in a Suffolk churchyard – 'dogs must be kept on leads. They must not desecrate the graves'. These people were bursting with life. At night, couples copulated over dead relatives. Babies were born in the tombs – yet no one thought of desecration. There was no Imam cursing the living for not respecting the dead. The dead were friends; as much a part of life as the living. They were expected to give their blessing to the activities of the living. In this sense the modern Egyptian had inherited the attitudes of his Pharaonic ancestors. He expected to share his life with the departed.

She liked the place. Andreas was at home there. He, too, saw nothing strange about sharing the dead's resting place. Perhaps the Greeks had a similar attitude towards their dead. She remembered seeing an article once describing how Greeks celebrated their feast days by picnicking amongst their ancestors in the cemeteries – celebrating life with the cheerful popping of corks. Perhaps the Christian celebration of the Eve of All Souls was a faint echo of this practice of sharing the joys of life with the dead.

They walked as far as the famous tomb of Qaytbay, the fifteenth-century jewel of Mameluke architecture. Here, Andreas wanted to stop and sketch the interior, with its intricate carvings of filigree flowers upon a star-shaped polygon; but the light was fading. They would have to return when there was more light. It was a magical place. The tombs – some with delicate minarets silhouetted against the darkening sky – had captured Charlotte's imagination.

'We'll have to come one morning and see the sun rise behind the Citadel. You could sketch these people waking up,' she said to Andreas, who was engrossed in the details of the tomb. He nodded. That expedition was one of many. The Old Cemetery would be a substantial chapter in her book, and Andreas' sketches would be much admired in the artistic circles of London and New York.

They were not yet lovers. It was as if the death of Alexander had created a barrier between them. They both worked furiously as if to forget their friend. Perhaps they wanted to justify their own lives. At night time Andreas threw himself down on his truckle bed, and turned his face to the window. He had lost his gaiety. His face, designed for laughter and irreverence was now set in a new determination. He scarcely noticed Charlotte. She would have loved to have slept near him – to comfort him when he mourned for his friend – but he gave no sign that he needed her. One morning, things changed.

She had got up early – as soon as the daylight penetrated the latticework of the window. She'd slept badly. Her mind had wandered off towards the chapter of the book she was writing – the chapter on Alexandria. She wanted to get up and see how it would turn out. Andreas was asleep; she wondered whether the typing would disturb him. He always slept so soundly that she doubted it.

She got up from her mattress, and dressed in a long cheese-cloth shirt. She quickly brushed her hair, and tied it back out of the way. Then she went into the kitchen and splashed some cold water over her face to remove the sweat. She then went back to the room where her typewriter was placed on an unsteady wooden table. She started to type, and soon became absorbed in her description of Farouk's palace at Montazah. Suddenly, she was aware of Andreas looking at her. He had turned over on his stomach and propped himself up on his elbows. He was laughing at her – his clown's face alight with affection and mischief.

'If you're going to work at this hour every day, we shall have to get you a separate room to live in, or else buy you a silent typewriter. I expect they make them somewhere, and we can send for one in New York, or Washington, and get it delivered at vast expense. I'll sell one of my oil paintings to buy it for you. You see how much I value my sleep?'

'I'm sorry Andreas. I had an idea, that was all. I'll stop and make some tea.'

'That's not enough. I shall need at least two cups of tea, and my breakfast in bed if I'm to forgive you.'

It was a long time since Andreas had teased her. They hadn't spoken much since their return from Alexandria. She decided to risk a rebuff. She got up from her machine and went over to where Andreas was lying on his stomach, with both feet sticking out of the blanket. He always slept with a blanket over him, in spite of the temperature. Lightly she flicked away this cover, and playfully tapped his bottom.

'It was time to wake up, anyway. You can make the tea now.' In a second, he had turned over and pulled Charlotte down on top of him. She hadn't realised his strength. Now it was his turn to pull up her shift and smack her hard on the bottom. At first she felt anger, and struggled to get free, but then everything changed. She wanted him to make love to her, and he felt the desire. She removed the shift herself, and drawing her curtain of hair around Andreas, she held him close. He was a strong and gentle lover. This was different from Hassan's cold-blooded sensuality. She felt Andreas' love and tenderness, and she loved him in return.

They lay there for some time when it was over. There wasn't room for both of them on the bed, but neither wanted to break the spell. Andreas put one leg on the floor to support himself. Charlotte lay on his chest, relaxed and at peace.

'I've been wanting to do that for a long time,' said Andreas after a while, 'but you never seemed interested. Also, I couldn't really believe that someone like you could be interested in a little fellow like me.'

'I've wanted to hold you like this for a long time now. But I suppose there was always the memory of Hassan that stopped me.' She buried her head on Andreas' chest to try and suppress the memory. Suddenly she felt ashamed; Hassan had never loved her. He had used her in the time-honoured way, and she had been too stupid, too inexperienced to realise it. Probably, he had thought her a very inferior prostitute. She certainly had never learnt her trade.

Andreas held her tighter. 'I know. My next task is to find out what happened to that crook. I hope he's in jail, for life. You are my lover now; and a wonderful lover you will be.' She liked the way he used the word 'lover' where Englishmen would use the word 'mistress'. It implied mutual loving – the feminist in Charlotte approved.

She moved suddenly, to look at Andreas, and he promptly fell onto the floor. The spell was broken! He looked ridiculous lying there on the worn carpet shaking with laughter. Charlotte rolled on top of him and they played together like children or puppies until they were out of breath and streaming with sweat. Charlotte was learning to laugh. Sex with Andreas was loving and satisfying, but also fun. Neither wanted to prove anything. Both loved each other's body; both wanted to satisfy the other. The clown made the intellectual laugh; the intellectual gave the clown a purpose in life. It was a remarkable partnership.

It was that morning after breakfast that Andreas went out, for once without his sketchbook.

'Don't wait for me; I might be a long time. Don't worry, I shall be all right.'

'Where are you going?' She was back at her typewriter; she felt like writing. She felt happy and confident.

'To find Khatib. Don't worry' – as he saw her look of concern – 'I'm a born coward; all clowns are. I only want to know if he's got his just deserts. Either the police, or the Devil will have claimed him by now. Let's hope it's the latter; then there's no fear of his resurrection!'

He was gone. From the window she watched him walk off down the street; then he dodged round a boy on a bicycle carrying loaves of bread on his head, and that was all. She forced herself back to work. There were lessons to prepare, and Mahmoud was coming for special tuition. He was turning out to be a serious and conscientious student, and his father was paying well for extra lessons. Already he was helping his family with the foreign letters.

Andreas came back in the evening. Charlotte had prepared the meal. She'd made the falafel herself, frying the meat in olive oil on the tiny cooker. She was using the local spices and the local cheeses, and was confidently producing Middle Eastern dishes. Andreas had taught her several Greek dishes, so she often enjoyed making an evening meal of an assortment of dishes well-laced with garlic and spices from the bazaars. It was a new skill.

He was tired, but content. She had learnt not to ask questions until he had washed under the pump, and had eaten a plateful of *mish* – dried cheese with spices which she had crushed into a paste, and had spread on the local bread. It was delicious with the rough red wine.

'He's gone; he's left the country. He flew to Athens and then Rome, and at the airport he was arrested by the Italian police for drug-running, and the London robbery. He's in an Italian jail for the moment; then I suppose he'll come back here to serve his sentence. It will be twenty years at least. It was in all the papers. It took me a long time to track down the information; I couldn't ask the police of course – otherwise I'd be in jail with him, but I have an acquaintance in the University. He's a law student and sometimes he used to play with us in restaurants in the vacations. He's too busy now. The lawyer is more important than the musician, but I knew he would help me. He had access to all the newspapers in the library. I had to wait about a bit whilst he was in a lecture, but as soon as he came out we had a drink together and I explained what I wanted. He went to the library as soon as he could. Look – he photocopied the articles.'

It was true. Hassan had been arrested and was waiting to be deported back to a Cairo prison. He was accused of dozens of offences, mostly for drug-running, and robbery; once with violence. He'd shot his way out of a tight corner; fortunately the official hadn't died, but had been paralysed from the waist down, and was still a cripple.

Charlotte read the articles with horror. How had she been

so stupid? Why hadn't she taken any notice of her friends? They had been suspicious of him ever since he had first introduced himself into Embassy circles. She had been blind and stupid.

She turned away from Andreas and sat down on her bed, like a child in disgrace. He looked at her and smiled. 'Yes, you've been stupid, but not bad. He must have been very attractive.' Was he jealous? Charlotte got up and went to him.

'Yes, he was attractive to me, then. I was inexperienced and trusting. I had known no one else. My life hadn't included emotional friendships up till then. Remember I was a student for years; an earnest one, with no time for parties and boyfriends. My friendships were all academic.' She thought of James Hamilton. Had he been in love with her? If so, she had been blind, or just totally unaware. Perhaps some women remained unawakened for most of their lives. Hassan had found just the right woman to help him in his criminal activities. No one else could have been as gullible, or as trusting as she had been.

Andreas drew her down on his knee. It was a special feeling. She had never been treated to this mixture of affection and playfulness.

'It's over now. You were never mentioned. He used you, that was all. Your only crime was loving too much. In future your main crime is to love a clown – a fool, who loves you too much.' He was stroking her hair – a gesture he found soothed her immediately.

'It's not a fool I love,' said Charlotte, 'but an artist – a good one, who is going to be appreciated by art connoisseurs in Cairo and Venice. Come on, let's eat this food I've prepared. Neither of us has done any proper work today. Tomorrow – on with the important things like writing and painting. Thank you for finding out what happened to that man,' she added as an afterthought. He had given up a whole day to make investigations.

Hassan was not mentioned again. Only later did she see the headlines in an Egyptian newspaper saying that an international jewel thief and drug-runner had been arrested at Cairo airport. He had been deported from Rome. He now faced trial, and a probable prison sentence of twenty years; but she had looked away, and hadn't told Andreas.

22

December; and the tourist season was at its height. The restaurant was full. It was lunchtime and the owner was rushed off his feet. Where else could you eat fish or grilled pigeon and gaze at the splendour of the Great Pyramid of Giza? Tourists are notoriously impatient, and today, the bright sunshine, and the exhilarating sightseeing made them exacting customers.

This restaurant was one of many which lined the road from Cairo to Giza. The road, once a dirt track, was now a stream-lined motorway, ablaze with neon lighting. All-night advertisements broadcasting their message – drink Coca Cola – travel by TWA – flooded the scene with dazzling light. Stridently, they commanded the world to buy western products.

But on the horizon the three pyramids stood aloof on their rocky plateau, impervious to the competition from the hordings. It was these tombs the tourists had come to see. Nothing could detract from their magic. They had no need of lighting. The mere sight of their shapes silhouetted against the evening sky reduced the tourists to silent wonder.

After the wonder came the need for refreshment. Like tourists everywhere, after the sightseeing, there was a rush for food and a rest. The restaurants were there to oblige. This one was one of many – there wasn't much to choose between them. But with that sixth sense which people on holiday seem to possess, the tourists flocked to this place. Even though most tables were full and the place next door was offering music as well as food, the visitors obstinately preferred to wait for a table, rather than risk going next door. The reason was always a mystery.

The owner knew he had only a limited time to make his killing. As soon as temperatures began to rise in the spring, the tourists would be off. Egyptians never came here. Maybe the odd businessman would bring a western customer to gaze at the splendour of Egypt's past, but on the whole the locals had their own places in Cairo or Alexandria. They didn't need to pay high prices to look at their own monuments.

The Christmas Season was approaching. All those people in the west who couldn't face a traditional Christmas in their own countries, and all those people who disliked the winter climate in Northern Europe came to Egypt in December. The first category was satisfied that at least Egypt had some connection with the Bible; it was the next best place after Israel or Jordan. After all, the Holy Family had spent a long time here. The second category, those who came for the climate, were amply rewarded. Egypt in December and January is perfect for anyone who doesn't like it too hot, and who likes to look at tombs and pyramids in comfort. With a temperature of 73° Fahrenheit in the daytime, it is just right. The British matrons even need their cashmere cardigans in the evenings, and the British male does not have to be deprived of his favourite sports-jacket.

Today, the British were much in evidence. The owner beamed his pleasure. It was just like old times, before Nasser upset the social order. These British were not the same as the old colonial types of the thirties, though. They weren't even the self-confident military types he was used to, either. These seemed to be more timid; taking rather too long to scrutinize the prices, and actually asking for bottled water. The women with the men were comfortable matrons in sensible shoes, with, of all things, raincoats over their arms! These women actually appeared to be wives, and wives of the men they were with. In the past, no self-respecting Army Officer ate lunch with his wife. The owner had soon learnt never to ask who was having lunch with whom. There was one occasion when a husband and wife had both been seen eating their pigeons at his restaurant; one with someone else's wife, the lady with a young officer. The husband had been important too – a Colonel at least. There hadn't been any trouble; both had waved at the other, and he'd been given a good tip by each of them, and a conspiratorial wink from the husband.

These new British had no style – they were lifeless. They

looked desperately bored with each other. They didn't drink, they didn't talk. They clutched their guide books, and looked worried when the bill came. On the whole he ignored them. They didn't spend any money, and they weren't fun. So they were served last, after the Americans, who at least made a lot of noise, and certainly spent money. He liked the Italians best. They liked a good time, expected good service, and could be a nuisance when the food was not to their liking. When they were happy, the place became a theatre. They could transport you to another world. They would call for music, and toss coins to the gully gully man, and shout things across to their neighbours. They were good for business, too. Even the gloomy British liked to sit near them. They radiated colour and excitement – both things lacking in the present-day British tourist.

The waiter was weaving his way through the maze of wooden tables, carrying huge dishes of grilled pigeons filled with spiced rice. Washed down with the local red wine, they were delicious. At the back of the restaurant, the cook was heaping charcoal on the open fire, turning the pigeons and loading up the skewers, keeping the supply going. It was only half-past two, halfway through the lunch period, and already they'd sold two hundred birds.

The smoke rose up like incense. The cook looked like a cross between Vulcan and a High Priest. The smell was heavy and penetrating . . . the fish, stuffed with thyme and rosemary, and the pigeons laced with garlic and sage sent up a mouth-watering cloud of smoke. It was the signal for all the stray dogs for miles around. Two suffragis with heavy sticks were posted at the entrance to fight off the scavengers. The restaurant was like a besieged fortress at these times. There was a wooden fence around the place and a hedge of thorns, but outside sat the besieging army. There were dogs of all breeds, a splendid illustration of nature's contempt for pedigree, and, of course, the ever-watchful, ever-silent crowd of shuffling beggars. Slowly, this army would advance towards the barricades – an imperceptible flood-tide. At last they reached the barrier. It was usually a dog, braver than his companions, which hurled himself at the fence, driven to desperation by the smell of the grilling pigeons. Sometimes the fence gave way, and in a second the Hordes of Midian went amongst them.

Then all hell broke loose. The horde had about five minutes to snatch whatever was edible before the defending troops could rally their forces. It was enough time to grab a few loaves, maybe seize a pigeon or two, snatch some bottles of beer and extract a few piastres from a terrified tourist. It was a nightmare which haunted the restaurant owner at nights when he would lie awake beside his fat, white Egyptian wife wondering when the dam would next be breached. He saw his profits wiped out in the next offensive.

If the worst came to the worst he could always blow his whistle; then the police would arrive, with dogs and whips, but this was only a last restort. On the whole he didn't like the police. They were better kept at a distance. The tourists didn't like having their meal disrupted, either. They didn't like the encircling encampment of the poor and the deprived. If the beggars got too insistent, they would get up and leave the restaurant, their food untouched. The middle-aged matrons from Surbiton didn't like to be reminded that Egypt was really only on the edge of the western world. The Third World was better kept out of sight.

Today, however, the attackers weren't yet rallying for an offensive. The restaurant owner had discovered that a cheaper way to keep the hordes at bay was to pay tribute every day before the first tourist arrived. It was a sort of Danegeld. The attackers weren't fussy. Yesterday's leftovers, bottles of flat beer, fish that was no longer fresh, were all very acceptable offerings. If enough was collected and distributed sparingly, then, provided the horde wasn't too huge, it could be kept at bay. The dogs were the main nuisance. The beggars, on the whole, weren't strong enough to brave the barricades; but a starving dog, a mixture of a Doberman and an Alsatian was fearsome. The owner longed for a shotgun; the sort of thing the suffragis used to shoot the pigeons. But the tourists didn't like seeing the dogs shot in front of their eyes. They'd even got up and walked away in disgust when, on one occasion, he'd had to use a gun to save his cook. They preferred the police to come and net the dogs like the gladiators of Ancient Rome, even though the dogs were later shot, or put down with an injection at the police station. On the whole they were shot; injections were expensive. It just wasn't fair, but he had long ago stopped trying to understand foreigners.

Charlotte and Andreas were sitting at a table in one corner of the restaurant. They had eaten their pigeons. Today, the owner had been generous, and had given them one each. Andreas was fast becoming a tourist attraction. Even Charlotte was popular, especially in the evenings, when the Americans and the British wanted western music after a diet of Arab music. Charlotte could play the sort of semi-folk music which they liked. The songs of Simon and Garfunkel, and John Denver went down particularly well. Her madrigal voice could easily adapt to the modern songs. It was strange singing *Are You Going To Scarborough Fair?* or *The Streets of London* under a hot Egyptian sky. But she was popular, and once she'd collected enough money to live on for a week. Much to the owner's amazement, she'd been called upon to play the whole evening. The belly dancer he'd been keeping in the wings was not needed. He'd been delighted. He hadn't had to pay Charlotte – the tourists paid for their own entertainment that night. They also seemed happy to do so. They also liked the insulting pictures which the strange Greek drew for their benefit. They even paid him good money as well. In fact, people were beginning to come to his restaurant, not for the pigeons, nor the gully gully man, but for these sketches by the little artist. So he fed them from time to time to keep them happy.

Not for the first time, he mourned the passing of the old days. The Old Colonials didn't know anything about art. Long-haired western girls didn't sit in the corner and play guitars. He'd even had to get her a microphone, because the tourists had complained they couldn't hear her properly. They were a happy couple though, and brought him a lot of business. They were also grateful for the food, and left when they were no longer wanted.

Today, Andreas had just finished a sketch of a solitary tourist. He was sitting to the right of them, and Andreas had been drawing his profile. He looked Italian – his shoes, his immaculate silk shirt, his Gucci tie, his perfect hair, all indicated the Italian male. Charlotte had noticed his hands – long white fingers, perfectly manicured. He dissected his pigeon with fastidious precision. He then removed pieces of the flesh from his teeth with a small ivory tooth-pick. No Englishman would have done this.

The man was pretending he hadn't noticed their interest. He'd ordered coffee, and continued to pick his teeth and watch the other tourists. He seemed at home. He'd probably eaten at the restaurant before. He didn't look like a casual visitor. Perhaps he was a businessman. The Italians did a lot of business with the Egyptians. Many of the letters which Charlotte translated for her friends in the bazaar were from Milan or Venice. But somehow, this man didn't look like an ordinary businessman. His hands were too white; there were too many rings on them. His wristwatch was magnificent; gold, as big as a small orange. It was a maze of tiny wheels, each one recording some piece of information. Charlotte remembered seeing these watches in Knightsbridge, and she'd marvelled that anyone would want to pay such an enormous sum just to carry a recording machine around on his wrist.

The stranger had the long, pointed face of an artist, or an art connoisseur. He seemed to radiate sensitivity. Perhaps he was a jeweller from Venice. They often came to buy ornaments from the bazaars. They bought the gold objects cheaply, and then took them back to Milan or Venice to get them mounted in their own country. Then they sold the pieces at four times the price they'd paid for them in the Muski.

Andreas finished the sketch. He passed it across to Charlotte who smiled when she saw it. It was one of his best. He had captured the fastidiousness of the Italian – the perfect hair, the manicured nails. He'd drawn him picking his teeth, revealing the full glory of the wristwatch. He'd used a fine pencil to draw all the wheels, which had added emphasis to the sketch. In fact, the rest of the picture was merely sketched in, using broad strokes of the charcoal. The eye was irresistibly drawn towards the watch. She laughed, and in her neat handwriting she'd written at the top of the paper. 'Modern Man'. Andreas had laughed with her.

Suddenly, the man got up from his table and came across to

them. Without a word he picked up the sheet of paper. Charlotte and Andreas immediately fell silent, like guilty school-children caught writing rude messages to their companions. He stood there, looking at the drawing. A tall man, lean and athletic, he seemed to radiate disapproval. Andreas stood up to take the paper away from him. He felt conscious of his height; it made him feel awkward and ashamed in the presence of this sophisticated westerner.

'I'm sorry,' he stammered in embarrassment. 'I only really wanted to draw your watch; it's truly wonderful. That's all. I didn't mean to be rude.'

The man looked at him in astonishment. Again, Andreas felt himself shrink away to nothing. He sat down in order to disguise his height. Charlotte knew what he was feeling and was ready to defend him, if the stranger should become insulting.

'Rude? What's rude about this? To an Italian there is nothing particularly rude about using a tooth-pick in public. An Englishman likes to use a toothbrush in private, but he will pick his nose in public. An Arab will happily spit in public. A middle-class English child will be told not to belch in public; to an Arab this is a sign of appreciation. Manners are only relative.

'It's very good,' said the Italian. Now he was speaking English with a strong Italian accent. 'You have drawn me well, and you have admired my watch. It cost me a lot of money in Milan. Why shouldn't you draw it?'

Andreas relaxed visibly. 'It is indeed a marvellous piece of machinery. I wanted to capture its intricacy, that's all.' Thus had the satirists of the eighteenth century flattered the tradesmen by drawing their possessions, whilst laughing at the owners. No one objected to flattery. Only Charlotte realised the mockery.

'I'd like to buy this,' said the man after a moment. 'It's better than any photograph. You have a real talent. How much would you be happy with?'

Andreas was used to this. He usually sold his sketches for one or two Egyptian pounds depending on how wealthy the customer appeared. This man looked well-off. The watch alone would have cost a fortune. He paused and rubbed his chin.

'It's taken me some time to finish it; but then, I've enjoyed doing it, and we have eaten well. My friend here fed us on pigeons today.' This was spoken to the café owner, who had come up to see what was going on. He didn't want any trouble, and this Italian looked wealthy. If the artist had insulted him, then the artist could go. His two suffragis could easily dispatch the man and his girlfriend. He set his face into a disapproving scowl.

'Why don't we say you can have it with my compliments and the price of our supper tonight.' He indicated Charlotte.

The man nodded. 'Fair enough. I suggest you eat at the Hilton tonight, or the Sémiramis.' He gave Andreas thirty Egyptian pounds. Andreas started back as if he had been offered a scorpion. The restaurant owner's face dissolved into a smile of relief.

'I can't take this,' said Andreas. 'It's more than I earn in a month.'

'My dear chap, you have talent. I have actually been watching you for a long time now. I own a gallery in Venice, and I'm here looking for paintings and drawings to exhibit. I've watched you and your friend here, and I've been waiting for an opportunity to speak to you. You should be thinking of better things than drawing for these people.' He waved a contemptuous hand around the restaurant, as only a sophisticated art dealer from Venice can wave his hand.

'Thank you for the compliment, but we have to live.'

The Venetian looked sympathetic. 'I know, I do understand. It takes time to earn money in your trade. But I can give you a future. You will have to come out of Cairo though, to find it.'

He took a small white card from the pocket of his immaculate suit. The card was made of stiff white paper – the sort of paper that Andreas would have given his right arm for. His name was engraved on it in gold letting. It read

Roberto Andrelli
MANDOLA GALLERY,
Via Arsenale,
VENEZIA

'Come and see me whenever you like. Bring me all your paintings and I will undertake to exhibit some for you. Why not come along tonight to the Sémiramis, with some of your work, and I can look at it over an apéritif. I might possibly buy some to take with me tomorrow. I think we can do business.'

23

The following December, James Hamilton stood with his back to the fire in the sitting-room of his house in Trumpington Street. The little Victorian fireplace glowed with heat. His housekeeper had lit a coal fire for him that evening. It was a cold night, with more than a hint of fog about. He walked over to the window and drew back the velvet curtains. Sure enough, he couldn't see the other side of the street. A yellow curtain had descended, muffling the sound of the traffic below. Fog was always a risk in Cambridgeshire at this time of the year.

He went back to the fire and poked it unnecessarily with the little wrought-iron poker with the brass handle, which Charlotte had given him two years before. He always kept it beautifully polished; a treasured possession. He was thinking of her tonight, as he always did when he had friends to dinner. They would miss her guitar playing. The same people were coming tonight who had been there on that last evening she had eaten dinner with him. Brian Matthews was an old friend. He and his wife Sheila had known him for years. They had all been students together and had all gone straight into University teaching. Sheila was now a Fellow of Newnham College, and was widely tipped to be the next Principal. They all liked good food and amusing conversation, and it had been one of James' dreams that Charlotte would make the friendship into a convenient foursome. He felt that then his life would be complete. He only needed a wife, and two good friends to see him through to the end of his days. He wasn't really sociable; but from time to time he stirred himself and invited the same people to dinner.

He walked over to the sideboard and poured himself a glass of sherry from the beautiful antique decanter. James had a fine artistic sense and had acquired a formidable collection of antiques. He couldn't resist eighteenth-century glass and porcelain. He looked forward to showing off his new coffee cups this evening. He'd bought them in York last summer, and this was the first time he would put them to use. His housekeeper was extremely nervous at the prospect of pouring coffee into them.

She came in just at that moment as James was admiring the colour of the sherry through the fine cut-glass. She carried a dish of black olives, the Greek variety with stones in them.

'A bad night,' she said. 'They'll all be late.'

James smiled and tried to look philosophical. 'Not necessarily. Only two are coming from Grantchester. The other two are local. They could come on foot if they wanted to. Don't put the fish pie into the oven until they're all here, though. It won't take long to heat through.'

He'd spent the afternoon making what he called 'fish pie', – a large platter of scallops and prawns covered with a cream sauce; a dish far removed from its humble namesake. An abstemious eater, James sometimes liked to dash into the kitchen and concoct a gloriously exotic dish which terrified the housekeeper who had to serve the food on these occasions. James liked cooking, but he also enjoyed talking to his guests, and disliked hovering between the kitchen and the dining room with a glass in his hand watching the soufflé bubbling in the oven. One cooked, talked, ate and drank; but it was impossible to do all at once. So Mrs Browne was asked to serve up, keep watch, and then clear up afterwards.

He helped himself to a handful of olives, spitting the stones into the grate and watching them hiss and bubble on the hot coals. It made him think of Christmas, and red-hot pokers plunging into the rum punch.

He always enjoyed these moments before the first guest arrived. It was like being in the theatre and waiting for the curtain to go up. The stage manager had done his work – the props were in place, and in a minute the actors would take up their positions. He thought briefly of the menu; all was in order. He left nothing to chance on these occasions. Even the mention that there might be fog this evening had caused him to substitute a cold starter instead of the smoked salmon soufflé. He knew that provided the menu was foolproof, he would be able to relax and enjoy his friends.

He heard the doorbell ring on the ground floor. The actors were arriving! He heard Mrs Browne go down the stairs and then the murmur of voices. It was Sheila and Brian — first, in spite of having to drive in from Grantchester.

'Hallo. Good of you to come in this weather. What's the visibility like?'

'Not too good; it's worse where we are. The river seems to attract the fog.' Brian walked over to the fire and warmed his hands.

'How comfortable your house is, James. I sometimes wonder whether we shouldn't sell ours and come into town. The motorway's a bit too near for comfort. There's something very relaxing about these Victorian town houses.'

James poured the drinks. He didn't have to ask what they wanted. He knew them very well. The little group settled down to a civilized evening.

The other two arrived — late, but they were not as familiar with Cambridge as the others. Achim was an earnest student from Munich. He and his girlfriend were both attached to James as research students. James was particularly fond of Karen. A lady in her early thirties, she reminded him of Charlotte; the same seriousness, the same elegant beauty. She too was slim with brown hair down to her waist; but there wasn't the same hint of restlessness or mystery which had so intrigued him with Charlotte. They resembled each other physically, that was all. Karen was practical and down to earth. She had a no-nonsense attitude to history. People in the past got themselves into terrible messes because they were so badly organised. If only Charles the First had been more efficient, he would never have lost his throne. Cromwell won because he was efficient, and knew how to organise an army. James smiled as he listeneed to her. She had become a fervent admirer of Cromwell ever since she'd come to Cambridge. One felt that if Karen had been around to advise Napoleon he would have won the Battle of Waterloo, and certainly wouldn't have invaded Moscow.

She was anti-church and anti-religion. She had little patience with the Middle Ages and, listening to her, James was glad that he had let her loose on the Middle East since 1922.

She had little patience with the religious beliefs of either Arab or Jew, but a great deal of passion for the justice of the Palestinian cause. He was now having grave doubts whether the paper she was going to read to the meeting of the Modern History Society next Wednesday was going to be impartial. She was far too emotionally involved with her subject. Achim was trying to calm her down.

The fish pie was delicious. Mrs Browne had obeyed her instructions and placed the great dish, with its bubbling contents, and golden-brown crust on the table in front of James at just the right moment. He smiled his thanks. He served a dry Moselle with the fish, and there was a good Sauterne to drink with the chocolate gâteau which he'd brought back from Fitzbillie's that morning. He wasn't good at desserts; in fact, he seldom ate any. Tonight, however, he relented and helped himself to a large slice of the cake, saying a silent prayer that his liver wouldn't suffer. James was obsessed with his liver. He had a mediaeval attitude towards it; it was the seat of the 'humours' – the bad ones at that, which could control one's mood for days at a time.

The conversation moved on to Cairo. Karen had been there last September. It had been her first visit and she was exclaiming over the wonders of the Cairo Museum.

'A remarkable place. But so badly organised! Do you know that a rod from Tutankhamun's treasure was once stolen from its showcase, and the attendants didn't discover its loss for years after? It is terrible. No one seems to have made an inventory of the contents of the cases. There are stones and tombs all over the place. It shouldn't be allowed.'

James was glad she'd moved away from the Modern Palestinians. He didn't like being harangued over the Sauterne – an essentially contemplative drink. 'Did you get to Sakkara?' he asked – glad that she'd moved back to Ancient Egypt.

'Yes, I went on horseback, and took a lot of photographs. But they don't do justice to the beauty of the place. I'm not a good photographer, in spite of the good camera which my father gave me for my last birthday. I seem neither to have the eye, nor the technical skill. The photograph still comes out too white or inky black. The Step Pyramid looks as though it was wreathed in fog.'

They laughed. For such a strong personality, Karen was remarkably modest. She had no confidence in her ability to do anything. She had the endearing habit of laughing at herself — a characteristic which made her popular with the British. She could sort out Bismarck's problems, but was totally unable to get to a lecture on time. Once James had eaten dinner cooked by her in her rooms in Newnham. It was an hilarious evening, with the rabbit pie burnt to a cinder, and full of bones. As she said, she'd picked the skinniest rabbit in the market. The jelly hadn't set in the dessert, because she'd forgotten to put it in the fridge in time, but everyone had forgiven her, and had had two helpings of mashed potatoes instead.

'Did you ever get to Egypt, James?' asked Achim. Sheila looked at James sympathetically. She wondered if he was ready yet to talk about Charlotte.

'No. I did think I might have gone last year, but my trip to the States went on longer than expected. I was anxious about a friend of mine who went out to marry an Egyptian, but as I heard no more from her, I presumed all was well. It was a highly suspicious affair. I didn't trust the fellow, but she was besotted with him, and I couldn't stop her from going out there. I hope she's happy.'

'Did she never write to you?' asked Sheila.

'No; she seemed to disappear. One day I might write to someone in the British Embassy — I suppose it would be the Consul — and see if anyone has heard about her. The chap seemed wealthy — one of these playboy types, so no doubt they are the leading socialites in Cairo society. I'm surprised if it has worked out well. Charlotte was not a playgirl. She was far too clever, and too sensitive.'

'In fact, she would have made an ideal wife for a University professor,' smiled Sheila.

James laughed. 'There was a time when I thought so. Now she's lounging around the Mediterranean. I hope she's not wasting her life, that's all.'

'The week before Christmas, I'm going up to London to see an exhibition of sketches and paintings about Egypt,' said Karen. 'It's in Wigmore Street. It's an exhibition by an unknown Greek called Andreas Angel . . . something or other.

The Times gave it a strong recommendation last week. I think it starts this week, but I can't get up there until after term is over. And then I have to visit a friend in Sussex first.'

James looked interested. 'Is it an exhibition in oils or water colours?'

'Both, I think. Also he has done a lot of sketches in charcoal of people and places, and details of Islamic architecture. The report in *The Times* seemed to praise these as much as the larger paintings, calling him an Egyptian Hogarth – except that he's Greek,' she added.

'I thought he'd done those sketches to illustrate a book on Egypt,' said Brian, who had read the report.

'Yes, that was highly praised too. I can't remember the details, but I just noticed the exhibition.'

Mrs Browne came in with the coffee. She was looking anxious, and James got up to relieve her of the tray. The cups were much admired, the coffee was just right, and James was satisfied with the evening. They took their cups over to the fire, which Mrs Browne had just stoked up. No one was going to stay late that evening. The thought of the fog outside was making everyone anxious.

'Why don't you stay the night?' James asked Brian. But they declined. They wanted to get back to Grantchester, and there was no indication that the fog would lift on the following day.

'You might have us here until Monday,' they laughed.

'That's all right. Sheila can bring me my breakfast in bed. I only eat toast and honey,' he added as Sheila looked worried. No one liked cooking in James' house. His standards were too high.

As the two Germans stood up to go, James remembered the exhibition.

'Let me know when you go to London, Karen,' he said. 'I might go to this exhibition. Wigmore Street, did you say? I could meet you there. I like sketches and caricatures better than paintings, as a matter of fact.'

Karen promised to let him know, and the party broke up. But James had been disturbed by the mention of Charlotte. For the hundreth time he wondered what had happened to her.

It was 21 December before James and Karen got to the exhibition in Wigmore Street. It was a cold grey day; snow had been forecast by the evening, and James had debated whether it was worth making the effort to get to the exhibition. The thought of his comfortable house in Cambridge was very seductive. But Karen, enthusiastic and brimming over with energy, had promised him lunch after the visit to the gallery, and she had turned up to his club determined to drag him along with her. She was an ardent culture enthusiast.

They arrived at the discreet little shop in Wigmore Street at eleven o'clock, just in time for a good look round, and then lunch at the Tandoori restaurant which Karen had found in the neighbourhood. James liked the look of the gallery. It was small and intimate – warm and softly-carpeted. Each painting was well-lit, not theatrically so, but just enough spotlight for him to see all the details.

In the window there were just two large oil paintings; both of them of the pyramids at Giza. They were extraordinarily beautiful, and he noticed that both had red dots placed discreetly in the corners. So they had been sold already, and no wonder, because he would have been delighted to own either of them. One was painted at sunset – the pyramids in silhouette against the red sun. A traditional view, but there was nothing cheap or sensational about that painting. The artist had painted with feeling. It was a romantic interpretation, but then what could be more romantic than the sight of the pyramids with the great red sun setting behind them?

The other canvas was of the same subject; only the time of day was different. It was dawn – the light misty-grey, tinged with pink. The pyramids were mere outlines on the horizon. The Sphinx stood out sharply, its face touched by the rising sun just appearing above the Moqattam Hills on the other side of the Nile. The picture was hard and mysterious, with a brooding romanticism. The artist had captured the mystery which will always surround the Ancient Egyptians.

Karen and James stood there looking at the paintings for a long time. They were a glorious promise of what might be in store for them inside the gallery. They pushed open the door, and were transported into a magic cave. Oil paintings glowed from every wall of the little room. It was crowded. It was a popular event, near Christmas, and the exhibition had received good reviews. The artist was doing well. Lots of pictures had red dots in the corner. He didn't know what the artist looked like, and gazing round at the throng of fashionable art lovers, he couldn't pick out any likely candidate. He must be somewhere in the background.

James had never been to Egypt, but no one could fail to be impressed with the artist's skill. Karen stood for a long time before a water colour of the Mosque of Ibn Tulun. It was the place in Cairo which had impressed her the most when she had been there.

'I wonder how much the paintings are fetching?' she asked James, as he came up to where she had been standing for the past ten minutes. The room was in semi-darkness, but the paintings were discreetly lit, and this one glowed with light – the hot light of midday in North Africa.

'We can find out in a minute. I think his prices could be high, although he's not yet well-known. It would probably be a good investment, though.'

He'd said the wrong thing. Karen whirled round and attacked him with a feminine ferocity which he wasn't used to.

'What an appalling thing to say! One never buys as an investment. Art is to be looked at, and admired, and is a source of mental refreshment. I suppose you would hide away a Turner in a cellar, and bring it out only when the market was right?'

Poor James! He had disturbed a hornets' nest. There was only one thing to do, and that was to flee. James was a mild man. He hated arguing, unless it was the strictly intellectual kind. And he hated emotion. Passion was beyond him. Faced with a fanatic, his only course of action was to flee.

Another room led away from the first room. This was more to his taste. The lighting was still subdued, but each sketch was beautifully mounted and lit. These were all natural studies of different Egyptian 'types'. There was the coppersmith hammering away at his brass trays. The leather-worker sat cross-legged on his mat, making slippers. There were lots of sketches of tourists, gazing at camels, watching belly dancers, eating in outdoor cafés, arguing with tour operators and guides. He was amazed at the quantity of sketches. 'He must work very quickly', he thought. 'He's got a good eye for the ridiculous. He's not unkind – merely poking fun at human vanity. It's the human comedy described in charcoal rather than in words.'

He walked along the wall of pictures, wondering how much the artist was charging for the sketches. He particularly liked a drawing of the coppersmith, a little man in turban and traditional gallabiya, surrounded by a mountain of pots and dishes. The artist obviously loved drawing the different shapes. James liked symmetry in his pictures. He liked the modern Cubists for this reason. He wasn't a romantic, but he would have liked to have been. He tired of romanticism, whereas the poetry and logic of form, whether in music or art, never bored him. He loved the logic of architecture, and the controlled passion of Bach. Coming home from a day's lecturing to undergraduates, he always played Bach rather than Beethoven. Logic soothed him; romanticism irritated him. It was one step towards anarchy, which he always feared. The emotion of romanticism upset his equilibrium.

He walked on. Suddenly, he stopped. Emotion, which he so feared, now took over. His heart thundered and his breathing became difficult. There, next to a sketch of a tomb in a place called the City of the Dead, was a drawing of Charlotte – Charlotte sitting in a faded velvet chair in the street, surrounded by children. The mediaeval gateway was in the background, but the artist undoubtedly meant the sketch to be a study of Charlotte Peel. The hair, the shoulders, the whole droop of the body was unmistakable. He looked around. The whole scene was becoming unreal. Why was Charlotte Peel in so many of the sketches? Because there she was – squatting on the sand writing in an exercise book. There she was eating pigeon, or some such small bird. There was a sketch of Charlotte lying on a bed, her hair tucked over one shoulder writing in the same exercise book. There she was playing her guitar, standing in front of a pyramid, and collecting money in a café. She was holding out a piece of material which looked like a scarf of some sort. He could see the fringes around the edge. Then he saw her again, sitting by an open window – the sort of window he always associated with Moslem houses. Outside, the light looked white – a shimmering heat. It was probably the height of summer. But where she was sitting it was mysterious and dark. A painting by Vermeer, but in charcoal. It was beautifully drawn. The contrast between the light and the darkness, the heat and the coolness of the interior of the room was beautifully conveyed in that most difficult of the artist's tools, charcoal.

Immediately, he wanted this picture. James, a man who seldom wanted to buy anything, was filled with covetousness. He looked round desperately in case someone came forward and placed a red dot on the corner of the seated Charlotte. Suddenly, he saw a little man come forward. He must have been watching James for some time. He had noticed his interest in the sketches. This man was small, no more than five feet four. His shoulders were powerful, and his chest broad. He had a slim waist and muscular legs which his tight trousers couldn't conceal. He looked like an athlete of some kind. James noted his face; friendly but wary. He'd suffered at the hands of his fellow men. But the large southern European eyes were looking at him quizzically.

'Do you like the sketches?' he asked, his accent foreign.

'They are very good,' said James. He was still agitated. 'But where did you find this subject? Do you know the girl?' Instinctively, he knew he was talking to the artist. In a room full of city types, and art connoisseurs, he was the only one dressed in blue jeans and a navy blue pullover. He looked like a yachtsman, but as that was impossible, then he must be the artist.

'I know her well,' said the artist with a smile. 'She's my wife. I met her in Cairo. She's an English lady. Tell me your name and I'll see if she's still here. She has to meet her agent at noon.'

Reality was receding for James. He gave his name to the little man. He couldn't be Hassan. Charlotte had never mentioned that he was an artist. Why was Charlotte going to see an agent? Did she paint pictures as well? Or had she started to be a writer?

Karen had come up to him. She was excited. She wanted to buy the painting of Ibn Tulun. She knew just where she was going to hang it in her rooms in Cambridge. She was aware that something was not quite right with James. He looked unusually agitated and he wasn't listening to her. He was looking towards the back of the room, where a little man had just disappeared behind a tapestry curtain.

'What is it?' she asked.

'It's Charlotte. She's here,' he said softly. 'The artist is her husband. Good God, it *is* Charlotte!' he exclaimed.

Charlotte came over to him. James gazed at her in astonishment. He had never expected to see her again. This was a different Charlotte from the one he remembered. The 'Miss Tragedy' had gone. This was a 'Miss Happiness' instead. She was dressed in a long caftan of some sort of emerald green brocade. Her hair was the same, cascading down her back. But she was now plump and rounded; the caftan disguising the bulk of her pregnancy. Charlotte was going to be a mother. He felt the physical pain of jealousy. It wasn't going to be his privilege to make her happy. Someone else had done that. This man, the artist, had transformed the intense intellectual girl he had once known.

She came forward confidently, and kissed him on the cheek, her eyes glowing with affection and happiness. Pregnancy suited her.

'James, how marvellous to see you. How lovely. So you've met my husband Andreas?' He nodded. He still couldn't collect his wits. Karen helped him out. She came forward and introduced herself, and then went on to say how she wanted to buy the painting of Ibn Tulun. Andreas went off with her, and Charlotte and James were left standing together.

'So much has happened,' said Charlotte. 'I went out to marry an Egyptian, and came back with a Greek. We are very happy,' she remarked unnecessarily.

'So I see.' James was collecting himself. 'I am delighted for you. When can we all meet?'

'We are in London until Christmas Eve, then we go to the cottage in Suffolk. Why don't we meet some time over Christmas? In January we have to go to Paris, and then Rome; so there isn't a lot of time. When shall we meet and tell each other our stories?'

'Come to dinner on Christmas Eve, and we'll talk then.'
'Around seven-thirty,' Charlotte was smiling.
'Yes, and bring your guitar.'
She laughed – a new, happy laugh. 'And James – you will be the first to have a copy of our book on Cairo. Thames and Hudson are bringing it out in the New Year. Andreas and I produced it together. I wrote the text, and Andreas did all the illustrations. It's those which will sell the book. He's had such a success in Venice and London.'

The other two had come back. 'It's entirely due to you my dear,' said Andreas, putting an arm around Charlotte's shoulders. 'I would have been lost without you. She saved me from idleness,' he said to James, who was still speechless with wonder.

'And he saved me from despair,' said Charlotte.

Christmas that year was happy for all of them. Charlotte was back in a part of the world she loved, with the man she loved, and whose child she was carrying. She was also back with her friends. A new life lay ahead of her – exhibitions in Rome and Paris, and the signs were there that the book would be a great success, but whether due to the text or the illustrations would always be a source of argument.

James was happy because Charlotte was happy. In the course of time he became a devoted godfather to the child that was born in February. They called him James, of course.